THE BILBURY CHRONICLES

By the same author

THE
BILBURY CHRONICLES

Vernon Coleman

Chilton Designs

Chilton Designs Publishers
Publishing House, Trinity Place, Barnstaple, Devon EX32 9HJ

First published in the United Kingdom by Chilton Designs in 1992

Reprinted 1996

Set by Bath Press Integraphics, Avon
Printed by J. W. Arrowsmith Ltd, Bristol

A catalogue record for this book is available from the
British Library

ISBN 0 9503527 5 6

To: Kath, Muriel, Ted & Terry

The Bilbury Chronicles

Vernon Coleman

CHAPTER ONE

There can be few more beautiful railway journeys than the one between Exeter and Barnstaple. The train moves slowly and stops at a dozen small hamlets on the way but the view from the window is overpoweringly rural: oak and silver birch, hazel nut and walnut trees provide shade and shelter for foxes, badgers and deer; thick, untrimmed hedgerows border lush, dark green meadows; thatched roof cottages sit alongside streams and bridle paths; herons haunt the shallows of the river Taw; dippers and kingfishers decorate the banks, rocks and overhanging branches and buzzards soar high overhead, unflapping and unflappable.

It was 1971 and an early autumn afternoon when I first travelled on that train and, as it chugged slowly and peacefully along the river valley, through Lapford, past Eggesford and into and out of King's Nympton, the glorious majesty of the scenery was the last thing on my mind.

You need to feel calm and relaxed to get the best out of this sort of journey. And I was feeling neither calm nor relaxed. I had no time for rich, red soils; plump hilltops crowned with copses or slowly swirling pools of meandering river water. I was on my way to my first job and to say that I felt nervous would be an understatement of grand proportions.

I had finally completed my training as a doctor just five days earlier. My registration certificate, collected by hand from the General Medical Council, lay unfolded and hardly dry in a large, study brown envelope at the bottom of my brand new, black leather 'doctor's bag': a badge of office which had given me confidence and pride when I'd bought it but which now seemed, by its very shiny newness to advertise my inexperience and professional innocence.

I'd got the job as Dr Brownlow's assistant after a telephone interview that had lasted somewhere between a minute and a minute and a half. My conversation with his receptionist, who had told me which trains to catch, had lasted only slightly longer.

Then, surrounded by the hospital wards and university laboratories where I'd trained, I'd been full of self assurance. Now, swaying gently from side to side on a train which was steadily lurching its way towards the unknown I felt almost overcome by great, cold draughts of incompetence and ignorance.

As the train took me nearer and nearer to my new job I gradually realised that practising medicine as a senior student in a ward staffed by experienced doctors and briskly efficient, starch fronted nurses was something entirely different to practising medicine out here in the wilderness. The real world was, I began to suspect, something that I might not be quite ready for.

In hospital my patients had mostly lain neatly in rows, dressed in their pyjamas and labelled with diagnoses and recorded symptoms. Advice and help was never more than a few moments away. Out here in the real world my patients were chopping wood, poaching trout, catering for holiday makers, driving trains and herding cattle. I looked around the unfamiliar faces sharing my carriage. Were any of these, I wondered, potential patients of mine? Did they have any idea how much I wanted them to stay well and healthy?

A large, red faced man wearing a brownish tweed jacket, old fashioned gaiters and a pair of heavy brown boots suddenly belched, temporarily interrupting his steady snoring to do so. A young woman wearing a dark blue overcoat and a small, blue felt hat looked across at him, sniffed and tutted, and then looked away. She clasped her gloved hands neatly in her lap and stared out of the window. She was in her late twenties or early thirties but her clothes made her look much older.

A young woman in her early twenties loudly shushed the two boys who were travelling with her. I supposed they were her sons. They seemed to find great humour in the sounds

2

emanating from the fat man's body and had to struggle to contain their amusement. A man in a grey suit buried himself in his morning newspaper. An elderly woman wearing a black dress, black coat, black hat and black shoes glowered around at all of us, as though holding us all responsible for failing to protect her from these social insults, before folding her arms across her chest as though defiantly barricading herself against our world.

The train, slowing down, started to follow a long, gentle curve to the left. Looking out of the window I saw a sign on the platform which told me that we had arrived at the end of the line: Barnstaple. This was it. Grown up reality, responsibility and heaven knows what else lay just a few miles away from here. My mouth felt dry and I could feel a squadron of butterflies becoming airborne in my stomach.

Politely, I waited until the other passengers had left the train and then picked up my black leather 'doctor's bag' and my cheap but capacious blue cardboard suitcase and shuffled along the corridor.

I was clambering down onto the platform when I realised that something had happened a few yards in front of me, half way between the train door and the exit from the platform. As I got closer to the crowd which had formed I realised that the fat man in the tweed suit, gaiters and heavy brown boots was the centre of attraction. He was lying flat on his back on the platform and even from a distance it was clear to a trained medical mind that all was not well.

'Excuse me!' I heard myself saying as I gently squeezed my way through between a tall, thin man in a brown trilby, and the elderly woman dressed all in black. I dropped my suitcase outside the circle but kept a tight hold on my 'doctor's bag'. It contained the instruments of my profession and without it I would have felt as vulnerable and as useless as a gunfighter entering the OK Corral without his pistols. 'I'm a doctor,' I explained diffidently, hoping that this confession would excuse my behaviour but not attract too much attention.

I had spoken quietly but the response was as immediate and as dramatic as if I'd shouted the words at the top of my voice. These magic words – 'I'm a doctor' – would, I was to discover in the fullness of time, part any crowd. The circle widened and I was aware of every eye being trained on me.

Every eye except two that is. The exceptions belonged to the young woman in the blue woollen coat and the blue felt hat who had sat across the aisle from me on the train. She was stooping beside the prostrate fat man in the tweed suit, having unbuttoned her coat to make kneeling easier.

'Give me a hand!' she said, without looking up but moving round so that she was behind the man's head. She nodded towards his feet.

I put down my black bag. 'Is he all right?' I asked, hesitantly. 'Shouldn't we do a few tests before we move him? He might have damaged his spine.'

'He's drunk,' said the woman in the blue coat firmly. As though anxious to confirm her diagnosis the fat man suddenly sat up. He opened his eyes and looked around him, lifted one hand as though he wanted to make a gesture of some kind and then collapsed flat on his back again with a loud burp. I found myself engulfed in a suffocating cloud of stale beer.

The woman in the blue coat sighed wearily as though none of this was new to her. 'Let's get him into a taxi.'

She lifted his head and shoulders and I lifted his feet and together we carried him out to the station forecourt. There were half a dozen taxis queuing there but the woman in the blue coat ignored the first three and headed straight for the fourth in line, a rather battered vehicle of indeterminate make that was heavily pockmarked with rust patches. To my surprise, the drivers who had been overlooked made no protests. The driver of the rust speckled car put down his newspaper, climbed out and opened the back door so that we could push our passenger in.

'Drunk again?' enquired the driver, helping us to manhandle the fat man into the taxi.

'It's the last Wednesday of the month,' answered the woman in blue as though this explained everything.

The taxi driver frowned.

'L.V.A. meeting in Exeter.'

The taxi driver grunted and nodded.

The fat man belched again.

I bent down, picked up one of the fat man's shoes that had come off as we had pushed him into the car and tried to fit it back onto his foot. Mysteriously, the shoe seemed several sizes too small. I dropped the shoe onto the floor beside the unshod foot, backed out of the car and stood up. The woman in the blue coat and the taxi driver were both standing waiting.

'His shoe had come off,' I explained, apologetically.

'If you're coming with us you'd better get your luggage,' said the woman in the blue coat.

I frowned. I didn't understand.

'You're Dr Brownlow's new assistant aren't you?'

I nodded. 'How did you know . . .?'

'There can't be all that many new doctors arriving at Barnstaple station today.' She walked round to the other side of the taxi, opened the front door and got in.

'Do you need a hand with your luggage, doctor?' asked the taxi driver. He handed me a grubby visiting card upon which was printed 'Peter Marshall – Taxi Driver'. Underneath was printed 'Funerals and Weddings a Speciality'. There was a Bilbury telephone number. When I'd had a chance to read the card Mr Marshall reached out and took it off me.

'No, thank you!' I said. 'There's only one case and a bag.' I suddenly remembered that I'd left them both standing in the middle of the platform. I turned away from the taxi and ran back into the station. Both the suitcase and the black bag were standing exactly where I'd dropped them. I picked them up and carried them over to the taxi. Mr Marshall had opened the boot, which was full of old oil cans, dirty pieces of rope, old newspapers and a large quantity of shrink wrapped toilet rolls stacked neatly in two large cardboard boxes.

'Delivery for the Duck!' explained the taxi driver cryptically, pushing the toilet rolls to one side. He had, I noticed for the first time, a very thin moustache on his upper lip. He wore a flat cap that had a greasy mark on the peak where he'd touched it countless times with thumb and forefinger and a badly creased suit that had rather a lot of stains on it. He took my suitcase and carefully laid it down in the centre of the boot. Too late I noticed that much of the boot lining seemed to be soaked with oil. He then placed my black bag on top of the suitcase.

I still felt more than a little uncertain about all this. 'You are going to Bilbury?'

The taxi driver nodded. 'That's where we're going, doctor. Don't you worry about a thing.' He opened the nearside rear door of the taxi for me to get in but the fat man in the tweed suit had collapsed sideways and was now taking up the whole of the rear seat. After trying to push him upright, and failing, Mr Marshall scratched his head and walked to the front of the car. 'Would you mind sharing the front seat with Mrs Wilson?' he asked. He opened the front passenger door and in lieu of a smile showed me his gums. He didn't seem to have any teeth at all. Much later I discovered that he had a set of false teeth but that he only wore them on occasions which he deemed 'special'.

The woman in the blue coat looked first at him and then at me. I stared at him and then at her. Mrs Wilson could politely be described as having a fulsome figure.

'I'm Kay Wilson,' said the woman. She swung her legs sideways, showing an indelicate amount of stocking top and bare white thigh, and clambered out of the taxi again. 'I'll sit on your lap,' she offered. I climbed into the taxi and took her place.

As I have already mentioned Mrs Wilson was not a small woman and her weight was not insubstantial. Fortunately, the springs in the taxi's seat had long since lost all their resilience and our combined weight meant that the seat sank close enough to the floor for Mrs Wilson to get her head into the car. Once inside she fidgeted about as though trying to get comfortable. Even through her thick woollen coat I could feel the bony structure of her firmly structured supporting undergarments. The air around me was thick with her perfume to which I suspected I was probably allergic.

'Mrs Wilson is our district nurse,' explained the taxi driver, turning the ignition key in an attempt to start the taxi's ancient engine. I realised then that the clothes Mrs Wilson was wearing were her official uniform. I extricated my right hand from between the handbrake and the side of the passenger seat upon which we were sitting and offered it to Mrs Wilson, inspired by a sudden sense of professional courtesy. We were in the act of shaking hands when we were both projected forwards as the engine caught and the car, which was in gear, suddenly jerked forwards. The district nurse was crushed against the car's worn vinyl dashboard and I, the more fortunate of the two of us, was crushed against the infinitely more pliant district nurse.

'Maybe we should fasten the seat belt?' I suggested.

Mrs Wilson, her hat now resting at an unlikely angle, moved her head so that she could look at me and raised an eyebrow doubtfully. Behind us I heard the fat man in the tweed suit cursing noisily. Judging from the pressure on the back of my seat he had rolled forwards onto the floor. I felt a sneeze developing and in an attempt to distract myself from such a potentially hazardous incident I wriggled around so that I could reach the dangling seat belt clip with my left hand. I then tried to pass the seat belt clip from my left hand to my right but this wasn't quite so easy. The main consequence of my struggle was that I pulled Mrs Wilson even closer to me than before. Deep out of reach and trapped in my trouser pocket I could feel my Swiss Army penknife pressing into my leg.

'Let me help you doctor,' said Mrs Wilson, taking the seat belt clip from my left hand and putting it into my right for me. She turned towards me when she'd completed this simple manoeuvre and I noticed that her face was looking distinctly flushed. She put her right arm around my shoulders and pulled herself even closer to me so that I could fasten the safety belt.

'Got it!' I announced proudly. This was no mean feat since the taxi was bouncing around like a fairground ride.

Mrs Wilson didn't seem too interested. Her eyes were closed and she was breathing heavily. My Swiss Army penknife was pressing even harder against my thigh and I could feel my leg going numb.

'Are you all right?' I asked the nurse.

Mrs Wilson smiled, nodded and murmured something inaudible. In the back of the car I could hear the fat man in the tweed suit talking to himself.

7

'What's an L.V.A.?' I asked the taxi driver.

Mr Marshall, hunched over his steering wheel as he urged his ancient taxi onwards past a touring caravan being towed by an underpowered motor car, turned towards me looking puzzled.

'I heard Mrs Wilson tell you that your other passenger had been to an L.V.A. meeting in Exeter.'

'Oh!' said the driver. He swung the steering wheel hard to the left and swerved back in front of the car, just in time to avoid crashing head on into a tractor that was coming towards us. 'The L.V.A. is the Licensed Victuallers' Association,' he explained. 'Frank is the landlord of the Duck.'

The Duck?'

'The Duck and Puddle. The pub.'

'Is that the Duck and Puddle in Bilbury?'

'That's the one,' nodded Mr Marshall. 'You'll be staying there, I expect.' He jerked his head backwards. 'That's your new landlord.'

*   *   *

The village of Bilbury lies about ten miles to the east of Barnstaple and about three miles south of the North Devon coast. Bilbury is one of the very few English villages that looks like a traditional village ought to look. The three most important buildings – the pub, the church and the village shop – all look out onto the village green; one and a half acres of lush, green grass that used to be kept closely cropped by the Bilbury goats but which is now cut six times a year by one of the local farmers working on contract for the County Council.

In addition to these three essential and conspicuous centres of public consumption and absolution the village green is overlooked by a couple of dozen cottages, while around its edge stand half a dozen towering oaks, two equally impressive horse chestnut trees and a single ash tree. A small stream meanders along one side of the green; at one end passing under the road in a hidden ditch and at the other flowing across the road to make a ford that in summer often dries to a trickle and sometimes dries completely but in winter has been known to flood to a depth of over eighteen inches.

When Mr Marshall's taxi drew up outside the Duck and Puddle public house I was in no condition to take in any of this. Inhaling concentrated draughts of Mrs Wilson's perfume for half an hour had left me rather light headed and my Swiss Army penknife had by now succeeded in deadening one of my femoral nerves more or less completely.

The taxi driver disappeared in through the front door of the pub, leaving the district nurse and I to disentangle ourselves from the seat belt as best we could. Neither of us had moved more than a couple of inches when Mr Marshall reappeared with a small, slightly built, worried looking woman in her early forties who was dressed in a pale pink jumper and a pair of very tight blue jeans. This, I was to discover, was Gilly Parsons, the landlady of the Duck and Puddle and the wife of the unconscious licensed victualler lying on the floor of the back of the taxi.

Mrs Parsons didn't seem surprised or alarmed to see her husband lying there. She reached in, took hold of a random handful of suit cloth and yanked him out of the car in a single, impressively smooth, movement.

Seemingly inspired by this Mrs Wilson made a supreme effort and, by swinging open the car door and grasping hold of the top edge with one hand, succeeded in pulling her head and shoulders out of the car completely. Unfortunately, although her coat and dress made every effort to follow her body and legs seemed unwilling to leave the taxi. I found myself flushing with embarrassment as I stared down at a mysterious and confusing vision of lingerie, buckles, silk stockings and white flesh.

By this time half a dozen villagers had left the pub and, all clutching pint or half pint glasses, were standing around watching. The tweed suited landlord of the Duck and Puddle had made a sudden and surprising recovery and was now standing looking doleful as his wife, hands planted firmly on her hips, told him what she thought of him. Three small and scruffy boys who had been throwing sticks up into a horsechestnut tree in vain attempts to dislodge early conkers abandoned their exhausting endeavours and joined the enthusiastic audience.

Eventually, the taxi driver came over and freed Mrs Wilson

9

from his motor car by the simple expedient of taking hold of her shoulders and pulling hard. She shot out of the car like a cork out of a champagne bottle and the two of them landed on the dusty road in front of the pub.

'You must be the doctor,' said Mrs Parsons, the landlady, turning away from her husband, ignoring the sprawling Mr Marshall and Mrs Wilson and approaching as I clambered out of the car.

'Yes!' I confirmed, standing up and then falling down onto the road alongside the taxi driver and the district nurse in one fluid and seemingly well practised movement. My Swiss Army penknife had succeeded in arresting the nerve supply to my right leg so successfully that it had been blissfully unaware of its duties when I had tried to stand on it. My arrival in Bilbury had not been quite as dignified as I might have hoped.

*   *   *

My room at the Duck and Puddle overlooked the village green. Mrs Parsons, who seemed disappointed to discover that her new guest was as prone to falling over as her husband and the rest of her customers, performed the usual rituals without enthusiasm. She opened the window and then shut it again. She opened the wardrobe, rattled the row of wire hangers which hung on a single, wooden rail, and then shut it again. She pointed to the sink and told me what it was, showed me how the taps worked and pressed a hand on the bed to demonstrate its pliability.

She then pointed out the bedside lamp, the tiny child's desk and chair that stood beside the window, opened and shut the drawers of the dressing table and pulled the cord which dangled over the bed to turn on the main light. As she left the room she used the light switch just by the door to turn the light off again. She paused just before she left. 'Dr Brownlow asked if you would be kind enough to call on him as soon as you have settled in,' she announced rather formally. Having passed this message on she looked around, as though taking a last minute inventory, turned away and closed the door behind her.

I shook the worst of the dust off my jacket, brushed my trousers with my hand and shared the contents of my blue suitcase between the wardrobe and the dressing table. Then I placed my brand new 'doctor's bag' on the desk by the window and limped back down the stairs again. My leg still wasn't completely recovered.

The pub had either been built in some long distant era when customers were a good deal shorter that I am or when watching customers crack their skulls against solid wooden beams was considered good sport.

Whatever the explanation I counted six possible danger points between my bedroom and the pub's front door. At two of these sites the landlord had attempted to minimise the extent of possible damage by tacking an old piece of carpet across the beams. The gesture might have been more effective had the carpet not been threadbare. On my first descent I succeeded in banging my head on every possible impediment.

'Excuse me!' I said to Mrs Parsons, now standing behind the bar and pulling a pint of locally brewed beer for an eager customer. 'Could you tell me how to find Dr Brownlow's?' Mr Parsons, the landlord, was standing at the far end of the bar and although erect he did not yet look entirely conscious.

'Turn right out of the front door,' Mrs Parsons answered, without lifting her eyes from her work. 'And then follow the road around the village green. Take the first lane on the right. It's signposted to Combe Martin. You'll see the gates and the drive leading to Dr Brownlow's house a hundred yards on your right.'

Murmuring my thanks I followed her directions faithfully and less than ten minutes later found myself staring at the largest pair of iron gates I'd ever seen. The gates, which were painted black and which stood wide open were suspended from hinges built into two huge stone pillars upon each of which rested massive stone griffins. On either side of the pillars a nine foot high stone wall separated the road from the grounds within.

I studied the gates and the pillars looking for a name, an inscription or some sign that this was what I was looking for. But I could find nothing. I stood still for a moment and stared up the driveway. Flanked by seventy foot tall poplars the drive looked to be several miles long. I could see no sign of any house. I didn't know much about country doctors but this all looked a little grand to me. Maybe, I thought, Dr Brownlow lived in part of the house. Or maybe he had a cottage in the grounds. Whatever the explanation I was pretty sure that I was at the right place unless Mrs Parsons had deliberately sent me off on a wild goose chase. I was comforted by the thought that she didn't look like a woman who enjoyed sending strangers chasing off after wild geese.

After walking for what seemed like a modest eternity I finally saw the house. It looked like something out of a horror film; the sort of place that Dracula or Dr Frankenstein might have found 'homely'. Built entirely of grey stone softened slightly by several acres of dark green ivy it wasn't so much a house as a castle. There was no moat but there were towers, battlements and mullion windows. Apart from the ivy the only colour breaking up the grey of the stone was provided by a Union Jack flag flying from a pole which was fixed at an acute angle to the front of the central tower. Directly underneath the flag, and flanked by two huge stone lions, was the front door. It was about twelve feet high, and was decorated with scores of very solid looking metal studs. Incongruously, a large ginger tom cat lay curled up beside one of the stone lions.

I couldn't see anything that looked like a doorbell so I knocked on the door with my knuckles. The door, which from the sound my knuckles made seemed about three feet thick, soaked up the sound I made with ease. Certain that my knocking had been a waste of time and effort I raised my fist to give the door a more appropriate hammering. But before I could land my first blow the door surprised me by opening.

The man who opened the door wore a black frock coat, black trousers, a white shirt and a black bow tie. He was tiny, wizened and looked at least eighty years old. Pulling the door open seemed to take up an awful lot of his remaining energy.

'I'm looking for Dr Brownlow,' I said hesitantly. 'Can you tell me where to find him, please?'

'This is Dr Brownlow's residence,' wheezed the old man, producing a silver card tray from behind his back. He held the tray out to me. 'Do you have a card, sir?'

I stared at the tray and then at him. I didn't have any visiting cards. I'd never been to a house where people asked you for visiting cards. I didn't think there were still any such homes in existence. The only people I knew who had visiting cards were salesmen for pharmaceutical products and life insurance policies.

'I'm afraid not,' I mumbled. I tried to look past the old man but it was impossible to see anything behind him except darkness. I told him my name and explained that Dr Brownlow was expecting me. The old man looked me up and down very carefully. 'I'll speak to Dr Brownlow,' he said. Then he shut the door.

Shortly after I'd decided that he wasn't coming back but just before I left the door opened again. 'Dr Brownlow will see you now, sir,' said the old man. He pulled the door wide open so that I could enter and then, the moment I was safely inside, closed it shut behind me. With the door shut it was so dark that I could hardly see anything and so cold that I shivered involuntarily.

The skinny old man turned left and shuffled along a corridor that looked long enough to park a train in. Since he walked slowly I had plenty of time to look around me. The corridor was about ten feet wide with a thin strip of threadbare red carpet running along its centre. On each side of the strip of carpet I could see the bare stone flags that made up the floor of the corridor. The walls of the corridor were decorated with huge old oil paintings, hung in battered but massive gilt frames.

We walked until I felt sure that we must be close to the county's border and then the skinny old man stopped, knocked on a huge oak door and put his ear to the panelling before opening the door and ushering me into an extraordinarily small room. The most remarkable thing about this room was that it was higher than it was wide or long. It was, I suppose, no more than twelve or fifteen feet square but the gap between the floor and the ceiling seemed to be at least twenty feet.

Sitting at a huge, scrubbed pine kitchen table in the centre of the room was a bald, plump man in his late sixties or early seventies who looked over his half moon spectacles as I entered and beamed broadly. Apart from a window set high in one wall the room was lined with shelves upon which stood rows of books and dusty, bound copies of old medical and scientific journals. Behind the seated occupant of the room stood an examination couch which was piled high with yet more books. Tufts of horse hair showed that the contents of the couch were making a determined effort to escape.

The room's occupant waved a hand in greeting. 'I'm Dr Brownlow. Thank you for coming.' He looked over my shoulder at the elderly manservant who was still hovering behind me. 'Thank you, Bradshaw,' he said. Then he looked at me. 'Would you like a cup of tea?'

'No, thank you!' I said. 'I'm fine.'

'Wise fellow,' whispered Dr Brownlow confidentially. 'Bradshaw has never got the knack of making tea and Ethel's out somewhere today.' He peered around me and raised his voice again. 'That's all, thank you, Bradshaw.'

I heard the door behind me click shut as Bradshaw left and realised that thirty square feet of solid oak makes a very different noise to the average modern door.

I looked around. 'Is this your study?'

'It's my consulting room,' answered Dr Brownlow. 'It used to be the gun room but it's one of the few rooms in the house that is small enough to keep reasonably warm in the winter.' He pointed the pen he was holding back over his shoulder towards two large electric fires which stood side by side behind him. Even though it was still only early autumn both fires were switched on. 'Sit yourself down,' he said, nodding to the empty chair in front of his table.

I sat down and suddenly had a bizarre vision of a long line of infirm patients struggling along the corridor down which I'd just walked.

'Patients come to the back door,' explained Dr Brownlow, as though reading my thoughts. 'It's a bit quicker.' He sighed. 'Hardly anyone comes to the front door any more. When they do Bradshaw always likes to give them the silver tray treatment'.

I nodded. 'I'm afraid I don't have any visiting cards.'

'No one ever has,' said Dr Brownlow. 'At least no one

14

I ever want to see. The last man who put a visiting card on that tray was a double glazing salesman from Bristol. He was so excited by the prospect of double glazing this place that it took me half a day to get rid of him.'

'It's a spectacular house,' I said.

'I like it,' said Dr Brownlow simply.

I could feel a little cramp developing in my left leg again so I stretched my leg out in front of me underneath the table. As I did so I felt my toes hit something soft. I heard a growl and pulled my leg back quickly and instinctively. I looked down but could see nothing.

'Don't worry!' said Dr Brownlow, comfortingly. 'It's only Max.'

'Max?'

'One of my dogs,' explained Dr Brownlow. 'He gets nervous eczema if he's away from me for too long.'

'What sort is he?' I asked, brightly. I get anxious in the company of dogs but I didn't think I should be worried about a dog which suffered from nervous eczema.

'A Dobermann,' answered Dr Brownlow. 'I've got two. They're lovely dogs'.

I felt myself going pale and my terror must have shown.

'They wouldn't harm a fly,' Dr Brownlow assured me. 'Are you settled in at the Duck and Puddle?'

'Yes. It seems very nice. Thank you.'

'Good. Ready to start work tomorrow?'

I swallowed hard. 'Yes.' I lied. I was beginning to have severe doubts about the whole thing. I tried to think of an excuse for running away but couldn't.

'I'd liked to have been here with you on your first morning,' said Dr Brownlow. 'But I've got to go to Exeter tomorrow.'

'What time does morning surgery start?' I asked with a voice I only half recognised.

'Nine. Then there will just be a few home visits afterwards. And the evening surgery is at five thirty. Simple. Miss Johnson will show you the ropes.'

'That's your secretary?'

'Secretary, receptionist, nurse – she does it all. Been with me for years. Knows everyone. Just ask her if you get any problems. She'll sort you out.' Dr Brownlow suddenly stood

15

up. He was shorter than I expected he'd be. 'I thought perhaps you wouldn't mind doing most of the night duties,' he said. 'I'm getting a bit past it now to be honest.' He started to move around the desk. 'Bit of a dicky ticker you know.'

I started to say something sympathetic but Dr Brownlow waved the comment away with a shake of his hand. He moved towards the door. 'Where did you park?'

'Park?'

'Your car.'

'I haven't got one,' I admitted.

Dr Brownlow seemed startled. 'Haven't got a car? You'll need one for tomorrow. Can't be a GP without a car.' He looked at his watch. 'I've got to go to Ilfracombe. I'll drop you off at the Duck.' He smiled at me. 'I'll do the night duty tonight and then you can take over from tomorrow.'

I nodded weakly.

He opened the consulting room door and turned right, going in the opposite direction to the way Bradshaw had brought me. 'That's Miss Johnson's office,' he said, pointing to a door split horizontally in two. 'It used to be the boot room.' He nodded towards another room, painted white and decorated with colourful health education posters. 'The patients sit in there.' A mixture of wooden chairs were arranged in a circle around the walls. 'Used to be the flower room.'

'Flower room?'

'All big houses have them. Somewhere for the gardener to lay out flowers for the house.'

'Yes. Of course.'

'It works quite well,' said Dr Brownlow. 'We've managed to make a self contained surgery suite down here.' He looked around, obviously proud of it all.

A moment or two later we were outside the back of the house. Dr Brownlow strode across towards a large coach house that had its own clock tower. He pulled open two huge wooden doors to reveal an elderly, black Rolls Royce.

'I bought it thirty years ago,' he said. 'It's a 20/25. The most reliable car ever built. I climbed in beside him and he drove me back to the Duck and Puddle. It was the first time I'd ever ridden in a Rolls Royce and, despite the car's age, I was astonished at its luxury and quiet, smooth power.

It seemed to me that general practice was going to be full of surprises.

*   *   *

I had a hundred things on my mind but my first task was to get hold of a motor car.

I'd passed my driving test when I was seventeen but had never owned a car of my own. I'd never had enough money and there had never been much need. When you're living, studying and working in a teaching hospital a car isn't exactly essential. I had £45 saved up in my bank account but Dr Brownlow's advertisement had promised to pay me £60 a week on top of my board and lodging at the Duck and Puddle so, for the first time in my life, I felt as rich as a king.

The problem was not so much finding the money to pay for a car but finding a car to buy. Innocently I thought that since £45 was a lot of money to me it would be a lot of money to a car dealer. Everything was made infinitely more difficult by the fact that I hadn't seen a garage since I'd arrived in North Devon.

Mrs Parsons had my evening meal ready when Dr Brownlow dropped me off and she seemed to have forgiven my rather bizarre arrival. Her husband, Frank, seemed to have made a miraculous recovery and was standing laughing and joking in the public bar.

'We usually serve our residents' meals in here,' said Mrs Parsons, showing me into the pub's small and totally deserted lounge bar. The main difference I could spot between the two bars was that in the lounge bar the red leather chairs and benches were a little less battered and scuffed and the ash trays smaller though there was no dartboard, no bar billiards table and no fire in the hearth. Later, I discovered that the beer was a penny a pint more expensive in the lounge bar.

I can still remember my first meal at the Duck and Puddle. Someone, probably Mrs Parsons herself, had written out the menu in neat handwriting on a piece of white cardboard and had lent it up against the cruet.

There was no choice. I had minestrone soup, followed by home made steak and kidney pie and chips and peas and I finished with a large bowlful of strawberry ice cream with a blob of Devon clotted cream balanced on top of it. Every mouthful was excellent; simple but nourishing pub fare. After the food I'd been used to eating in hospital I thought I'd died and gone to heaven.

When I'd finished I took the remains of my pint of beer ('You get one pint of beer with every meal except breakfast,' Mrs Parsons had told me. 'Anything more you'll have to pay for yourself.') into the public bar.

'Just passing through the village?' asked Frank Parsons, the landlord, when I asked him to refill my glass.

'I'm staying here,' I reminded him.

He looked at me, a frown on his face.

'I arrived this afternoon,' I explained. 'We came together from the station.'

'Oh, you're the doctor!' said the landlord, a broad grin developing on his face. 'I'm sorry about that!' he apologised, putting my refilled glass back down in front of me. He leant forward a few inches. 'I never remember anything much that happens when I go down to an L.V.A. meeting,' he confided. 'All a bit of a blur you know.'

I wasn't surprised but didn't say so.

'Though from what I heard you must have had a few jars before you got here, eh?'

It was my turn to frown and look puzzled.

'The wife told me,' he said, 'Arse over cap before you got in through the door!'

'Oh that! I had cramp in my leg. It was my Swiss Army penknife.'

The landlord exploded in laughter. 'That's a good one!' he exclaimed cheerily. 'Must remember that one. Cramp in the leg, eh? Swiss Army penknife?' He leant forwards again and touched the side of his nose with his forefinger. 'Don't you worry, doctor!' he assured me. 'The wife's the very soul of discretion and you can trust me.'

I handed him a pound note to pay for the drink. I had no small change in my pockets. The landlord pushed the note back across the counter towards me. 'I'll put it on the slate for you,' he said. 'You don't want to be worrying with money every time you want a drink.' He leant forwards across the bar counter again. 'And you don't need to worry even if word does get out that you like a drop,' he said. 'There's no one round here who's likely to take offence. Saving perhaps the vicar.'

'Do you know where I could find Mr Marshall?' I asked him, taking a sip from my glass. It was good beer.

'Mr Marshall?' repeated Mr Parsons, thoughtfully. He pursed his lips, screwed up his eyes and then shook his head. 'I don't think I know anyone called Mr Marshall,' he said sadly.

'The taxi driver,' I explained. 'Mr Marshall the taxi driver. I think he lives in the village.' I paused. 'He brought us all over from Barnstaple.'

'Oh, Pete!' said the landlord, grinning. 'I didn't know you meant Pete!'

'Does he come into the bar?' I asked.

'He does and he doesn't,' said the landlord enigmatically. 'But usually he does.'

'Do you know if he's likely to be in tonight?'

'I couldn't say precisely,' said Mr Parsons. 'Do you want a taxi then?'

'No!' I shook my head. 'But there are a couple of things I need to see him about. First, I never paid him for this afternoon's journey. And second I wanted to ask him if he knows anywhere around here where I could buy a car.'

'Oh, don't you worry about Pete's bill!' Mr Parsons reassured me. 'He'll run up a tab for you. No problem. You don't want to be finding cash every time you want to go somewhere do you?'

I suppose I ought to have been worried by all these tabs I was running up but to be honest I found it all rather pleasant. It made me feel part of the village.

'Excuse me,' said a voice I hadn't heard before. I turned towards it and saw a tall, well built man in his twenties. 'I couldn't help overhearing you say that you want to buy a car.' The speaker was wearing a scruffy, brown leather jacket, a pair of well worn, oil stained jeans and a faded tee shirt that managed to look grubby even though it was black. He

19

had an unruly mop of curly, jet black collar length hair that he was beginning to lose.

'That's right,' I nodded.

'What sort of car are you looking for?'

'I don't know,' I confessed. 'Something second hand. Fairly cheap I'm afraid. But I need it urgently. Are you a dealer?'

'Me? A dealer?' He laughed. 'I wouldn't trust a car dealer as far as I could kick one.'

'No,' I said, 'I suppose not.'

'How much can you afford to spend?'

'No more than £45,' I told him. 'That's all the money I've got.'

The man in the leather jacket sucked in air between his teeth. The sum didn't seem to impress him. He picked up his glass, which was empty, and stared into it as though reproaching it for being empty.

'Can I buy you a drink?' I asked, responding readily to the cue.

'That's very kind of you,' said the man in the leather jacket, seemingly surprised by my generosity. 'Very kind of you indeed. Be rude to refuse. I'll have a pint of special if that's all right with you.'

I turned towards the landlord who had been chatting to an elderly man who wore a grey mackintosh and a brown homburg and who was drinking half a pint of stout but he'd started to pull the pint of special before I had chance to pass on the order.

'My name's Robinson,' said the man in the leather jacket, holding out a hand. 'But people call me Thumper.'

I shook his hand and introduced myself.

'You're the new doctor?'

I nodded.

'Pleased to meet you!' said Thumper, taking my hand again and pumping it up and down.

I rescued my hand and massaged it gently in an attempt to get some blood flowing through the tissues again.

'You need something with a bit of class,' said Thumper. 'It wouldn't do for the new doctor to be driving round in any old wreck.'

'I don't think it matters too much what it looks like,' I

20

said. 'The important thing is that it's reliable'.

'Reliable isn't enough!' said Thumper. 'Drink up. I know just the thing for you.' He picked up his glass, lifted it to his lips and slowly but steadily drank it dry. When it was empty he put it down on the bar, wiped the froth off his lips and walked towards the front door.

In an ancient Ford pick up truck that had what looked like metal farm gates welded to the back and front, Thumper drove me to a farm in the nearby village of Parracombe. The truck shook like a fairground ride and sounded as though it had several terminal problems.

'Wait here a moment!' he told me, skidding to a halt in a muddy forecourt and sending chickens, cats and dogs flying and scurrying in all directions. He leapt out of the cab and disappeared into the farmhouse.

When he emerged a few minutes later he had a huge and rather bad tempered looking man with him. Thumper smiled and waved for me to join them. I opened the cab door and jumped down into a deep mixture of mud and manure.

'Come and look at this,' said Thumper, letting the farmer go ahead and whispering to me conspiratorially. 'You'll love it and I can get you a terrific deal on it!' We followed the farmer into a large barn where two old tractors and a car were stored. The car was large and it had undoubtedly once looked very elegant. The bodywork had originally been painted pale blue but the chickens had redecorated it in their own unique and original style.

'Does it go?' I asked. I tried to sound optimistic but my doubt must have shone through.

'Does it go?' repeated Thumper. 'Its a classic! A masterpiece of engineering. These will be collectors' items in a few years time'.

'What sort is it?' I asked, peering at the inside of the car through windows that were grey with dirt.

'What sort is it?' Thumper asked the farmer.

The farmer shrugged.

Thumper climbed over two bales of straw and a few oil drums so that he could look at the back of the car. He reached out and rubbed at the car's name plate. 'It's a Humber,' he announced. 'Very smart.'

'Are there any keys?' I asked Thumper. 'Can we see inside?'

'Any keys?' Thumper asked the farmer.

The farmer looked confused.

'Keys?' repeated Thumper. 'To open the doors with.'

The farmer still looked puzzled. Thumper tried the driver's door. The catch was a little stiff but the door opened fairly easily.

'I think he must have mislaid the keys,' said Thumper. He bent down, fiddled about somewhere close to the pedals and produced two pieces of wire. 'Let's try it, shall we?' He twisted the two wires together but nothing happened. 'Battery might be flat,' he admitted. 'I'll bring my truck across. You get into the driving seat.'

Five minutes later the Humber coughed reluctantly into life, courtesy of two connecting leads and the battery in Thumper's truck.

'There you are!' shouted Thumper, above the clatter of the engine. 'Told you! No problem! When you want to stop it just pull those two wires apart. When you want to start it again just re-connect them'.

The farmer stared in surprise as the old Humber rattled and shuddered. I sat inside it, shaking and shuddering with it, and looked around. The inside of the car must have been very smart when it was new. The seats were real leather and the dashboard contained an impressive looking array of dials.

'Radio too, eh?' said Thumper, peering in through the door which I'd left open. He leant a little closer. 'I think I can get it for £75,' he whispered.

I looked at him in horror. 'I've only got £45!' I reminded him.

Thumper waved a hand. 'Don't worry about it,' he said reassuringly. 'I'll sort it out and you can owe me the cash.'

'But . . .' I began.

'No problem,' Thumper insisted. 'You can pay me next week.'

He unfastened the 'jump' leads from the Humber's battery, slammed the bonnet lid down and walked over to the farmer and gave him something. I didn't see what it was. The farmer looked disappointed but Thumper shrugged his shoulders and jerked his thumb in my direction.

I drove the Humber back to Bilbury behind Thumper's old Ford truck. It never even occurred to me that I needed road tax or insurance and if I'd thought to look at the state of the tyres I would have probably insisted on walking instead.

*   *   *

CHAPTER TWO

I was awake at seven the following morning. I got up, flung the curtains aside and gazed with undiminished delight at the sight of the Bilbury village green. On the far side of the green I could see Mr Marshall, in his capacity as village shopkeeper, laying out the fruit and vegetables in front of his shop. I discovered later that he rose at four every weekday morning to drive into Barnstaple to fetch fresh produce and to collect the mail for the village. While his wife sorted out the post, ready for him to deliver, he laid out the apples, oranges, bananas, carrots, onions, potatoes, cabbages, cauliflowers and sprouts in wooden trays outside the shop.

My room had its own private bathroom (it was the only bedroom in the pub to be so well served) and so while I shaved I ran myself a piping hot bath. This was a wonderful luxury to which I was totally unaccustomed. At the hospital where I'd worked most recently I had had to share a bathroom with half a dozen others.

Scrubbed and shining I dressed carefully in my best grey flannel trousers and a woollen shirt with a fine red cross check pattern. My only jacket, a Harris Tweed sports coat had a large ink stain on the lining but as long as I kept it buttoned up no one would ever notice.

'Would you like a full breakfast?' asked Mrs Parsons when I stepped rather hesitantly into the lounge bar. There was a strong smell of beer and tobacco everywhere. It seemed strange to be in a pub so early in the morning.

I must have looked confused for Mrs Parsons spelt out exactly what she meant. 'Porridge or cornflakes; bacon, egg, sausage, tomatoes and fried bread; toast and marmalade;

24

coffee or tea.'

I was impressed. I'd never had a *proper* English breakfast before. For six years, while I'd been studying as a medical student and then working as a junior hospital doctor, my breakfast had consisted of little more that a cup of warm coffee – usually made by putting a spoonful of instant coffee powder into a chipped mug and then adding hot water from the tap.

Mrs Parsons mistook the silence for dissatisfaction rather than joyful anticipation. 'I can always do you a couple of boiled eggs or scrambled eggs on toast if you'd rather.'

'No! No!' I said quickly. 'The full breakfast sounds terrific.'

'Porridge or cornflakes?'

I chose porridge.

'Coffee?'

'Yes, please. Black.' I'd never taken milk or sugar in my coffee since neither had ever been available when I'd been a student.

'I like to see a man have a good appetite,' said Mrs Parsons, looking satisfied with herself before she scurried back into the kitchen. She brought the porridge out to me within minutes. While I ate it tantalising smells wafted out from the kitchen and overcame the smells of stale beer and cigarette smoke left over from the night before. Soon, bacon and coffee were the only smells I could detect while the only sound I could hear was the glorious sizzle of bacon cooking in its own fat.

'Did you enjoy that?' asked Mrs Parsons, half an hour later as she refilled my coffee cup for the third time.

I picked up the linen napkin from my lap, wiped toast crumbs away from around my mouth, smiled and nodded at her. 'It was lovely, thank you.'

'Good!' said Mrs Parsons, who looked genuinely pleased. She nodded towards the clock on the far side of the room. 'I don't want to rush you,' she said. 'But what time is Dr Brownlow expecting you?' You don't want to be late on your first morning, do you?'

I turned and looked at the clock. It was five minutes to nine. The morning surgery was due to start in five minutes time.

While I'd been concentrating on breakfast the weather had changed completely. This was, I eventually realised, typical of North Devon. One minute the sun would be shining and the sky would be blue and cloudless. Then, within minutes and with no apparent warning, the sky would turn black and it would be pouring with rain. I rushed upstairs, brushed my teeth and collected my black bag and my raincoat. I was half way down the stairs again before I remembered that I now owned a motor car.

The Humber was still where I'd left it, parked directly in front of the pub. I climbed in, put my black 'doctor's bag' on the front passenger seat and joined together the two wires that Thumper had arranged for me. It never even occurred to me that the old car wouldn't start and the car, whose battery had clearly been given a new, albeit temporary, lease of life by the previous evening's journey, justified my faith in it by bursting into life with just one touch of the wires.

Cautiously, I selected reverse gear and backed out onto the roadway. Once I was facing the direction in which I wanted to travel I realised that the windscreen needed wiping.

After turning on the headlights, the direction indicators and the cigar lighter I eventually found the switch which operated the windscreen wipers.

Unfortunately, the operation was only partly successful.

The windscreen wipers moved up from their recumbent position and swept the windscreen once but that was it. That was the successful part. At the end of their arc, when they should have returned to base, the wipers chose to make a break for freedom. One after the other they simply flew off to the right leaving tiny metal stalks to make the pointless return journey.

I toyed with the idea of stopping to look for them but I was late, the windscreen wipers had disappeared into a thick hedge and it was raining heavily. I decided to struggle on without them.

I suppose there must have been a time when motor cars didn't have windscreen wipers. But I can't imagine how drivers managed. Maybe the man who carried the red flag in front of all horseless carriages also carried a brush with which to wipe the windscreen clean from afar. Or maybe our motoring predecessors simply stopped and stayed wherever they were when it rained. Whatever the truth of the matter I got to Dr Brownlow's surgery in one piece only by opening the window, sticking my head out and navigating through almost closed eyes.

By the time I'd found my way round to the back of the house it was twenty past nine. I parked the Humber, picked up my black bag and rushed in through the back door to present myself at the receptionist's window.

'Sorry I'm late!' I said, breathlessly, poking my head into Miss Johnson's office.

The woman sitting at the desk in there was about fifty five, tall, slim and white haired. She wore a pink tailored suit over a white blouse with a high neck. A single row of pearls hung over the top of her blouse. She had a pair of gold rimmed spectacles perched on the end of her nose and a thin gold chain hung from each arm of the spectacles and was draped around the back of her neck.

Miss Johnson looked at a small, wooden, framed clock on her desk, looked at me and then looked back at the clock. I still can't describe the look, though I got to know it well. It wasn't rude or even overtly critical. It was tinged with sadness, disapproval, disappointment and despair. But there was a strong element of contempt in there too.

I introduced myself. 'I'm Dr Brownlow's new assistant.' Water dripped off my head and I could feel my shirt sticking to my back but that was sweat rather than rain.

With a sigh Miss Johnson put down the thin, gold propelling pencil she was writing with. Gracefully, she stood up and walked across to a cupboard on the far side of the room. She took out a freshly laundered and neatly folded white towel and brought it across to where I was standing.

'I think perhaps you'd better dry your hair before you start your surgery,' she said.

Only after I'd dried and combed my hair would Miss Johnson show me into Dr Brownlow's surgery.

'Are there many patients waiting?' I asked her, opening my black bag, taking out my stethoscope and draping it around my neck.

Miss Johnson looked horrified. I suspected that Dr Brownlow, like most older doctors, used to let his stethoscope hang around his neck by the ear pieces, with the tubing dangling down the centre of his chest. 'One or two,' she replied, refusing to commit herself. 'I suspect they want to have a look at you.'

'Is there an appointments system?' I asked her.

Miss Johnson looked puzzled.

'Are patients given fixed times when they'll be seen?'

'I should think not!' said Miss Johnson rather stiffly. 'They come and they wait and the doctor sees them when he's ready.' She turned her wrist and looked at her watch. 'Its a good job there isn't an appointments system isn't it?'

When she'd gone I opened the top drawer of the desk. It contained a bottle of blue-black ink, three golf balls, a box of paper tissues, a corkscrew, half a dozen drug company sponsored scrap pads and an old stethoscope with a very long piece of red rubber tubing separating the chest piece from the ear pieces. The rubber tubing had been repaired with two bicycle inner tube patches.

I felt very nervous and uncertain. In hospital all the patients lie in neat rows; sterilised, bandaged, wrapped and labelled. Every doubt or uncertainty can be tackled with the aid of expert, specialist advice. The community within the hospital is a closed one, governed by written and unwritten rules. Each professional is a member of the ruling team. Doctors wear white coats, nurses wear uniforms and patients wear pyjamas. Doctors stand upright and patients lie down flat on their backs. The rules are simple. Doctors do the doing and patients are there to be done unto.

I didn't know what rules governed life in general practice but I strongly suspected that there were none. I knew my patients wouldn't come in labelled. They wouldn't arrive at the surgery dressed in their pyjamas. They wouldn't lie down meekly and placidly, speaking only when spoken to. They might, I suddenly realised, have the temerity to ask me questions! What would I do if I didn't know the answers? What if they complained of strange symptoms which I didn't understand?

On a hospital ward a doctor knows what his patients are suffering from. He knows what needs to be done. Most of his patients come ready sorted by general practitioners. Now I was a general practitioner. I was going to have to do the sorting. All I knew was that the people I would see would be unhappy about their health.

I settled myself back in Dr Brownlow's swivel chair, an ancient and wonderful piece of furniture which was suffering from a noisy form of arthritis and which squeaked steadily whichever way I moved. I had not been in a doctor's surgery since I'd damaged my knee some fifteen years earlier. It felt strange to be sitting on the other side of the desk with only a few short years in medical school behind me and a pine desk in front of me.

Suddenly, I realised that I'd been sitting waiting for several minutes. Wondering where the first patient had got to I thought I'd better go and find out.

'I haven't seen any patients yet!' I said to Miss Johnson. She was sitting at her desk again.

'Have you pressed your buzzer?'

'What buzzer?'

She explained that I would find a buzzer underneath the desk. She spoke in a tired voice, as though explaining something to someone very dim. She told me its whereabouts in a 'where else would you expect to find it' voice. 'When you press it a light comes on in the waiting room and the patients hear a sound. When they see the light and hear the sound they know that you are ready for them.'

'How do they know who's next?' I asked her.

Miss Johnson looked at me as though alarmed. 'They just know,' she said, her patience clearly wearing thin. 'Everyone knows when it's their turn.'

I nodded. I could feel beads of sweat breaking out on my face. 'Perhaps I'd better just start.'

'That would be a good idea,' agreed Miss Johnson. 'I did tell them that you had been delayed by an emergency on your way to the surgery this morning but I've no doubt that they heard you come in.'

'Right!' I said firmly. 'Thank you. Thank you very much.' I turned away. 'Oh, where are the instruments kept?' I asked before I left.

'The instruments?' said Miss Johnson. She gave me another

29

one of her looks. This one would have been appropriate if I'd made an indecent proposal. 'What instruments?'

I shrugged. 'Auriscope. Ophthalmoscope. Electrocardiogram. Patella hammer. Tuning fork. That sort of thing.'

'Dr Brownlow's stethoscope is in his drawer,' said Miss JohnⳐn. 'I don't think he needs any other instruments.' Her manner made it pretty clear that she felt that instruments were the refuge of less than adequate doctors. 'Anyway,' she said, nodding towards my own shiny new stethoscope, 'you seem to have brought your own instrument with you.'

I went back to the surgery, sat down, felt under the desk, found the buzzer and pressed it. I felt about as well prepared for the job I was supposed to be doing as I would have felt for a job driving a train or flying an aeroplane. I had spent several years studying the history and epidemiology of leprosy, schistosomiasis and a whole host of rare blood clotting disorders. I knew how to identify fat cells under a microscope and I'd spent long hours in the operating theatre pulling on retractors, snipping stitches and watching as surgeons pulled out gall bladders or amputated rotting limbs. I pressed the buzzer and changed my life.

These days I understand that young doctors going into general practice are trained for the work they are destined to do. It was not always thus. I realised with a sudden, cold wave of horror that I was a fraud. In hospital I'd felt secure in the knowledge that even when I didn't know something I could get help quickly. It had all been more of an intellectual game than anything else. When I got a diagnosis right I got points. Here it was all for real. Life or death.

Sitting there, in Dr Brownlow's chair in Dr Brownlow's surgery, I felt terrified, alone and totally incompetent. I was a qualified doctor but I had no idea what to do. I was legally entitled to ask these trusting souls to take their clothes off and subject themselves to the most intimate of examinations but I no longer had any confidence that I would know what to do if I spotted a symptom.

Pressing that button was the most courageous thing I'd ever done.

As the door opened the black bakelite telephone on Dr Brownlow's desk began to ring. I picked it up with my left hand.

'You can take your finger off the buzzer now,' said Miss Johnson, reverting to her 'talking to the idiot' tone. 'Unless you want them all to come in at once.'

'Thank you, Miss Johnson,' I said, taking my right forefinger off the buzzer and replacing the telephone on its cradle. I looked up at the figure who'd entered the surgery and who was now standing just inside the still half open door.

'Please sit down,' I said, standing up myself and at the same time pointing to the chair on the other side of the desk.

My first patient sat down.

He looked about forty years old, wore a smart though rather old fashioned blue suit and a green and blue patterned tie that looked as if it had been a Christmas present from a female relative. He carried a tweed cap which he circled endlessly between his fingers. His hair was covered in cream to make it lie down neatly and a small piece of sticking plaster just in front of his left ear showed that he'd used a fresh blade in his razor that morning. He carried with him a small beige envelope. This, I realised, was his medical records envelope.

We stared at one another for a few moments. I wasn't sure what I was supposed to say. 'How can I help you?' sounded a bit too much like a shop assistant.

'What's wrong with you?' I asked him at last.

'The back!' replied my patient, economically. He reached around his chair and supplemented this supply of verbal information by rubbing what he could reach of his spine.

'Oh, dear!' I said. 'I'm sorry to hear that. Is it bad?'

The man nodded.

'How long have you had it?' I looked at the front of his medical record envelope and found his name. 'Mr Porter?'

There was a long, long pause. This was obviously not such an easy question.

'Quite some time, doctor,' said Mr Porter eventually.

It was my turn to nod while I desperately tried to think of something else that I could ask him. In hospital it was much easier. There were always other people around to ask questions if you ran out of things to say.

'I thought perhaps I ought to have a few days on the box.'

'On the box?'

'The sick.'

I still didn't understand.

'A week perhaps?' suggested Mr Porter.

Suddenly I realised what he wanted. 'You'd like some time off work?'

Mr Porter grinned and nodded. His false teeth parted from his gums as he smiled giving him a strange, rather frightening look.

'What is your job, Mr Porter?'

'Gardener.'

'And whereabouts is the pain worst?' I asked.

Mr Porter, who looked puzzled, reached behind him and rubbed at the bottom of his back again. 'And down me legs.'

The penny dropped. 'Sciatica!' I said triumphantly.

Mr Porter nodded happily.

'Rest!' I said firmly. 'You need to rest.'

Mr Porter smiled but didn't move.

'Perhaps I ought to examine you?' I suggested. I looked around. The horsehair stuffed examination couch was piled high with books and boxes. And the room was so crowded with furniture and books that there was nowhere to move them. The only immediately available flat area was the desk. I moved the leather edged blotter that sat in the middle of it. 'Just lie down for a moment, please!' I told Mr Porter.

He looked at me as if I'd gone mad.

'I want to examine you,' I explained.

'But it's my back!' Mr Porter protested.

After some cajoling he finally agreed to lie down on the desk. When he'd walked into the room he'd looked fit enough but climbing up onto the desk seemed to cause him tremendous pain. He groaned and held his back and generally made it pretty clear that he wasn't fit for any form of physical activity. When I tried lifting his right leg to see how much the nerve was being irritated Mr Porter groaned and rolled about on the top of the desk.

'It seems pretty bad,' I agreed.

Eagerly and with more agility than he had shown when climbing up Mr Porter climbed down off the desk and sat down again. 'Can I have a note now, doctor?'

'A note?'

'For the sick.'

'Of course!' I agreed. I looked around but could see nothing suitable upon which I could write a note. And what was I supposed to write? I wished my medical school lecturers had spent less time teaching me about trypanosomiasis and more time teaching me how to write sick notes.

'I shan't be a moment, Mr Porter,' I promised, heading for the door.

I went straight through to the office where Miss Johnson was busy filling in forms. She looked up and stared at me over the top of her spectacles. 'Is there a problem, doctor?'

'I need to write a sick note,' I explained. I no longer felt quite so embarrassed about the extent of my ignorance. I'd long since gone way past the point of no return. 'But I'm not sure what to write or what to write it on . . .' My confession tailed off into silence.

'You'll find a book of national insurance certificates in the top left hand drawer of Dr Brownlow's desk,' Miss Johnson told me. 'Just fill in one of the certificates and hand it to the patient.'

I rushed back into Dr Brownlow's consulting room, found the certificate pad and scribbled out a sick note for a month. Mr Porter seemed quite pleased. When he'd gone I felt exhausted. Being a GP was harder work than I'd expected. I went back out to Miss Johnson's office.

'That seemed to go OK,' I said brightly. 'Satisfied customer I think.'

'Good!' said Miss Johnson flatly.

'I suppose it must be nearly time for coffee?'

Miss Johnson didn't say anything but stood up and walked past me to the door. She walked along the corridor and opened the door to the waiting room. Having followed I peered past her. It was absolutely packed. There were at least thirty people in there. There was so much steam rising from so many coats that it was almost impossible to see the far corner of the room at all. No one was speaking but everyone looked up expectantly when the door opened. Without saying a word Miss Johnson shut it again.

I followed her back to the office feeling slightly faint. Thirty. *Thirty!*

'It took you fifteen minutes to deal with Mr Porter,' said Miss Johnson. 'At the rate you're going you won't have finished the morning surgery before it's time to start the evening surgery. And I've already got three home visits booked in for you.'

I worked it out. If I spent fifteen minutes on each patient it would take me seven and a half hours to work my way through the patients who were waiting. And that was assuming that no more came. Miss Johnson was right – patients would be arriving for the evening surgery before I'd finished the morning surgery.

Feeling weak I hurried back into the surgery and pressed the buzzer again.

'It's my Johnnie!' said a very large woman, striding speedily into the room. 'He's got his tonsils again.' She didn't bother to sit down but just stood in front of me blocking out the light. She had several chins and wore a rubberised riding cape which still had small puddles of water collected in folds around her neck. The cape had a hood attached to it which she had pushed back.

I looked around for Johnnie but I couldn't see him. Unless he was hiding underneath the cape he wasn't anywhere to be seen.

'Where's Johnnie?' I asked. It seemed a reasonable question but I hadn't been at the job long.

'I'm not bringing him out in this!' exclaimed the large woman defiantly. 'Not with his tonsils.'

'No!' I agreed quickly. 'Of course not.'

'I'll just take a proscription for penicillin.'

'A proscription?'

'For his penicillin. Dr Brownlow always gives him penicillin.' She handed me a medical records envelope with John Albert Saunders-Lee written on it. A quick glance showed me that Johnnie had been given several lots of penicillin in recent months.

'He's been waiting to have them out,' said Mrs Saunders-Lee. 'He's been on the waiting list for months.'

I honestly didn't know what to do. Handing over drugs for a patient I hadn't seen didn't seem quite right. But Mrs Saunders-Lee was quite right; it was absurd to expect her to bring her young son out in this weather. And if she stayed at home and waited for me to visit him he'd probably be waiting for days. I decided to start young Johnnie on penicillin. I carefully wrote down the word 'Penicillin' on Johnnie's medical records. As I did so I remembered that I hadn't written anything down on Mr Porter's medical records. I made a mental note to scribble something down later.

'Fine!' I said to Mrs Saunders-Lee. 'That's OK then.'

'Where's the proscription?' Mrs Saunders-Lee folded her arms defiantly. Her coat crackled.

'I've written it down on here,' I explained. I held up her son's medical records for her to see.

'Yes!' she said. 'But where's the proscription?'

I still didn't really understand. In hospital when I'd wanted to prescribe a drug for a patient all I had to do was write down the details on the medical notes. A nurse would come round later and give the patients whatever drugs had been ordered. It may sound unbelievable but no one had explained to me that in general practice the doctor has to hand the patient a piece of paper to take to the chemist. Remember, I hadn't even seen inside a GP's surgery since I'd been a child.

'Excuse me for a moment,' I said to Mrs Saunders-Lee. I darted out and found Miss Johnson again.

'Mrs Saunders-Lee wants a proscription for her son,' I explained. 'What do I do?'

Miss Johnson looked at me very suspiciously. 'Are you sure you're a doctor?'

'Absolutely!' I said indignantly.

Miss Johnson explained that what Mrs Saunders-Lee wanted was a prescription and that I would find a whole pad of virgin prescription forms in the same drawer in which I'd found the sick notes.

'Just write out the instructions for the chemist on the form and hand it over to the patient,' explained Miss Johnson, rather wearily.

'Thanks!' I said. I started to head back towards the surgery but stopped and turned. 'Are there any more forms I need to know about?'

Miss Johnson sighed and glanced towards her own desk. 'I once filled in 47 different types of form in a single day', she said. 'But you've discovered the two most important.'

I thanked her, went back into Dr Brownlow's consulting room and wrote out a prescription for Johnnie Saunders-Lee. I handed the prescription over to his mother.

'While I'm here,' said his mother, studying the prescription carefully before stuffing it into some deep, dark recess beneath her cape. 'I'd like a check up. I'm going to see my sister in Carlisle next month and I want to make sure I'm all right before I go.'

* * *

Somehow I struggled through the morning surgery and eventually Miss Johnson came in to tell me that there were no patients left to see.

'Thirty!' I said proudly. 'I must have speeded up a bit.'

'Seventeen of them gave up and went home,' Miss Johnson explained.

'I managed to keep the home visits down to three,' she added handing me three medical record envelopes.

'Thank you.'

'I'd like to have you back in time for the evening surgery,' she explained drily. 'Now that word's got out that you've started there'll be a lot here.'

'Oh!' I said, blushing lightly. I must have looked rather pleased with myself.

'They'll know you're a soft touch,' explained Miss Johnson quickly. 'They'll want to take advantage of you before you learn the ropes.' She smiled sweetly at me. 'Will you be going back to the Duck and Puddle for your lunch before you start on your visits?'

I looked at my watch. It was quarter to two. 'I am a bit hungry. I'll just pop back for a quick bite.'

'Just as long as I know,' said Miss Johnson. 'In case anyone needs you.'

I suddenly realised that from now on I wasn't going to be allowed to go anywhere without telling Miss Johnson or the local telephone operator where they could find me.

I went outside to where I'd left the Humber. It was still pouring with rain. As I got in and bent down to reconnect the wires to start the engine I heard someone tapping on the side window. I looked up and tried to wind down the window. It moved about an inch before it got stuck.

'Sorry to bother you, doctor,' said a stern faced man whom I half recognised. 'But I'd be grateful if you'd park your car a little further away.' He pointed to a muddy area behind the stables. The man was wearing a voluminous waterproof jacket and a pair of waterproof trousers.

'Certainly! I'm sorry,' I said, assuming that I must have parked in someone's way.

'It's the oil, doctor,' explained the stern faced man, almost apologetically. He looked down. I opened my door and looked down. I could see a large patch of oil spreading out from underneath the car.

'Sorry!' I said again. Then I remembered where I'd seen the man before. It was Bradshaw – Dr Brownlow's butler.

I closed my door, heard a click as the window winder fell off onto the floor and bent down to reconnect the wires which would start the engine. Then, very slowly, I drove back to the Duck and Puddle for lunch. The absence of windscreen wipers and my inability to wind down my window so that I could look out meant that I had to lean forwards all the time and keep my nose pressed against the windscreen in order to see where I was going. Inevitably, this meant that the windscreen soon steamed up and by the time I reached the pub I could see almost nothing.

Mrs Parsons had, she told me with apparently genuine regret, sold my hot lunch to a commercial traveller from Bristol, but she made me a huge plateful of sandwiches. They were unlike any sandwiches I'd ever eaten before. The bread was soft and freshly baked. Inside it was doughy and moist and outside it was crisp. The ham was home cured and cut in half inch thick slices. The cheese was cheddar and tasted of cheese instead of plastic. And the chicken breast was succulent and tasty.

I ordered a pint of best bitter to help wash it all down and by the time I'd finished I felt truly refreshed and no longer in the slightest bit envious of the commercial traveller from Bristol. When I looked at my watch it was twenty to three. I had, I thought, plenty of time to do the home visits before the evening surgery started.

'Where is the nearest petrol station?' I asked Frank Parsons, after I'd drained the last inch of beer from my glass. As I'd driven back to the pub I'd noticed that the petrol gauge in the Humber was reading close to zero.

Frank drew in his breath and shook his head in that way people have when they know that they're about to give you bad news. 'That'll mean a trip to Combe Martin,' he announced, as though I'd asked him where I could buy rocket fuel. He told me to take the main Barnstaple road to Black-moor Gate, to turn left and to follow the main holiday route into Combe Martin. 'There's a garage on the outskirts of the village,' he told me. 'By the way,' he added, 'judging by the amount of oil you left outside our front door this morning you might need some oil as well.'

* * *

'Do you think I ought to have it serviced?' I asked the petrol station attendant when he'd filled the tank with petrol and the engine with oil.

He looked puzzled. 'What's up with it?'

'Nothing much,' I said. 'Well, the windscreen wipers don't work – there aren't any to be honest – and I have to start it by twisting two bits of wire together but it seems to go all right.'

'So what do you want us to do with it?'

He had me there. 'I'm not sure,' I admitted. 'But don't you do routine servicing? Check the tyres and brakes? Stuff like that?'

He put the petrol pump back into its holster and walked round the car. It was still raining and the garage's narrow canopy provided inadequate protection against the driving rain. He kicked the front nearside tyre with the toe of his boot and scratched his head. 'You ain't got no tax disc,' he pointed out.

I followed his gaze to the corner of the windscreen where most cars carry a tax disc. Mine had none.

'I've only just bought it,' I said. 'I never thought about tax.' As I spoke I realised that I hadn't arranged any insurance either. I was beginning to think that I'd spent too long working in hospital where I didn't have to worry about any of life's unpleasant realities.

'The tyres are bald,' he added.

I bent down. There still seemed to be some tread on them.

'They aren't completely bald,' I protested.

The garage attendant shrugged. 'I've seen worse,' he admitted.

'Do you have any windscreen wipers you can sell me?'

'For this?'

I nodded.

He shook his head. 'I've got some wipers on a Ford Consul that you can have.'

'Will they fit?'

'Maybe.'

'Will you try?'

He turned away and walked over to a car wreck that was parked at one side of the garage. It was only vaguely recognisable as a Ford Consul. He reached over and tore off both windscreen wipers with his bare hands and then walked back with them.

'You want me to fit them?'

'Yes, please.'

The wipers would not fit, of course. But the garage attendant wasn't about to be put off by such a trivial difficulty. He pulled a length of wire out of his overall pocket and used it to bind the windscreen wipers to the stumps that were still attached to my Humber. He used a pair of pliers which he took from another overall pocket to twist the wire around the wipers securely.

'Try that.'

I tried it. To my astonishment it worked. It didn't look pretty and it didn't work perfectly but it was much, much better than having no windscreen wipers at all. I paid him for the wiper blades and the petrol and oil and set off to do my home visits.

Finding people in hospital is easy. Even if you don't know which ward they are on you can still find them within seconds by ringing up the administrators, who keep comprehensive files showing where all their patients are. It's quite rare for a hospital actually to lose a patient.

39

Finding people in a town is relatively easy. Most streets have names and most houses have numbers. With the aid of a good, local street map it is fairly easy to find your way around. And even if you do manage to get lost you can nearly always find someone prepared to give you directions.

But finding people in the country is not easy. The difficulty is increased when you're a stranger, when it's raining, when your car windows are steamed up and when you're in a hurry.

The first patient on my list was Keith Harper and he was, according to his medical records, six years old. His address was Mulberry Cottage, Bilbury.

Finding Mulberry Cottage wasn't made any easier by the fact that very few houses in the village had their names on them. There were no street signs and no house names for the simple reason that everyone in the village knew where everyone else lived. Buying and erecting expensive metal or wood name plates would, for them, have been a waste of money. The very few name boards that did exist had been allowed to fade, get dirty or become so overgrown with brambles that they were impossible to read.

After searching for an hour I ran out of petrol. The Humber stuttered, coughed and then died ingloriously in a lane so narrow that I couldn't open the doors to get out. When I checked the petrol gauge and saw it registering 'zero' I couldn't believe my eyes. I'd put ten gallons of petrol into the car and had done no more than thirty miles. Racing cars and jet aircraft probably do more to the gallon.

I was rescued by the arrival of a tractor which appeared behind me.

Even though I couldn't get out of the car I managed to squeeze my head out of the passenger window (mine didn't open) far enough to shout to the driver to tell him what had happened and to ask him to give me a push out of the lane.

'You want the garage?'

'Yes!'

I took off the handbrake and allowed the tractor to push me out of the lane towards the main road from Blackmoor Gate to Combe Martin. There, on a slight downwards incline, the tractor stopped. In my mirror I saw the driver jump down onto the road and walk forwards towards me. I pulled on the handbrake.

'I'm turning right here,' he said. 'But from now on its all downhill.'

I thanked him, let off the handbrake and coasted down the hill to the garage. There I had the tank filled and I got the attendant to lend me three spare cans, filled with petrol, which I stowed in the boot.

'I don't suppose you know where Mulberry Cottage is, do you?' I asked the attendant as I paid him. 'It's in Bilbury.'

He told me. I'd passed it at least half a dozen times. It was a hundred yards from the Duck and Puddle.

I drove back, parked and knocked on the door of Mulberry Cottage.

A woman in her early thirties answered the door. She was wearing a housecoat covered in pink flowers and had her hair wrapped up in a matching pink scarf.

'Mrs Harper?'

She shook her head.

'Does Mrs Harper live here?'

Another shake of the head.

'This is Mulberry Cottage?'

A nod.

'I'm looking for Keith Harper,' I explained. 'He's six.'

'He's not here.'

'I'm the doctor,' I said. 'I'm told that Keith is poorly.'

'There's no one in.'

'Do you know where they are?'

'Mr Harper is at work.'

'Do you know where Keith is?'

'He doesn't live here.'

'Do you know where he does live?' It was hard work.

'He lives with his mother.'

'Doesn't his mother live here any more?'

'No. They're separated.'

'Do you know where she lives?'

'Yes.'

'Could you tell me, please? Someone asked for me to call and see Keith. He's not very well.'

The woman folder her arms underneath her bosom and held her head to one side to stop the plume of smoke from

41

her cigarette interfering with her view of me. 'You're a doctor?'

It was my turn to nod.

'You're a bit young, aren't you?'

'I've just started work.'

'With Dr Brownlow?'

I nodded again. I was beginning to get the hang of the conversation.

'And you want young Keith?'

Another nod from me.

'They've split up.'

'Yes. You told me.'

'I work for him.'

'Mr Harper?'

'I wouldn't be here if I worked for her, would I?'

'It could be urgent,' I told her. 'I'd be grateful . . .'

'On the Combe Martin road,' she said. 'Called 'White Larches'.' A half inch length of ash fell from her cigarette and broke up on her apron. She brushed it away. 'She's renting.'

'Is it easy to find?'

'If you know where it is.'

'I don't know the area very well.'

'Down towards Combe Martin.'

'Is it anywhere near the petrol station?'

'If you get to the petrol station you've passed it.'

I thanked her, got back into the Humber and drove back towards Combe Martin.

To my surprise and relief I found the cottage without too much difficulty. Its white washed walls bordered the edge of the road and it had a large sign outside which read 'White Larches – Bed and Breakfast'.

I parked in a lay-by fifty yards down the road, took my black bag and went back to the cottage. There was no bell so I knocked on the front door with my bare knuckles. It was still raining and I was by now soaked to the skin.

'Yes?' I heard someone shout. I looked up. A woman's head was peering out of a window directly above me. 'I'm sorry, we aren't taking any holiday-makers,' she said before I could say anything. 'My little boy isn't well.'

'I know,' I shouted back. 'That's why I'm here. I'm the

doctor. I've come for Dr Brownlow.'

'Dr Brownlow isn't here. I'm still waiting for him to arrive.'

'No. I mean I've come in place of Dr Brownlow.'

'Why hasn't Dr Brownlow come?'

'I'm his assistant.'

The head looked unhappy.

I swallowed hard. 'I'm sorry,' I said. 'But Dr Brownlow isn't available today.'

There was a loud sigh. 'I suppose you'll have to do then.' The head disappeared. 'The door's open.' I heard it shout.

I opened the front door and looked into the cottage. The front door led straight into the one large room that served both as a dining room and a lounge. The furniture was fairly new and cheap and although it was clean it was battered. It looked as though it had all been bought second hand in a job lot at a house auction. At the far side of the room one door led into a small, neat kitchen while another door, half open, revealed the beginning of a narrow staircase.

Tentatively, I stepped into the room. It felt slightly strange to be walking into a stranger's home. Clutching my black bag I stood there, just inside the door, for a few moments. I've always been rather shy and I suddenly felt waves of terrible anxiety sweeping over me. I deliberately left the door open behind me because I felt that at any moment I would need to make a run for it.

'Are you coming up?' shouted a voice from upstairs.

I really did want to run away. I wasn't ready for any of this. What was up there? What was wrong with Keith? Suddenly the enormity of my responsibility loomed large in my mind. This was, I decided, even more terrifying than conducting a surgery. There I did at least have Miss Johnson to help me. Here I was utterly, completely and totally alone.

At last I managed to find the strength to move my legs towards the staircase. As I started to climb the narrow steps I looked up and saw Mrs Harper peering down at me. She was about thirty, was wearing a dark purple jumper, purple corduroy jeans and pale blue slippers and had long, dark brown hair drawn back into a pony tail. She looked worried.

When I got to the top of the stairs she led me into a small bedroom which contained a bed and a stripped pine chest of drawers. There wasn't room for any more furniture. Several colourful paper mobiles hung from the ceiling and a toy garage complete with a dozen metal toy cars took up most of the available floor space. A small, unhappy looking boy lay in the bed.

'Watch where you put your feet,' said Mrs Harper. 'There are toy cars everywhere,' she explained. 'I keep falling over them.' She tried to smile but her eyes still looked worried.

'What's wrong with him?' I asked.

Mrs Harper looked at me hard. 'I was hoping you'd tell me that,' she said, rather sharply I thought. I winced and cursed myself. (I should have learnt from that but I never did. I asked the same question and got the same answer ten times a day, every day for years.)

I tried again. 'What symptoms does he have?'

'He's been under the weather since yesterday,' said Mrs Harper. 'I thought he was putting it on but he was due to go to a party last night and he didn't want to go so I knew he must be poorly.'

I sat on the edge of Keith's bed, picked up his wrist and took his pulse. He smiled at me rather nervously and I smiled back at him. I tried not to look nervous though I'm not sure that I succeeded. His pulse was a little fast and he looked pale and rather sweaty. I pulled back the bedclothes and asked him to unfasten his pyjama jacket. I was hoping to spot a rash but there was nothing abnormal to see.

'How's his appetite?' I asked his mother.

'He hasn't eaten much.'

'Has he been sick?'

'No.'

'Any diarrhoea?'

'I don't know. Have you had any diarrhoea, Keith?'

Keith clearly didn't know what we were talking about. Clumsily I tried to ask the same question in nursery language. He went red and shook his head furiously.

I listened to his heart and lungs, checked his glands and looked into his throat and ears. I could find nothing at all wrong with him apart from the fact that he clearly didn't look very well.

'I don't know what it is,' I said at last.

'When will Dr Brownlow be back?' asked Mrs Harper.

It was my turn to go red. 'I'm not sure,' I said. 'I don't think there's anything much we can do today. I'll call in again tomorrow and have another look at him.'

'Aren't you going to give him anything?'

'I can't think of anything useful that I can give him,' I confessed. 'I don't want to prescribe a drug until I know what's wrong with him.'

Mrs Harper sighed rather loudly.

'I'm sorry,' I said. I could feel my face burning. I put my stethoscope back into my bag, made my way back down the narrow staircase and left. I had intended to ask Mrs Harper to give me directions of how to find the next house I had to visit but I didn't dare display any more ignorance. What little confidence I had had when I'd entered the 'White Larches' had now entirely disappeared. Outside it was, inevitably, still raining heavily. I pulled my collar up and hurried back to the car.

* * *

CHAPTER THREE

I arrived back at Dr Brownlow's surgery at fifteen minutes to six and hurried in to find Miss Johnson sitting in her office filling in forms.

'Are there many people waiting?' I asked her, breathlessly.

'Twenty. And they're getting rather restless.'

'I'm sorry I'm late!' I apologised. 'I got a bit lost.'

'Lost? But you only had three visits.'

'I know. I'm sorry.' I hurried off to get myself settled down behind my desk. As I looked around the by now almost familiar surroundings I felt a strong spasm of confidence breaking through. After all I now knew where the buzzer was and I knew how to sign someone off on the sick and how to write out a prescription. I felt that I'd learnt a lot.

To my surprise the evening surgery went quite smoothly. When I finished, at twenty minutes past eight, Miss Johnson told me that Dr Brownlow wanted to have a few words with me before I left. I found him in his dining room. He was just finishing his dinner. A huge round stilton cheese stood in the middle of the table and a bottle of 1948 Taylor's port stood beside it.

'How did it all go?' he asked me. 'Good first day?' He told Bradshaw, now dressed in his butler's uniform again, to bring another glass and an extra plate.

I told him that I felt as though I'd done a year's work in a day. 'How do you cope?' I asked him. 'How does any GP cope without going insane?'

Dr Brownlow just smiled. 'Did Miss Johnson look after you?'

'Very well!' I said. 'I couldn't have managed without her.

46

Though I'm afraid I don't think I impressed her very much,' I added.

'Don't you believe it!' said Dr Brownlow. 'She thinks you're wonderful. She'll be telling you about her feet before you know where you are. When she tells you about her feet you'll know you've got it cracked.'

'I've got a thousand questions to ask you,' I told him. 'I don't know where to start.'

Bradshaw had brought another glass and a plate. Dr Brownlow poured me a glass of port and dug out a spoonful of cheese. I'd never seen anyone serve stilton with a spoon before. It tasted good. So did the port. It was like drinking velvet.

Suddenly I remembered Mrs Harper. I asked Dr Brownlow if she'd rung him.

He snorted and refilled his glass.

'I'm afraid she didn't seem very pleased with me,' I said. 'I couldn't diagnose what was wrong with her son. I think she'd like you to see him.'

'She said that you'd told her that you'd go back in to see him again tomorrow?'

I nodded.

'I told her that you're an expert in children's diseases,' said Dr Brownlow with a twinkle in his eye. 'And that if you couldn't make a diagnosis then I certainly wouldn't be able to.' He picked up a lump of stilton from his plate and popped it into his mouth. 'There are always people who'll try to play one doctor off against another,' he told me. 'But I'm not having any of that.'

I realised that Dr Brownlow was protecting me and I felt grateful.

'Do you ever see a patient and find it difficult to know what's wrong with them?' I asked him.

'At least fifty per cent of the time I *never* know what's wrong with people,' admitted Dr Brownlow. 'Any doctor who says he can always make a diagnosis is either a liar or a fool.'

'Thanks!' I said quietly. He'd made me feel a lot better. I caught sight of a grandfather clock on the far side of the room. 'I'd better get back to the Duck and Puddle,' I told him. 'I think Miss Johnson has already arranged for any emergency calls to be put through to me there.'

Dr Brownlow nodded. 'Ring me if you need me,' he said suddenly and unexpectedly. 'I won't ever interfere but I'll always help you if I can.'

I'd started to move away from the table but I stopped for an instant, looked at him and thanked him. Then I moved towards the door. I was nearly there when Dr Brownlow spoke again.

'I know I said I wouldn't interfere,' he said. 'But I've just remembered. I already have.'

I waited.

'Frank Porter,' said Dr Brownlow. 'You signed him off sick.'

I remembered. He'd been my first patient. He'd had a bad back.

'He's my bloody gardener!' said Dr Brownlow. 'He's had a bad back since he was a kid. He's always trying that one when the weather's a bit miserable.'

'Oh,' I said, weakly.

'He'll be back at work tomorrow,' said Dr Brownlow. 'I made him tear up that sick note you gave him. My rhododendrons need looking after.'

I left him pouring himself another glass of port. The strange thing was that although he was alone in a huge dining room he didn't seem alone at all. He was one of the first people I'd ever met who seemed totally self contained.

*   *   *

CHAPTER FOUR

Mrs Parsons made me gammon, egg and chips for supper and served it in the deserted lounge bar. 'The locals never drink in here,' she confessed. 'The beer is too expensive.'

After supper I had a bath and then retired, exhausted, to bed. My bedroom at the Duck and Puddle didn't have a telephone but there was a telephone in the landlord's bedroom and Mrs Parsons had agreed to answer it and to fetch me if there were any calls during the night. I seemed to have been asleep for no more than a minute when I felt someone shaking my shoulder. I turned and found myself staring into the beam of a powerful torch. I reached up, found the long light cord that dangled above my bed and pulled it. I rubbed my eyes as the light came on.

'Sorry to have to wake you,' whispered Mrs Parsons. 'But there's a call for you. It's Mrs Francis.' My landlady was wearing a long, pink, flannelette nightgown with a paisley patterned dressing gown on top of it. The dressing gown was tied tightly at the front but it only came down to her knees and two foot of nightdress hung down below it. She had three curlers in the front of her hair and the absence of make up gave her a pale, ghostly look.

I flung back the bedclothes only to remember, too late, that, as usual, I hadn't been wearing any pyjamas when I'd got into bed. I swiftly picked up a pillow and used it to preserve what was left of my professional dignity. It's very difficult to be dignified in the nude.

'I'll wait for you outside on the landing,' said Mrs Parsons quietly.

I quickly pulled on the same clothes that I'd been wearing

the day before.

'Ssshhhh!' said Mrs Parsons, when I joined her on the landing a few moments later. She put a finger against her lips. 'Frank is still asleep!' she whispered. 'He hates being woken up.'

I nodded and she led the way to their bedroom. I tiptoed behind her. Frank Parsons was fast asleep and snoring loudly. I picked up the telephone.

'Hello?' I whispered. 'What can I do for you?'

'Who's that?' asked the voice at the other end. 'I'm trying to get hold of Dr Brownlow.'

I explained.

'It's my husband,' said Mrs Francis. 'I'm not happy with the look of him.'

'Would you like me to come round?'

She said she would so I got her to give me instructions on how to get there, put the telephone down, thanked Mrs Parsons and then went back to my room to get my coat and my black bag.

Two minutes later I was in my car, wiping the mist off the inside of the windscreen. It was still raining. To my delight the car started immediately when I twisted the two pieces of wire underneath the dashboard together.

I left the Duck and Puddle with an impressive, rubber wasting squeal. My adrenalin was flowing for this was my very first emergency visit as a general practitioner.

Mr and Mrs Francis lived in a large house on the outskirts of the village and Mrs Francis had given me precise instructions on how to find it but I had nevertheless asked her to turn some lights on in the hope that this would help me find the house more easily. In my innocence I'd hoped that I'd be able to home in on the lights like a moth fluttering towards a candle. Being new to general practice I wasn't yet aware of the extraordinary fact that even in the country there are lights burning in numerous houses well after midnight.

Fortunately, the instructions I'd been given proved accurate and it took me no more than fifteen minutes to get to the Francis's home which turned out to be an old rectory, built in the nineteenth century. The English countryside is littered with large Victorian rectories. Clergymen a century or so ago must have been very wealthy and must have had very large families. I parked outside the front door and rattled the door knocker.

'Come in, doctor!' whispered Mrs Francis. People always whisper late at night, even in their own homes. 'Do you know,' she said, 'I thought that your wife sounded just like Gilly Parsons at the Duck and Puddle.'

'I'm not married,' I told her, following her up the stairs to the master bedroom. 'That was Mrs Parsons.'

Mrs Francis stopped on the step above me and turned round. 'You were at the Duck?' she said. She obviously hadn't realised that her call had been automatically transferred from Dr Brownlow's number.

I admitted that I had, indeed, been in the pub when we'd first spoken.

'It seemed to take quite a time for you to get to the telephone.'

'Mrs Parsons had to wake me,' I explained.

'Oh!' said Mrs Francis, who looked rather more startled than seemed entirely reasonable under the circumstances.

She carried on upstairs and I followed her into the bedroom. Her husband was lying flat on his back, coughing and wheezing. He looked miserable. I put my black bag down, sat down on the edge of the bed and felt for his pulse. I put my stethoscope down on the bed, took out my pocket torch, aimed it down his throat and asked Mr Francis to say: 'Aaaaarrhhh.'

It didn't take long to discover that Mr Francis was suffering from asthma. I was about to tell him this when he looked up at me, wheezed, and, with some difficulty, told me that he had asthma and that he had suffered from it for most of his life.

'Right!' I agreed. I rummaged around in my bag and found a glass phial of aminophylline.

'Dr Brownlow usually gives me aminophylline,' wheezed Mr Francis noisily.

'Does that help?' I asked him.

He nodded.

I took the aminophylline out of my bag, filled a syringe with the fluid and started to roll up his pyjama sleeve.

Mr Francis grasped my wrist and shook his head furiously.

I looked at him, stopped and waited.

'Dr Brownlow usually puts it into the other arm,' wheezed Mr Francis.

I rolled up the other pyjama sleeve and injected the aminophylline. Mr Francis's breathing started to improve almost immediately.

'Where are you going now, doctor?' asked Mrs Francis who'd been standing silently at the bottom of the bed.

'Back to the Duck and Puddle,' I said.

'Oh!' said Mrs Francis, surprised. She recovered quickly, however. 'Give my love to Gilly. And tell her not to forget the jam making competition.'

I said I would.

On my way back to the pub the Humber broke down.

* * *

I was asleep when Mrs Parsons came into my room the following morning but I woke when she put a cup of tea down on the bedside table. She was still wearing her night clothes but the curlers had gone.

'It's half past seven,' she announced, drawing back the curtains. 'Dr Brownlow did say that I wasn't to let you oversleep.' It was still raining and a harsh wind was driving the rain hard against the bedroom window.

I yawned, stretched, rubbed my eyes and did all the other things I do when I'm woken up. My bed was warm and soft and I felt tired and very comfortable.

'Were you late getting in last night?'

I nodded. 'It was after four o'clock. I had to get the garage in Combe Martin to come out. Something to do with the rotor arm.'

'How was Mr Francis?'

'I think he was OK when I left,' I replied. 'Mrs Francis sent you her best wishes and told me to tell you not to forget about the jam making competition.'

'Bless her!' said Mrs Parsons. 'She's got a heart of gold.' She paused and I could tell that the compliment was about to be qualified. 'Though she does love to gossip.' She stood at the end of the bed with her arms folded across her chest and smiled at me. 'I expect the reason she told you to remind

me about the jam making competition was because she wants
to make sure I'm there so that she can quiz me about you.'

I must have looked alarmed.

'Don't worry!' Mrs Parsons assured me. 'I won't tell her
anything too incriminating. Besides you're lucky. Everyone
in the village is talking about Mike Trickle. He's just moved
into Bilbury Grange.'

'Mike Trickle?'

'The man off the television,' explained Mrs Parsons. 'You
must have seen him.'

I hadn't. Long hospital hours meant that for several years
I hadn't had much free time. The free time I had I'd spent
sleeping rather than watching television.

Mrs Parsons seemed a little disappointed by my ignorance.
'Well, he's very famous anyway,' she assured me. 'He has
his own chat show and comperes a quiz programme too.'

'What's he doing in Bilbury? It's a long way from London.'

'Oh, I don't expect he's going to live here all the time,'
said Mrs Parsons. 'It'll be just a holiday home for weekends
and such like.' She glanced at the small clock on my bedside
table. 'Come on!' she said suddenly. 'There isn't time for chatting. You've got to get up and off to the surgery. And I've
got to get down and see how the new girl is doing.'

'New girl?'

'Patsy,' explained Mrs Parsons. 'She's one of the girls from the
Kennett farm. She should have your bacon under the grill by now.'

Mrs Parsons was right. As I hurriedly shaved and then
dressed the smell of bacon cooking wafted upstairs and helped
give me the strength to keep going. I felt exhausted not just
because I hadn't had much sleep but because of the endless
series of problems I'd encountered. When I'd taken the job
I had, I confess, rather thought that life as a country GP
would be something of a leisurely business. I'd seen myself
pottering about the countryside in an open topped Bentley,
stopping here to pick up a brace of pheasant, there to accept
a gift of a freshly caught trout. I hadn't realised that it would
be such hard work. I couldn't help wondering if it was ever
going to get any easier.

Still, not everything was bad and life at the Duck and Puddle
did have its compensations. Breakfast was one of them. It

was so good that I was almost late again. As I started my third cup of coffee I glanced at my watch and discovered that it was twenty to nine. I put down the cup, ran upstairs to collect my coat and bag and left the pub on the run.

'Good morning, doctor!' said Miss Johnson with a wry smile as I raced past her office. I looked in as I went past and saw with some relief that the clock on her desk said just two minutes to nine. 'Mrs Harper's been on the phone already,' said Miss Johnson following me into the surgery. 'She wants to make sure that you haven't forgotten that you said you'd go back and see her son again.'

'I haven't forgotten!' I promised. 'How many patients are there in the waiting room?'

'There were a dozen there at half past eight,' said Miss Johnson. 'I haven't counted since then.' She sighed. 'I sometimes wonder where all these ill people come from. Living in the country is supposed to be healthy but I think that's a myth.' She shuffled a pile of forms that she was holding. 'Have you heard that Mike Trickle has bought a house in the village?'

When I said I had she looked a little disappointed.

*   *   *

My first patient that day was a woman in her mid twenties. She had shoulder length light brown hair, lightly freckled cheeks and astonishingly blue eyes. She took off her raincoat and draped it over the back of the chair before she sat down. She wore a pink cardigan with buttons all the way down the front and a loose red velvet skirt. She leant across the desk and handed me her medical records envelope.

'Miss Thwaites?' I said, taking the notes from her and reading the name printed across the top.

She nodded. 'Anne.'

'What's the problem?'

'I want to lose some weight.' She looked down. 'I've put an awful lot of weight on in the last few months. It's really depressing.'

'Have you changed your diet at all?'

She shook her head.

'Exercise habits haven't changed?'

'No.'

54

'Have you tried dieting?'

'I tried a diet I found in a woman's magazine,' she told me. 'The grape and banana diet.'

'Did it work?'

She shook her head. 'I hate grapes and bananas give me indigestion so I hardly ate anything and got very hungry the first day.'

'Do you know how much you weigh?'

'According to the scales in the chemists I'm nearly eleven stones,' she said, and blushed. 'That's terrible isn't it?'

'How tall are you?'

'Five foot five. I was less than ten stones this time last year and I thought that was bad enough.'

'You haven't noticed anything else?'

She looked puzzled. 'Like what?'

'Any other symptoms?' I wanted to make sure that there was no strange hormonal explanation for her increase in weight.

Miss Thwaites shook her head. 'Oh, no! I feel fine. In fact I don't think I've ever felt so healthy.'

'Right!' I said, with far more confidence than I felt.

No one had ever taught me anything about dieting. I had studied at medical school for six years but no one had ever so much as told me how many calories there are in a slice of bread. 'Just a moment,' I said. 'I'll see if we've got some diet sheets.' I rushed out to Miss Johnson's office.

'Diet sheets?' she said. 'Yes. I think there are some around here somewhere. Dr Brownlow usually just tells them to eat less but I think one of the drug company representatives did leave a pile of diet sheets a couple of years ago.' She rummaged around in a drawer that was packed with leaflets, booklets and drug samples. 'Here you are!' she said gleefully. She held up half a dozen crumpled diet sheets. 'How many do you want?'

I took two so that I'd have one spare.

'Does Dr Brownlow have any weighing scales?' I asked Miss Johnson, before I left.

'Oh yes!' she said.

'Do you know where they are?'

'Frank's got them for his vegetables.'

I must have looked puzzled.

'Frank the gardener,' explained Miss Johnson. 'He uses the scales to weigh the best produce.'

I took the diet sheet back to Miss Thwaites and suggested that she weigh herself again next time she was in Barnstaple. 'Come back and let me know how it goes,' I said.

*　　*　　*

The rest of the morning went fairly smoothly and at the end of it I congratulated myself. Maybe being a family doctor wasn't going to be all that difficult after all. I looked at my watch. It was only twelve o'clock.

'Shall we have a cup of coffee?' I asked Miss Johnson.

'Certainly!' she said, rather kindly. 'And I'll bring you a biscuit,' she promised.

While she was away getting the biscuits I busied myself reading some of the morning's mail. I was interrupted by a visitor. It was Mrs Wilson, the district nurse with whom I'd shared the taxi ride from Barnstaple station. She was wearing the same blue coat and she had the same small, blue hat perched on the back of her head.

'How are you settling down?' she asked me, sitting down. 'Quite a week for our village!' she said, before I could answer. 'Two of you coming in one week.'

'Two of us?'

'You and Mike Trickle,' explained the district nurse. 'Don't tell me that you hadn't heard?'

'Oh yes,' I said weakly. 'He's off the television isn't he?'

'Off the television!' said Mrs Wilson. 'He *is* the television in our house. My Len thinks he's wonderful.'

'Len?'

'My husband,' explained Mrs Wilson. 'He's a policeman.'

'That's handy,' I said. I meant nothing by the comment but it seemed to touch a raw nerve as far as Mrs Wilson was concerned.

'Handy!' she said. 'He does the washing up and the ironing but he couldn't put a shelf up if his life depended on it.'

'Still,' I said, 'it's nice that he does the washing and the ironing.'

'Only because he likes to wear my pinny,' said Mrs Wilson. I thought she was being cryptic or humorous. I was to discover that she was merely being incautious.

Just then Miss Johnson reappeared with a small wooden tray upon which sat a cup of white, milky coffee and a plate full of biscuits.

I thanked her. I did wonder whether I ought to offer Mrs Wilson a cup of tea but Miss Johnson had gone before I had time to say anything.

'Would you like a biscuit, Mrs Wilson?' I said, offering her the plate.

She took two. 'Less of the Mrs Wilson,' she said. 'It's Kay to you.' She winked at me. 'Especially after our ride in Pete Marshall's taxi.'

I studied the skin that was forming on the coffee that Miss Johnson had brought in. I wondered what on earth I was going to do with it. I certainly couldn't drink it.

'Don't you like it milky?' asked Mrs Wilson.

'Not really,' I admitted. 'How did you know?'

Mrs Wilson laughed. 'The look on your face!' she said. 'You'll have to become a better poker player if you're going to survive in general practice.' She reached across and took the cup of coffee off the tray and put it down on the desk in front of her. 'Do you want any of those garibaldis?'

'Garibaldis?'

'The biscuits with the dead flies in them.'

I looked down. 'Help yourself.'

'So,' she said, as she munched away at one of the biscuits, 'you've struck out with Mrs Harper already?'

I blushed. 'Oh. You heard?'

'Don't worry,' she said. 'There isn't much that goes on around here that I don't get to hear about.' She took a sip from the coffee. 'Still, don't worry yourself too much.'

'She and her husband are divorced I believe,' I said, feeling that I ought to contribute something to the conversation.

'Separated,' Mrs Wilson corrected me. 'She couldn't stand his carrying on.' She lifted the skin off the coffee and draped it over the edge of the saucer. 'He was never very subtle,' she said. 'He had affairs with the last two barmaids at the Duck and Puddle.' She sniffed and took the last biscuit. 'Still,'

57

she said, 'they were no better than they looked.'

'Talking of Mrs Harper, I suppose I ought to get on and do my visits,' I said. 'I promised her that I'd call in again this morning.'

'When are you going to come and see us then?' she asked, her mouth full of biscuit.

'That's very kind of you,' I said. 'But . . .'

'They can put your calls through to us if old Brownlow has got you doing all his emergency work,' said Mrs Wilson. 'What are you doing tonight?'

'I don't think . . .'

'Good!' said Mrs Wilson. 'Don't forget to tell Gilly at the Duck and Puddle that you're having dinner with me. I'll make us something special.' She drained the rest of the coffee, took a small piece of skin from her tongue, smiled at me, winked and left.

* * *

Keith Harper was worse. He now had really bad diarrhoea and his mother still wasn't happy.

'I asked Dr Brownlow to come and see him.' she told me as I examined Keith's chest again. He was pale, his heart was beating rapidly and his eyes had a glassy look. I nodded.

'He said you're in charge,' said Mrs Harper.

'I'll do the best I can,' I promised. My store of confidence was draining away again. I gave up trying to find something wrong with Keith's chest and rummaged around in my black bag. 'I'd like to test your urine,' I told Keith. 'Do you think you could get to the toilet?'

It wasn't easy but he managed it. I'd done the test in despair more than hope. I hadn't expected to find anything. But the test showed that Keith's urine was loaded with sugar.

'Are there any cases of diabetes in the family?' I asked Mrs Harper.

She thought for a moment and then shook her head. 'Not that I can think of.' She looked startled. 'Is that what it is? Is Keith a diabetic?'

'No!' I said. 'Not necessarily. But he does have some sugar in his urine.'

'A lot?'

58

'Quite a lot,' I confessed. 'I'd like to get him into hospital for some tests.'

'Shall I go and call an ambulance?' demanded Mrs Harper, beginning to panic. 'What shall I pack for him? Will they let me stay with him? What will I do about the cats?' The questions poured out.

'Have you got a telephone?' I asked her.

She shook her head. 'There's a public call box in Combe Martin.'

I thought quickly. 'I'll go back to the surgery,' I said. 'I need to ring the hospital first to arrange for Keith to be admitted. It'll only take me a few minutes. You get a small case ready for Keith – pyjamas, soap bag, that sort of thing – and an ambulance will be here to pick him up. It won't be here for half an hour so you've got plenty of time.'

'Is he going to be all right?' There were tears in Mrs Harper's eyes.

'Yes.' I told her, with far more certainty than I felt. I drove back to the surgery as fast as I dared. The poor old Humber was developing more strange new rattles with every mile it travelled.

*   *   *

As a young, very junior hospital doctor I had answered calls from general practitioners many times and, like all young, inexperienced hospital doctors, I'd treated such telephone calls with some disdain.

Most hospitals are short of beds and junior doctors who do the admitting are expected to be selective. Senior consultants don't like their beds to be blocked by elderly, infirm or chronically ill patients. They prefer interesting, dramatic patients. Besides, hospital doctors – even the youngest and most inexperienced – tend to look down on general practitioners. Doctors who work in hospital regard themselves as being on the frontiers of medicine. They regard general practitioners as old fashioned, generally incompetent and troublesome. This contempt is enhanced by a certain amount of envy because most general practitioners earn more money than most hospital doctors.

This was the first time I'd been the initiator of a call designed to send a patient into hospital.

The doctor who answered the phone at the other end sounded about eleven years old.

I gave my name and explained that I wanted him to admit a patient.

'How old is he?'

I told him.

'What's the diagnosis?'

Here I was not on such solid ground. 'I'm not sure,' I confessed. 'But provisionally it's diabetes.'

'On what grounds?'

'His urine is loaded with sugar.'

'You've done a urine test?' asked the eleven year old, apparently surprised at such a display of technical excellence.

I said I had.

'Why can't he attend the out patient clinic?'

'I think he needs to be admitted now,' I said. Suddenly, I noticed that Dr Brownlow was standing just inside the door, grinning. He'd obviously been listening to my conversation.

'Having trouble getting a patient admitted?' he whispered.

I nodded and put my hand over the mouthpiece of the telephone. 'Keith Harper,' I said. 'I think he might have diabetes.'

'Ask him if he's prepared to take the responsibility if the boy doesn't get admitted and dies,' said Dr Brownlow, nodding towards the telephone receiver.

I lifted my hand from the mouthpiece. 'Look,' I said, as firmly as I could, 'I've got a boy who's ill. I think he needs to be in hospital. Are you prepared to take on the responsibility for refusing to accept him as a patient?'

There was a silence. 'Send him in,' sighed the junior hospital doctor, outflanked and outmanoeuvred by my employer. 'What's his name?'

I gave him the details and then rang the ambulance service and arranged for them to pick Keith up as soon as possible.

'That was incredible!' I said to Dr Brownlow, when I'd finished.

'Responsibility is the magic word,' explained Dr Brownlow. 'It's the only thing a GP has in abundance. Legally and morally we're responsible for our patients for twenty four hours a day and for three hundred and sixty five days a year. The buck truly stops here.' Dr Brownlow sat down on the edge of the desk. 'The trouble with our society is that responsibility and authority have become separated,' he went on, warming to his theme. 'The people with the authority to do things no longer have any responsibility for what they do whereas the people like us who have the responsibility no longer have any real authority.' He rubbed his chin thoughtfully. 'Most of the people who have the power to make our lives difficult – social workers, policemen and so on – spend their lives trying to avoid any responsibility. When they do get any they do their level best to pass it on to the next person. For them it's like a huge game of pass the parcel. No one wants to be stuck with the responsibility when the music stops. We're stuck with so much responsibility that we can't ever get rid of all of ours.'

I nodded. It all made sense.

'So, when you can't get someone to do something just tell them that you're passing some of your responsibility onto them,' said Dr Brownlow. He leant forward. 'The ultimate weapon,' he confided, 'is to tell them that if the patient dies you'll put them down as one of the contributing factors when you write out the death certificate.'

'Can you do that?'

'Of course!'

'And it works?'

'Works?' laughed Dr Brownlow. 'I can get any hospital administrator eating out of my hands with that trick.'

I was still admiring Dr Brownlow's manipulative skills when Miss Johnson knocked on the open consulting room door. She looked worried.

'What's up, Doreen?' asked Dr Brownlow. It was the first time I'd heard her first name used and it seemed strange. I hadn't even thought about her having a first name.

'There's been a phone call from Anne Thwaites,' said Miss Johnson. 'She says she's been getting bad tummy pains and would someone go and see her as soon as possible.'

'Thwaites?' I said. 'Wasn't she in the surgery this morning?'

'That's right,' said Miss Johnson. 'I think you gave her

a diet sheet.' She sounded disapproving.

Dr Brownlow looked at me, smiled and then looked at Miss Johnson. 'What's up, Doreen?'

'Well, it's not my place to say,' replied the receptionist. 'But I thought she looked pregnant.'

'Pregnant?' I said, sounding as astonished as I felt. I'd never even thought of the possibility of her being pregnant.

Dr Brownlow reached out and put a hand on my shoulder. At least he had the decency not to laugh at me. 'You'd better go and have a look at her.'

* * *

To my astonishment it had stopped raining. The sun wasn't exactly shining and the sky was still predominantly grey but it definitely wasn't raining. I began to realise just how attractive the countryside in North Devon must be in the sunshine. The beech and hawthorn hedges were thick with blackberries hanging off laden brambles and the swallows were already massing together on the telephone wires. I couldn't help wondering what they used before the telephone was invented.

Anne Thwaites lived in a tiny cottage on the edge of Exmoor. It could only be approached along a narrow, muddy track. The last few days' rain had left huge puddles on the track and the huge, heavy Humber skidded and slid along sideways as it struggled to get some traction on the mud. Several times I thought I was stuck but each time I managed to keep the wheels moving by slipping the car into second gear and lowering the speed.

The cottage itself was surrounded by ramshackle sheds in which various rusting pieces of farm machinery were stored. Most of the sheds had originally had slate roofs but the slates had long since been replaced with pieces of corrugated iron, most of which had gone rusty. A lone oak tree stood just behind the cottage; its trunk and branches shaped by the wind. Half a dozen rhododendron bushes sheltered a small vegetable patch but the wind had pushed the bushes over until they stood at an angle of forty five degrees to the ground. On the windward side their leaves were burnt brown.

As I drove carefully into the courtyard I could tell by the bumps that it had at some time in the distant past been covered with cobble stones. Today, however, the cobbles were covered with a thick layer of mud and water. I looked for the highest piece of ground I could find so that I could get out of the car without sinking up to my ankles in mud. I realised that I would have to buy some wellington boots for the winter months, and keep them in the car.

Within minutes of my appearance three dogs appeared; two of them were Welsh collies and the third was an Alsation. All three dogs were filthy and they barked furiously, paying most of their attention to the side of the car on which I was sitting. I didn't stop the engine straight away but sat for a moment looking at the dogs and trying to pluck up courage to get out of the car. The two collies didn't look too frightening but the Alsation bared its teeth and growled rather than simply making a lot of noise and I got the impression that it meant business. The collies looked as if they just wanted to frighten me off; the Alsation looked as if it wanted to eat me.

Looking around in desperation I noticed that at the front of the cottage there was a large porch, built to provide some protection from the wind, rain and snow. I put the Humber back into gear and manoeuvred it as close to the porch as I could. Then I stopped the car, opened my door into the porch and stepped into a small, secure area. Ahead of me was the front door. On each side of me I was protected by the stone walls of the porch. And the entrance to the porch was blocked off by my car which protected my rear. As the three dogs howled and barked in protest I hammered on the front door with my fist.

No one answered but behind me the Alsation was trying to climb up over the Humber's front bumper. I decided not to wait to see if he made it but to go straight into the cottage. I opened the front door, let myself in and then closed the door firmly behind me. 'Hello?' I called. 'Anyone in? Miss Thwaites?' I was standing in a tiny hallway. On my left and on my right there were two solid pine doors, both shut. Straight ahead of me there was a narrow staircase. I stood still and listened carefully and then I heard a woman's voice. It wounded very weak. 'Is that you, doctor?' The voice came from the room on the left.

I opened the door and stepped into a tiny living room.

A roaring log fire crackled in the fireplace and the room looked very neat and cosy. Miss Thwaites was sitting in an armchair. The chair had virtually no springs left and her bottom seemed to be no more than an inch or so off the floor. The room was boiling hot.

I said 'hello' and smiled at her.

'I'm sorry to have to call you out, doctor,' apologised Miss Thwaites. She grimaced and rubbed her hands on her tummy. 'But I keep getting these terrible pains.'

'When did they start?'

'Soon after I left the surgery. I caught the Lynton bus and got off at Darracott Farm. The pains came on while I was walking up the lane.'

She still had her shoes on and they and her legs were spattered in mud. I knelt down beside her chair and took hold of her hand. Her pulse was fast but quite strong. I felt her tummy and with some shame realised that Miss Johnson was absolutely right. Miss Thwaites was very, very pregnant.

'Are the pains getting worse?'

She nodded.

'And closer together?'

Another nod.

I opened my bag, took out a foetal stethoscope, pushed up her skirt and leant down so that I could listen to her abdomen. I could hear the baby's heart beating.

'What is it, doctor?'

'You remember that diet sheet I gave you?'

'Yes.'

'Well rip it up. You're not going to need it.'

She frowned. 'I don't understand.'

'You're about to lose all your excess weight very quickly.' She clearly still didn't understand.

'You're going to have a baby!' I told her bluntly. 'We've got to get you into hospital.'

'A baby!' She smiled. 'Oh, that's lovely!'

It wasn't quite what I'd expected her to say but at least she hadn't gone into hysterics and the fact that she wasn't married didn't seem to strike her as the slightest bit relevant. Just then she had another contraction. The contractions were coming thick and fast and I had to make a very rapid decision.

Should I telephone for – and then wait for – an ambulance or should I bundle her into my car and drive her to the hospital myself? I decided that it would take an ambulance at least half an hour to reach us and that we didn't have half an hour to wait. The car seemed the only sensible solution.

I told her what I was planning to do then rushed out to the porch to move the car forwards a couple of feet so that I could open the back door and get Miss Thwaites into it. Surprisingly, the dogs had given up and were standing on the other side of the courtyard looking miserable. Even the Alsation had stopped barking. When I went back into the house Miss Thwaites was on the telephone.

'I'm trying to reach my husband,' she whispered, putting her hand over the phone.

'I didn't know you were married!' I replied, thoughtlessly.

'Well, I suppose we're not really,' she blushed. 'Not in so many words.' I heard someone answer at the other end. 'Could you get Thumper, please?' she asked. She put her hand over the mouthpiece again. 'That's my husband,' she explained. 'We live together so it's all right to call him my husband, isn't it?'

'Yes!' I said, emphatically. 'I'm sure it is. Of course it is. That's not Thumper Robinson is it?'

She nodded. 'Do you know him?' She seemed pleased.

Before I could answer Miss Thwaites turned her attention back to the telephone. 'Is that you Thumper?'

I could hear the voice at the other end of the phone confirming his identity.

'It's me,' said Miss Thwaites. 'I'm going to have a baby.'

Thumper said something and Miss Thwaites blushed and giggled. Then she grimaced and held her tummy as she had another contraction. She held the phone out to me. 'Would you have a word with him?'

'We must hurry up,' I whispered to her, taking the telephone. 'Hello?' I said. 'Is that you, Thumper?'

A voice I recognised said it was.

I told him who I was. 'I'm going to take your wife into the hospital. Can you meet us there?'

'Well, it's a bit difficult at the moment,' he said.

'Why's that?'

'I've just set the balls up.'

'Balls?'

'Snooker,' explained Thumper. 'My mate's put his money in now.'

'Well, when you've finished that game,' I said, getting rather exasperated.

'We've agreed to play a best of seven frames match,' said Thumper. I heard him call to someone else in the pub. 'Dick!' he called. 'My floozy's having a baby. Can we make it the best of five?' There was a pause then he came back to me. 'We've cut it down to the best of five,' he said. 'I'll see you at the hospital later.'

'That's very good of you,' I said, trying to be sarcastic.

'Not at all,' said Thumper who clearly didn't appreciate the finer aspects of sarcasm. 'A man's got to take his responsibilities seriously.' There was another pause as something obviously occurred to him. 'You're not driving Anne to the hospital in that Humber are you?'

I said I was.

'Well you look after her!' said Thumper. Then he said something else I didn't catch and put the telephone down.

'Come on!' I said to Miss Thwaites. 'Let's go!' I started towards the door.

'The fireguard!' she said. 'Thumper goes mad at me if I go out without putting the fireguard up.'

I moved back and put the fireguard into position.

'Should we feed the goldfish?' she asked.

'I think the goldfish will be all right for a few hours,' I said.

'Shouldn't I pack some things?'

'We'll get Thumper to bring you some stuff in.'

'But he's playing skittles tonight!' protested Miss Thwaites.

I took her elbow and ushered her out to the car.

* * *

We got away from the cottage safely and successfully negotiated the muddy track without getting stuck. Our problems arose on the narrow lane which should have taken us straight on to the main road into Barnstaple.

Most of the lanes which traverse North Devon are single track. When they were created, a hundred years ago or more, farmers driving their carts to town were unlikely to meet much traffic coming from the opposite direction. These days when two vehicles do meet head on there is usually a passing space or a convenient gate no more than a hundred yards away. Local traffic isn't usually in too much of a hurry.

I was in a hurry. I'd delivered babies, of course. Every medical student has to take responsibility for at least ten pregnant women. But there is a vast difference between helping a woman deliver her baby in a sterile, purpose built suite which is packed with the very latest stainless steel equipment and staffed by experienced and skilled midwives, and delivering a baby in the back seat of a fifteen year old Humber.

When I saw the flock of sheep advancing slowly towards us along the lane my heart very nearly stopped. Desperately, I put the car into reverse and turned my head so that I could see where we were going. But we weren't going anywhere. The Gods must have felt in a mischievous mood that morning for behind us there was a herd of cattle, advancing down the lane at a quarter of a mile an hour.

I'd been close to panic before. But not this close. A teacher of mine once told me that in times of absolute disaster you should try to think of how things could get worse. 'It'll help put things in perspective,' he said. 'Things are rarely as bad as they seem. Try to imagine the worst possible scenario and you'll find that life isn't so bad after all.'

I'd found a flaw in his theory. I'd reached the point where things can't get any worse. And what do you do then?

The groans from Anne Thwaites in the back of the car convinced me that there was no point in trying to carry on. We weren't going to get to Barnstaple before the baby was born. The baby was going to be born here. I disconnected the wires under the dashboard and the engine stuttered to a halt. I got out of the car, opened the back door and looked in.

'How are you feeling?'

Miss Thwaites answered with a groan. I tried to squeeze into the back of the car to examine her tummy but there just wasn't room.

'What's up?' I heard someone behind me ask. I backed out of the car and turned round. The man who'd been walking with the cows was standing behind me, peering over my shoulder. 'She all right?'

'She's having a baby,' I told him. 'We were trying to get to the hospital but . . .' I shrugged.

Behind the sheep the driver of the tractor had stopped and was climbing down onto the road. It was a girl. She too came over to talk to us.

'Hello Anne!' she said. It was an impressive piece of identification since all you could see of Anne were her legs and her knickers.

Miss Thwaites groaned.

'I think we'll have to get her out of the car,' I said. 'It's a bit too cramped in there.'

'Take her into the field,' suggested the man who'd come with the cows. Every time he spoke his false teeth popped out and he had to pull them back into his mouth with his tongue. He nodded towards a nearby gate. One of his cows nuzzled me gently from behind.

'Who are you then?' asked the girl who'd got off the tractor. 'Where's Thumper?'

'I'm the doctor,' I said. 'Thumper is playing snooker.' Neither of them seemed at all surprised by this.

'I'll take the seats out,' said the man with the mischievous dentures. He reached into the front of the car and pulled at the driver's seat. The bottom part of the seat came away in his hands.

'At least the weather's fine,' said the girl, looking at the sky. And I realised then that it *could* be worse. It could be raining. 'I'll get the seat from the other side,' she said, clearly keen to do something to help.

Miss Thwaites, almost forgotten in the midst of all this energetic activity, groaned again. I reached into the car and pulled her gently towards me. 'Don't worry!' I said. 'Everything's going to be all right.'

She looked up at me. Her face was pale and sweaty and her hair was plastered to her scalp. 'I'm glad you're with me,' she said. 'I feel safe with you.'

I silently wished that I had her confidence and I carried

68

her down the lane to the gate over which the girl and the cowman had thrown my car seats. I had to tiptoe through the mixture of sheep and cows in order to get there. I wasn't surprised at the smell but the noise did surprise me; I could hardly hear myself think for the baaing and the mooing.

'I'll get some hot water,' said the cowman as I laid Miss Thwaites down on the impromptu couch. I bent down beside her and was goosed by a short but stout thistle.

'Is she going to be all right?' he asked in what he probably thought was a whisper. Even above the noise of the cattle and the sheep I could have heard him if I'd been standing a hundred yards away.

'Of course!' I said, emphatically. 'Women have been giving birth for centuries. It's perfectly natural.'

'Won't you need scissors and things?' Miss Thwaites asked. 'Something to cut the cord?'

'There's some in my black bag.' I said. I ran back to the car to get them. As I did so I passed the girl from the tractor who seemed to be picking flowers out of the hedgerow. It seemed an odd thing to be doing. The Humber was full of sheep who seemed to be trying a variation on the old 'how many students can you get into a telephone box' routine.

As I left the car I noticed that the cowman's legs were sticking out from underneath the front end. I hesitated for a moment, thought about stopping to see what he was doing, and then hurried back to my patient.

'It's coming!' Miss Thwaites shouted as I approached. Then she cried out in sudden pain. I sprinted towards her and then threw my bag down onto the grass as I knelt beside her. I took out my foetal stethoscope and listened to the baby's heart. It seemed to be fine. I picked up Miss Thwaites' wrist and felt for her pulse. That felt fine too. I turned to get a pair of rubber gloves out of my bag and noticed that in my haste I'd left the gate open. Half a dozen cows and several sheep were already in the field, advancing steadily towards us. Just then it started to rain. It wasn't heavy but it was rain.

I pulled on my rubber gloves and bent over Miss Thwaites. 'Push!' I told her. I hadn't even examined her internally but there didn't seem much point at this stage and even though

69

I was wearing rubber gloves I wasn't keen on introducing any unnecessary infections into the area.

Miss Thwaites pushed herself up onto one elbow and tried to say something. I couldn't hear for the noise the sheep and the cattle were making so I bent my head and asked her to repeat it.

'I've still got my knickers on,' she told me. 'Don't they need to come off?'

'I think that would help,' I agreed, struggling to repress images of a baby bouncing up and down for eternity on its own private nylon trampoline. I helped her remove her knickers and took advantage of the opportunity to see what was happening down there. I could just see the baby's head.

'Push!' I shouted. 'It's coming! Push!' I put one arm around her shoulders and used the other to help keep her knees up and well apart.

The rain was pouring down now and the grass upon which I was kneeling was becoming soggier by the second. Just then the cowman reappeared holding a large plastic container that had at some stage contained fertilizer. Steam was coming from the open top.

'Hot water!' he said, proudly. His teeth nearly escaped from his mouth this time and he cursed vividly. 'I'm sorry about the teeth,' he apologised. 'These aren't mine. I borrowed them from my mother.' He took the teeth out and grinned at me edentulously. 'Mine broke,' he explained. He stuffed the borrowed dentures into his jacket pocket.

'Where did you get the hot water from?' I asked him, nodding towards the steaming hot fertilizer container.

'Your radiator,' he said proudly. He didn't bother to explain where he'd found the container. He beamed at me. 'Hot water,' he explained. 'You need hot water for babies don't you?' He put the container full of hot water down beside me and then pulled a huge clasp knife from the same pocket into which the teeth had disappeared. 'Knife for cutting the cord,' he said.

Miss Thwaites screamed and grasped hold of my wrist with her hand. 'It's coming!' she shouted. 'I can feel it coming.' I peeped. She was right. The baby's head was very nearly out. It seemed a much easier birth than any of the ones I'd attended in hospital, where the mothers had invariably been surrounded by huge amounts of expensive, sophisticated equipment. Just then the shepherdess reappeared clutching a bouquet of flowers. It seemed a nice touch. She knelt down beside Miss Thwaites. 'Chew on these,' she said. 'They'll help with the pain.' I stared at her, stared at the flowers and then looked at Miss Thwaites who now had her mouth wide open though no sound was coming from it. I peeped down in between her legs and could see that the baby's head was entirely visible.

'Keep pushing!' I shouted uselessly. Behind me I could feel something warm and solid pressing against my back. I turned my head and saw that a sheep had come up to see what was going on. I tried to shoo it away but it wouldn't go.

Attracted by the noise and the activity a large black and white cow wandered over. It urinated loudly and healthily, showing a remarkable bladder capacity, and then I jumped a yard into the air as I felt its rough tongue licking the side of my head.

'I can see the baby,' said the shepherdess, still clutching her bunch of wild flowers. Her hands looked red and swollen and I noticed with horror that the bunch included quite a few nettles. 'It's a boy,' she said.

The baby delivered itself. All I had to do was cut the cord and help deliver the placenta. I tied the cord with a length of red twine that the cowman pulled out of his pocket.

'Can I go home now?' asked Miss Thwaites, when it was all over. It was still raining and we were all absolutely soaked but none of us minded. The new mother looked absolutely radiant.

'I think you ought to go along to the hospital,' I said. 'Just for a check up.'

'I feel fine,' Miss Thwaites insisted. She pouted. 'I don't want to go into hospital.'

'The baby needs a check up,' I said firmly. I picked Miss Thwaites up and carried her back towards the car. She was carrying her baby and the cowman was carrying my black bag.

The Humber looked and smelt disgusting. Two sheep were lying down in the back and the car reeked of them. The front seats were still in the field. The shepherdess got her sheep out of the car and wiped up most of the mess with her bare hands. The cowman went back for the seats.

It took ten minutes for the two of them to clear the road of animals sufficiently for me to drive past and continue on towards Barnstaple but I had forgotten that the cowman had removed the contents of my radiator and despite the rain the Humber overheated and came to an ignominious halt just outside Shirwell, five miles from Barnstaple. We telephoned Mr Marshall, the Bilbury taxi driver and he took us the rest of the way.

As we drove up to the hospital entrance Miss Thwaites turned to me and whispered something. I didn't catch what she said and had to ask her to repeat it.

'I've just remembered,' she said, giggling. 'I left my knickers in that field.' She giggled again. 'Still,' she added, 'It isn't the first time I've left my knickers in a field.'

I blushed heavily and helped her out of the taxi.

'Don't worry about the bill, doctor,' said Mr Marshall. 'I'll put it on your account.' He smiled. 'I'll wait for you,' he promised.

*   *   *

Thumper was waiting for us and he grinned broadly when he saw Miss Thwaites and his new son.

'What a day!' he said. 'First I win £2 at snooker and now I'm a dad!'

I left them hugging one another and Mr Marshall drove me back to Bilbury.

'Isn't that your car?' asked Mr Marshall, as we passed my sad looking Humber. Steam was still coming from the bonnet.

'Yes,' I said miserably. It hadn't been a good investment. I wondered if it was worth bothering to get a garage to go out and collect it.

'Back to the Duck and Puddle?'

'Yes, please.' I was soaked and my trousers were covered in mud. I smelt of cows and sheep. I wanted a bath and needed to change my clothes.

By the time I got back to the pub it was 4.30pm and all I had time for was a quick wash before slipping on some fresh clothes. Then it was time to take Mr Marshall's taxi to Dr Brownlow's for the evening surgery. I was physically exhausted, mentally drained and financially broke. I was so tired that when my first patient came into the surgery that evening I very nearly succumbed to the temptation to give him a bottle of cough medicine and to send him on his way unexamined.

*   *   *

Hubert Donaldson looked just like the classic English tramp is supposed to look. His navy blue raincoat was tied around the waist with a piece of parcel string and his straggly, greasy hair was long and out of control. He had a well developed beard that looked as though it probably had a fair amount of wildlife living in it and a pair of shoes that looked as if they were designed to keep his feet cool in summer and wet in winter. He complained of a cough and a bit of pain in his chest. I told him to sit down and asked him a few questions about his medical history. He told me that he was in his late fifties, that he usually slept out of doors and that he had been perfectly fit and healthy for most of his life. He admitted that he smoked twenty or thirty cigarette stubs a day but insisted that most of the cigarette ends he picked up were tipped.

The smell from the other side of the desk was not encouraging and I had no real desire to explore beneath the raincoat but I felt duty bound to do so.

'What?' demanded Hubert. 'You want me to undress?'

'That's right,' I said.

'I haven't taken my clothes off for years,' he insisted. 'I can't even remember what I've got on.'

'Well, if you want me to try and get rid of that cough you'll have to let me examine you.'

Beneath the raincoat were several thick wads of newspaper. As Hubert carefully laid these down on the floor I glanced at the dates and saw that most of them were eighteen months old. After the newspapers there came a couple of sweaters (full of holes) a few more newspapers and then, finally, a grey woollen shirt came into view. That concealed nothing more than an ageing yellow vest.

73

'Can I keep my trousers on?' asked Hubert, now beginning to shiver, despite the fact that the temperature in the surgery was comfortably warm.

I nodded.

He grinned.

I smiled, nodded again and stood up to listen to his chest.

'I'd like you to have a chest X ray,' I told him when I'd finished.

'Do I have to go to the hospital for that?' asked Hubert, beginning to dress himself again.

'Yes. But they won't keep you. It'll only take a few minutes.'

Hubert looked suspicious.

'They won't keep you,' I assured him. I wrote out the X ray form and then helped him finish dressing. 'Come back and see me in three days. I'll have the X ray report back by then.'

I suddenly had a thought. 'How are you going to get to Barnstaple?'

Hubert looked at me as though surprised that I should even need to ask. 'I shall walk,' he said with dignity.

I took my wallet out and offered him some money. 'For the taxi fare.'

He refused it.

But I did manage to save him the cost of a prescription for the antibiotic I wanted him to take by finding a sample bottle of something suitable left by a drug company representative.

'Don't forget!' I told him as he left. 'I'd like to see you in three days.'

'I'll be here,' promised Hubert.

*   *   *

CHAPTER FIVE

'Good evening, doctor!' said the next patient. 'I'm Lionel Francis.' He held his hand out across the desk and gave me the benefit of a broad smile that must have paid for at least one dentist's summer holidays for several years. He clearly expected me to know who he was. He wore an expensive grey suit with a broad chalk stripe, a maroon shirt with a white collar and around his neck had something that looked like a Garrick club tie but wasn't. He was grossly overweight and his waistcoat looked uncomfortably tight. He had a small pink rosebud in his buttonhole and smelt very strongly of something so powerful that I decided that it was probably designed exclusively for use by men who are having affairs and want to smother the scent of their mistress's perfume.

I took the proffered hand and looked at him blankly.

'I'm a friend of Dr Brownlow's,' Mr Francis continued. 'We're in the same line of business. I run a small chain of chemists shops in the area.'

I murmured my congratulations and asked him what I could do for him.

'Don't you remember me? You visited me.'

I looked up and felt a flush of embarrassment as I recognised him. He'd had pyjamas on when last I'd seen him. 'How's your chest?' I asked.

'That's what I've come about. I've been asthmatic for years but it's been getting worse. I get breathless very easily and I've even coughed up a little blood a couple of times recently. I thought that perhaps the time had come to get you to do a few tests. Maybe an X ray?'

'Sounds a good idea,' I agreed. 'Would you take your jacket

and shirt off so that I can listen to your chest?'

Mr Francis stood up and started to undress. 'The wife wanted me to get Brownlow to send you round to the house but I thought you were probably busy enough so I thought I'd pop along here with the ordinary patients.'

'That's very kind of you,' I said. Quite unreasonably I decided that I didn't like Mr Francis very much. 'Have you had any other symptoms? Or is it just the cough?'

'Just the cough.' Mr Francis carefully hung his jacket over the back of the chair.

'Any pains in your chest.'

'Nothing to speak of.'

'Have you coughed up any phlegm?'

He shook his head and folded his waistcoat neatly.

'But you do get short of breath?'

'Especially when I'm on the golf course!' laughed Mr Francis, draping his tie over the chair. He looked down at his waistline as he unbuttoned his shirt. 'I need to lose a few pounds,' he admitted. He was being generous to himself. He needed to lose a few stones.

I examined the fat chemist's chest but could find nothing of any consequence, though he undoubtedly had an unpleasant and persistent cough.

'I can't find anything but I want you to have an X ray,' I told him, filling in an X ray request form. 'If you take this along . . .'

'Yes! I know what to do!' Mr Francis nodded. 'Charles Jarvis and I play golf together at Saunton Sands.' He looked across at me. 'Do you know Charles?'

I finished filling in the request form while he dressed. When he'd finished I held the request form out to him. 'No, I don't think so.'

'He's the top radiologist in the area,' Mr Francis told me. 'Very good at his job and a cracking good golfer.' He took the form off me and stood up. 'You must meet him sometime. Do you play golf?'

I shook my head.

'We must get you into the club,' smiled Mr Francis. 'You can't be a proper doctor until you play golf.' He finished tying his tie. 'When will you get the results back?'

I told him that I thought they'd be back in about three days.

*　　*　　*

My heavily solicited promise to have dinner with the district nurse and her husband hung over me like a large black cloud. At the end of the evening surgery that day all I really wanted to do was to go back to the Duck and Puddle, spend an hour soaking in a hot bath and then spend an hour in the deserted lounge bar eating a solitary evening meal. My quiet but perfect evening would then end with me falling into bed and sleeping for ten hours.

But there was little chance of any of that. As soon as the last patient left the evening surgery I said goodbye to Miss Johnson and walked outside to where my car should have been standing. Only then did I realise that the Humber was still standing helpless somewhere out on the road to Barnstaple. I was about to start the long and weary walk back to the pub when a figure appeared out of the dusk.

'Good evening, doctor!' said Mr Marshall. 'Can I give you a lift anywhere?' He waved a hand in the direction of his car which was, I could see now, standing just a few yards behind him.

A small voice at the back of my mind warned me that this was all getting very expensive but I was too tired to care. 'The Duck and Puddle, please, Mr Marshall!' I said, wearily walking round to the passenger side of his car and getting in. I was so tired that when the taxi drew up outside the pub a few minutes later I was very nearly asleep. We had been parked for several minutes before I realised that we'd arrived at our destination.

'Why didn't you tell me that we were here?' I asked the taxi driver as I staggered out of the car.

'You seemed tired, doctor,' said Mr Marshall. 'I didn't like to wake you.' He handed me my black bag which I'd forgotten. 'Are you going anywhere else this evening?' he asked hopefully.

I looked at my watch. 'I'm supposed to be having dinner with Mrs Wilson and her husband.' It was already ten minutes to eight. I didn't know what time dinner was due to start

77

but it couldn't be long. 'Could you wait five minutes? I'll just have a quick wash and then I'll be ready.'

Mr Marshall beamed. 'Certainly, doctor,' he said. 'My pleasure.'

It would be a lie to say that I raced into the pub but I moved as quickly as I could. I didn't have another jacket to put on but I had one clean shirt left.

'Mrs Wilson tells me that you're having dinner with her,' said my landlady, whom I bumped into at the bottom of the stairs. For a moment I thought I detected a hint of something in her voice though I was too tired to decide whether it was surprise, disapproval or warning.

I nodded and smiled. 'But I won't be late back,' I assured her. 'To be honest I feel a bit tired.'

'What shall I do if there are any more calls for you?' asked Mrs Parsons.

'The telephone operator knows,' I said. 'They can put any calls through to Mrs Wilson's number.'

Mrs Parsons nodded. 'Don't forget to take your key. And if you're not coming in to breakfast I'd be grateful if you'd let me know.'

It seemed a strange thing to say but before I could reply she'd disappeared.

Outside, Mr Marshall was waiting for me. I climbed into the taxi, put my black bag down by my side and then sat quietly back as he drove me round the village green and stopped outside a cottage directly opposite the Duck and Puddle. We were no more than two hundred yards away from where we'd started.

'Why didn't you tell me it was so close?' I asked him, feeling rather aggrieved as I clambered out of the taxi.

'You didn't ask me!' protested Mr Marshall, indignantly. 'I'm just trying to provide a service,' he snapped rather crossly. 'And at night!' he added. Then he reached across, pulled the passenger door to with a bang and accelerated away to his shop, another fifty yards up the road. I felt rather guilty and tried to call after him to apologise but he'd gone.

Mrs Wilson's cottage was one of five that were all joined together and all painted white. They all had thatched roofs, all seemed to have pretty little gardens and all were protected from the road by a picket fence that was painted white. There were no street lamps around the village green so I could see all this only by the light of the moon. It was, therefore, with some difficulty that I eventually found the small gate in Mrs Wilson's piece of fencing. I walked up her narrow front path and knocked on a heavy oak door that was studded with iron work. No one in Bilbury seemed to have much faith in modern, flimsy doors.

*   *   *

At first I didn't recognise the woman who opened the door. She wore an extremely short blue dress that failed to come within hailing distance of her knees. But it was the top half of her dress which was most difficult to ignore. There were no straps and without any visible means of support the dress seemed to be offering Mrs Wilson's extremely ample bosoms for examination. I found myself unwillingly transfixed by the peculiar sight of what looked rather like two large, pink blancmanges served up on blue plates.

Mrs Wilson had also managed to build her hair up into some sort of strange and insecure looking edifice on the top of her head and she had glued a pair of massive but patently false eyelashes onto her upper eyelids. These artificial additions were so heavy that they pulled her eyelids downwards and in order to see Mrs Wilson had to hold her head back. The effect of this was, of course, to push her startling bosom even further forwards.

'Hello!' she said. She'd even changed her voice, which was now quite a bit lower than normal. She held the door back and positioned herself in the doorway in such a way that in order to get into the cottage I had to squeeze through an impossibly small gap between the far door post and her menacing chest.

Once inside I stood nervously in front of a plump looking sofa covered in a bright chintzy material. A large mackerel tabby cat sat at one end of the sofa. A mixed tabby sat at the other end. The whole room had a definite woman's touch. Mrs Wilson closed the door and moved into the room towards me. Her skirt was so tight that it made movement exceedingly difficult. Things weren't helped by the fact that she was wearing black, patent leather shoes that were supported by huge stiletto heels. 'What can I get you to drink?'

'A tonic water would be very nice,' I replied.

'Come on now, you're not driving,' insisted Mrs Wilson. 'I saw you arrive in Pete Marshall's taxi.'

'But I'm on duty,' I reminded her, pointing to my black bag which I'd put down on the floor. 'I don't want to get reported for turning up to an emergency call smelling of alcohol.'

'Round here they're more likely to report you for *not* turning up smelling of alcohol!' laughed Mrs Wilson. But she did pour me a tonic water. 'I'll just have to go and get some ice and lemon,' she said, disappearing in the direction of what I took to be the kitchen. 'Sit yourself down and make yourself at home,' she called over her shoulder.

I sat down on the sofa, between the two cats, and looked around. Half the room was designed as a living room, with a sofa and a matching easy chair positioned around an open fire place, and part of it was designed as a dining room, with an oak dining table surrounded by four chairs. The table had been set but there was something odd about it that I couldn't quite put my finger on at first. The walls were decorated with prints of wild flowers and there were two huge displays of artificial flowers on either side of the fireplace. The windows were covered with rich, red velvet curtains which hung right down to the floor. Several copies of a woman's weekly magazine were stacked neatly on a coffee table which stood between me and the fireplace.

'You've decorated the room beautifully,' I called to the absent Mrs Wilson.

'Oh, I can't take the credit for it,' she replied. 'My husband is in charge of that sort of thing.'

'Oh,' I said. I was genuinely surprised. And then I realised what was wrong with the dining table – it was set for two not for three.

'Where is your husband?' I called. I could hear Mrs Wilson thumping noisily in the kitchen. I assumed that she was trying to get ice out of an ice tray. I remembered her saying that her husband was a policeman.

'He's on duty tonight,' came the reply. 'He won't be home until tomorrow morning.' There was a pause and then she reappeared in the doorway. 'He does a lot of night duty,' she said with quite a smile on her face. 'It suits us both,' she confided. She winked at me.

'He won't be joining us then?' I asked, feeling rather like a fly who's wandered into the middle of a web.

'I'm afraid not,' sighed Mrs Wilson, putting a silver plated coaster down on a small delicate looking table that stood near the sofa and then putting my drink down on top of the coaster. 'Just the two of us, I'm afraid.' She put her own drink down next to mine, placing it on another coaster. 'I thought it might be nice for us to get to know one another,' she said. 'Since we're going to be working together.' She moved one of the cats out of the way and sat down beside me before I could say anything in reply.

As she sat down Mrs Wilson's skirt rode up her thighs, displaying her stocking tops and an inch or so of naked thigh. She then crossed her legs, making things considerably worse. I tried not to look. She looked down and pulled pointlessly at the hem of her skirt. 'This skirt is a bit short,' she said unnecessarily. She shuffled a little closer so that our thighs were touching. I tried to move away but I had nowhere else to go. I didn't like to move the other cat which seemed very comfortably settled. 'But I like the colour,' she said, stroking the material with her fingers. 'And it feels nice too,' she added. 'Try it!'

Obediently, but tentatively, I reached out and touched the hem of her skirt, as though testing it to see if it was hot. Mrs Wilson giggled. 'Don't be silly,' she said. 'I'm not going to bite you.'

'Thank you for reminding Mrs Parsons that I wouldn't be having dinner at the pub tonight,' I said, desperately trying to change the subject and tactfully trying to remind Mrs Wilson that we were supposed to be having dinner together. I was starving hungry.

'Oh, that's all right,' said Mrs Wilson. 'My pleasure.' She made another useless attempt to pull down the hem of her skirt. 'I know you've been busy today,' she said.

'Terrible day!' I said. 'I haven't stopped. I didn't even have any time for lunch.'

'Don't worry!' said Mrs Wilson. 'I've got some nice macar-

81

oni cheese in the oven.' She leant against me and I felt myself starting to wheeze again as a cloud of her perfume enveloped me. 'I expect you'd like to relax a little before you eat,' she said. 'I know I would.'

I couldn't think of anything to say that wasn't rude or didn't sound greedy so I didn't say anything. Even the meal promised to be a disappointment. I hate macaroni cheese. I was staring straight ahead but I could feel Mrs Wilson's head leaning on my shoulder. 'Isn't this lovely?' I heard her whisper. 'So peaceful and relaxing.' A thick strand of hair had escaped from her hair piece and was hanging over her left eye.

'Very,' I heard someone croak in a voice that sounded vaguely like mine.

'Let's drink to your future here,' said Mrs Wilson. She leant across me, reaching for her glass. Everywhere I looked there seemed to be nothing but acres of pink chest. I felt physically endangered by it.

Mrs Wilson grasped her glass but instead of taking it back to her mouth she rested the hand that was holding it on my left knee. I felt her other hand resting on my neck. I could feel my heart pounding in my chest as though desperate to break free and I could feel beads of sweat beginning to break out on my forehead.

'The countryside round here is beautiful, isn't it?' I heard someone say in a voice that no longer sounded even vaguely like mine.

'My husband is a transvestite,' said Mrs Wilson suddenly. 'He likes dressing up in women's clothes,' she explained, as though I might not understand.

'I bet it gets very windy in the winter,' I heard someone reply.

'Personally,' breathed Mrs Wilson, 'I like a man to be all man.' Her left hand was now stroking my neck and her right hand, still holding her glass, had moved off my knee and onto my thigh.

'There must be lots of nice walks here,' someone said, in a squeaky voice that I did not recognise at all. 'Especially if you like walks,' they added rather lamely.

'I came home one day and found him dressed up in my

underwear,' said Mrs Wilson, leaning even closer. 'I like sexy underwear,' she murmured. 'But I prefer to be wearing it.' She moved her lips closer to my ear. 'You should see what I'm wearing now,' she whispered throatily.

I know my mouth opened but I can't remember what came out of it.

Mrs Wilson's right hand moved further up my thigh and suddenly the contents of her glass were emptied over my trousers. I was so tense that the shock of the cold liquid on my leg made me jump.

'Oh, silly me!' said Mrs Wilson, glancing down. 'Never mind,' she said. 'Take them off. I'll dry them in the airing cupboard.' She put her glass down and reached for my waist with her right hand.

I was desperately trying to catch hold of her hand, which seemed to have acquired the properties of a ferret, when I heard a sound which I had never thought I would be so pleased to hear. When people talk glibly of 'being saved by the bell' they have no idea how wonderful it is to be so saved. 'The telephone!' I cried, looking around for the responsible instrument. 'Quick! It might be a patient.'

'Oh damn!' said Mrs Wilson crossly. 'And just when we were beginning to enjoy ourselves.' She reluctantly stopped struggling to unfasten my trousers and I took full advantage of the respite, firmly moving her hand to one side and then standing up. 'Where's the telephone?' I asked her.

Mrs Wilson nodded towards a small, low table in a far corner of the room. Desperate lest the caller gave up before I could reach the instrument I flung myself upon it.

'Yes?' I cried, as though it was I who was in need of emergency help.

'Can you come over to the Duck and Puddle straight away?' asked a voice I recognised but couldn't place. 'Someone needs help.'

'I'm on my way!' I shouted, slamming the phone down and making for the door. 'Emergency!' I told Mrs Wilson who was still sitting on the sofa where I'd left her. 'Must go I'm afraid. Terribly sorry.'

'Damned patients,' said Mrs Wilson crossly. Then she tried to smile. 'Will you come back when you've finished?'

I shook my head sadly. 'I'm afraid it sounds as if it could take a long time to sort out.'

'But what about the macaroni cheese?' I heard Mrs Wilson cry plaintively as I left.

I didn't stop running until I reached the Duck and Puddle. 'Where's the patient?' I demanded breathlessly, as I burst through the door into the bar.

I was greeted with cheers, cat calls and whistles.

I looked around, puzzled.

'It's Thumper,' said Frank Parsons, the landlord. 'He was taken a little queer.'

'Who are you calling queer?' demanded Thumper, who was standing at the far end of the bar and who seemed perfectly healthy, though perhaps slightly inebriated.

The landlord looked at me, shrugged and apologised. 'He seems to have recovered,' he said. 'I hope we didn't interrupt anything.'

'You mean there isn't an emergency?'

Frank shook his head and then started laughing. 'I wish you could see your face,' he said. 'I don't think I've ever seen anything quite like it.'

'I do feel another turn coming on,' said Thumper, pretending to faint forwards onto the bar.

'Maybe you ought to stay in case he has another attack,' said Frank.

'I think perhaps I should,' I said, to more loud cheers and whistles. And then I caught sight of Mrs Parsons at the back of the bar. 'I know it's a bit of a cheek,' I said. 'But I'm starving hungry. I'd be very grateful if you could rustle up a cheese sandwich or something.'

'I can do better than that,' promised Mrs Parsons. 'I've got a lovely pie ready. Shall I serve it up in the lounge bar as usual?'

'I'll eat in here if that's all right with you,' I said. 'I need to keep an eye on Thumper.'

'What made you ... er ... how did you guess what ... er ... ?' I asked Frank, as his wife hurried off in the direction of the kitchen.

Frank leant forward. 'Let's just say that Kay Wilson has got a bit of a reputation for being rather a man eater.'

'No offence to yourself,' added Thumper. 'But it didn't seem hardly fair to leave the two of you together all evening.'

'I'm very grateful,' I said. And then I remembered that the telephone exchange was still putting genuine emergency calls through to Mrs Wilson's number. Life was getting complicated.

'I'll get the wife to have a word with Phyllis on the telephone exchange,' said Frank, when I'd explained the problem to him. 'Leave it to me.'

'Excuse me, doctor,' said Mr Marshall the taxi driver, sidling over to me. 'Couldn't help noticing that you haven't got your black bag with you.'

I looked down. He was right. I'd left it at Mrs Wilson's.

'Do you want me to pop back and pick it up for you?' he asked.

'I'd be grateful if you would,' I said. 'Perhaps you'd be kind enough to explain that I'm stuck here with an emergency.'

'No problem,' he promised with a sly smile. 'You leave everything to me.'

I turned back to the bar. 'Can I have a pint, please, Frank?' I asked, no longer caring what patients might smell on my breath.

'My treat!' insisted Thumper, on my right. He raised his glass to me. 'Just want to thank you for everything you did today. Very grateful, doctor.'

'That's OK,' I said. 'My pleasure. Are they both all right?'

'Wonderful, the pair of them,' replied Thumper. 'The hospital want to keep them for a day or so but they'll both be home soon.' He shook his head in disbelief. 'What a surprise. When I left home this morning my bird was going up to the surgery to get help with losing a bit of weight. Within a day you've got all her excess weight off her and given us a baby into the bargain.'

Frank put my pint down in front of me and I drank the new baby's health with the father.

'Actually,' said Thumper, moving a little closer. 'Anne asked me to ask you if you'd mind if we named the baby after you.'

'After me?'

'Well, you brought him into the world,' said Thumper. 'We

thought it might be rather appropriate.'

'I'd be very flattered,' I said, blushing. Nothing like it had ever happened to me before.

'Of course, it'll only be a second name,' said Thumper. 'His first name will be Jack. We wouldn't want to lumber him with a poofy name like yours for day to day use, would we?' He paused. 'No offence,' he added quickly. 'But what's all right for a doctor isn't really going to be any use to a son of mine, is it?'

'Why not?' I asked. 'He might grow up to be a doctor!'

Thumper stared at me over his beer glass. 'You're right!' he said firmly. He thought for a moment. 'Jack can be his second name,' he said.

'There you are, doctor,' said a quiet voice behind me. I turned round to see Mr Marshall put my black bag down on the floor by the side of my bar stool.

'Thanks very much.'

'No problem. Would you like me to pick you up in the morning to take you in to the surgery?'

'Yes, please,' I sighed. 'Thank you very much.'

'I'll be outside at 8.30 then, doctor,' said the unctuous Mr Marshall.

'I heard about the Humber,' said Thumper, leaning across and putting a hand on my forearm. 'Sorry about that.'

I shrugged. 'It was a bit expensive on petrol,' I said.

'Wasn't the right car for you,' said Thumper, shaking his head.

'Best I could afford,' I said miserably.

'We'll do better than that for you,' insisted Thumper. 'I'll pick you up after morning surgery tomorrow and take you down to the car auction at South Molton.'

'I haven't got any money,' I protested.

'Don't you worry, doctor,' said Thumper. 'We'll sort something out for you. You're as good as family now.'

It felt good.

*　　*　　*

Although she had served me my breakfast for two days I'd forgotten the name of the girl who was working at the Duck and Puddle. I hadn't really taken all that much notice of her although I had noticed that she was very pretty. As she put my breakfast down in front of me the next morning I heard sobbing.

I looked up. She had light brown hair, cut quite short, and the most beautiful green eyes I'd ever seen. She looked a couple of years younger than me. Tears were rolling down her cheeks.

Then I smelt the burning. I looked down and saw that everything on the plate in front of me was burnt to a crisp. Someone had tried to scrape the burnt bits off the bacon and the toast but the damage was too great to be repaired.

'Don't worry!' I said, cheerfully. 'I like my breakfast well cooked.' I turned the blackened sausage over to discover that the underside was even worse. It made a solid, wooden sound as it rolled across the plate. The girl lifted up her apron, covered her face with it and then ran off towards the kitchen. I half stood up, uncertain about whether or not to go after her. Eventually, I decided it was probably better not to. I sat down again, picked up my knife and fork and started to cut a corner off a piece of crunchy fried bread.

'You can't eat that!' said Mrs Parsons, sweeping up my plate off the table before I could do my knife any serious damage. She was still wearing her dressing gown and nightdress. The curlers were still in place too; once again there were just three of them, all at the front as though it was only the front that mattered.

'It's OK!' I said, weakly.

'Patsy's a bit upset this morning,' whispered Mrs Parsons, tipping her head in the direction of the kitchen.

'What's the matter?' I whispered back.

'Her father's poorly,' explained Mrs Parsons. 'And she's worried about him.'

'Why don't they call the doctor in?'

'You're the doctor,' said Mrs Parsons. 'Well, Dr Brownlow is. But Patsy's sister believes in some sort of herbalism based on flowers and they won't have a doctor on the farm.'

Mrs Parsons looked down at the plateful of burnt food that she was holding. 'I'll go and do you some fresh,' she promised, and disappeared towards the kitchen.

As I sipped at my coffee I could hear whispering in the kitchen and a few minutes later Mrs Parsons reappeared carrying a plate containing two eggs, two sausages and two pieces of fried bread. 'I'm afraid that was the last of the bacon,' she apologised.

'Don't worry,' I said. I hesitated. 'If Patsy thinks her father will see me I'll gladly call in and see what I can do.'

Mrs Parsons put a hand on my arm. 'I hoped you'd say that,' she said. 'I'll have a word with Patsy.'

As I wiped up the last of my egg with a piece of fried bread Mrs Parsons emerged from the kitchen towing Patsy behind her.

'Go on!' urged Mrs Parsons to Patsy. She turned to me. 'She's shy!' she mouthed.

'Would you please come and see my father?' Patsy asked me at last. She had stopped crying but her eyes still looked puffy and red. 'I've just spoken to him on the phone and he says he'll see you.'

'Of course,' I said, wiping my mouth with my napkin. 'Where do you live?'

Patsy gave me the address of their farm on the other side of the main Barnstaple road and I promised to call in there as soon as I could.

*　　*　　*

I'd intended to go to see Patsy's father at the end of the morning surgery but I'd forgotten that I'd arranged to meet Thumper. To my surprise he hadn't. His battered old truck was parked outside the surgery when I'd finished.

'Pete Marshall was waiting for you,' said Thumper. 'So I sent him away.'

'I hope he wasn't offended!'

Thumper laughed. 'Pete? Offended? He'll probably charge you for the journey out here anyway.'

'I really haven't got any money,' I warned Thumper, as I climbed into his truck. 'This is very good of you but all my cash went on buying that Humber.' I paused and frowned. 'Do you think I ought to arrange for someone to move it?' I asked him as he accelerated away.

'Don't worry about it,' said Thumper. 'It's all under control.'

I looked at him. 'What do you mean?'

'A mate of mine drove his truck into it last night,' said Thumper. 'It's a write off now.'

'Thanks,' I said drily. 'How does that help?'

'It's an insurance job now,' explained Thumper. 'Simple. Car like that in good condition has got to be worth at least £150–£200.'

'But it wasn't in good condition!' I said. 'It was in terrible condition.' And then a more important thought occurred to me. 'And I hadn't even had time to get it insured.'

'Don't worry about it,' insisted Thumper. 'You can claim off my mate's insurance.'

'But won't he mind?' I asked. 'He'll lose his no claims bonus, won't he?'

'He works for a big haulage company,' said Thumper. 'They always pay up on claims under £200. It's not worth their while to make a fuss about it.'

This was all getting a bit too much for me. 'Isn't this fraud?' I asked him, quietly, looking around to make sure that no one was listening.

'Fraud!' laughed Thumper, as the Ford bounced into and out of a huge pot hole. 'You're just getting some money off an insurance company. That's not fraud.'

'But . . .' I began.

'Look,' said Thumper, 'I don't know of anyone round here who's ever had any house or car repairs done without making an insurance claim.' He looked across at me and grinned. 'You just leave it all to me,' he said.

I sighed and shook my head. Life in the real world was getting more and more confusing by the day.

'Are you hungry?' asked Thumper, as we hurtled south-wards. He looked at his watch. 'We've got another hour before the auction starts and it's only ten minutes from here.'

'I could eat,' I agreed. 'If you know somewhere good.'

'Do you like trout?'

'Yes,' I answered, assuming that he knew of a good fish restaurant or, more likely, of a pub that served fish.

Thumper swung the steering wheel round and swerved off the road and into an open gateway. Then he drove straight on across a meadow. I turned and stared at him. 'Is this a short cut?'

'Sort of!' he answered. 'The river's down here.' We bounced and jolted our way across the field and came to a halt a few

yards away from a shallow, fast running river. As soon as
the truck came to a halt Thumper jumped out. 'Let's catch
ourselves some lunch, then!'

I climbed out and looked into the back of the truck. I could
see no sign of a fishing rod or, indeed, a fishing line of any
sort. I turned round and saw, to my surprise, that Thumper
was taking his clothes off. 'What on earth are you doing?'

He looked across at me. 'Going fishing!' he replied, as
though the question was daft. Naked, he walked across the
grass and knelt down at the water's edge.

'But how?'

He turned round and put a finger to his lips. 'You catch!'
he told me.

Puzzled but fascinated I crept up behind him and watched
as he waded into the river, heading towards a large rock
around which the water divided. Just underneath the rock
there was a small, dark, still pool of water. Crouching,
Thumper waded out into the river. It was quite shallow and
hardly covered his knees. Slowly, he bent even lower until
his body was parallel with the water surface and his hands
were just below the surface. Then, steadying himself on his
left leg he pushed his right foot forward until it slid underneath
the rock. Things then happened so quickly that I didn't have
time to see anything properly. All I knew was that there was
a splash and Thumper seemed to fall forwards into the water.
Moments later he stood up with two fingers of his right hand
stuck firmly into the gills of a large trout and with his left
hand wrapped around the fish's tail.

'Catch!' he called, throwing the fish towards me.

I'd never tried to catch a flying trout before and it really
is the sort of thing you need to practise. I got one hand to
it but the fish was far too slippery to hold onto and it slid
between my fingers and fell onto the grass where it threw
itself from side to side in quiet desperation. Just in time I
realised that it was making its way back towards the river.
Knowing that I wouldn't be able to hold onto the trout with
my bare hands I tore off my jacket and threw it over the
fish. I turned round, hoping for a little applause from Thumper
but he was bent down in the water again, clearly looking
for a second fish. When this one came flying through the air

I was ready for it and caught it in a piece of sacking that I'd retrieved from the back of the truck.

'That'll do, won't it?' asked Thumper, wading back towards the bank.

'How on earth did you do that?' I asked him, very impressed. I'd heard of people being able to 'tickle' and then catch trout with their bare hands but I'd never really believed it was possible.

Thumper grinned at me. 'Nothing like fresh trout cooked in the open,' he said, drying himself on his shirt. 'Shall we have them with some boiled potatoes?'

I laughed. 'Where are we going to get potatoes from?'

Thumper didn't answer but pulled on his underclothes and trousers and slipped his jumper back on. Then he killed the two trout neatly with a flick of his wrist, wrapped them in his wet shirt and put them carefully into the back of the truck.

We drove across and out of the meadow and then continued for another half a mile towards South Molton. Suddenly, Thumper jammed his foot on the brake and the truck squealed to a halt. 'Wait there! I won't be a minute,' he shouted, leaping out and sprinting across the road. He climbed over a fence and disappeared into a field. A couple of minutes later he reappeared with an armful of potatoes.

'New ones are better but at this time of the year you have to take what you can get,' he said, tossing the potatoes into my lap and them climbing back behind the steering wheel.

'Where now?' I asked him, laughing. 'Peas? Beans? Almonds?'

'No time,' said Thumper, shaking his head. 'There's a good place for a picnic a bit further along the road.' He drove on for another mile or so and then once again swerved into a field. This was bumpier and muddier than the first one and the truck skidded and slewed round as its wheels struggled to get a grip on the soft grass. We stopped at the far edge of the field and I found that we had met the river again a little further along its banks.

'Do you know what wild mint looks like?' asked Thumper.

'I think so.'

'There's usually some growing in that hedge. See if you can find some while I get some twigs together for a fire.'

When I got back, clutching two sprigs of freshly plucked mint, Thumper had lit a small fire by the edge of the river. The two trout were threaded on bits of wire that Thumper had taken from the back of his truck and the potatoes were boiling in one of the truck's hub caps that had been filled with river water.

It was one of the best meals I've ever eaten in my life. Fresh trout and fresh potatoes cooked in the open air. For pudding we collected blackberries from the hedgerow around the meadow.

'No coffee?' I asked, as Thumper pushed the hub cap back into place.

'No time,' replied Thumper, looking at his watch. 'We ought to get on to the auction.' He stamped on the fire and kicked the remaining smouldering twigs into the river. It wasn't until some time later that I discovered that catching fish from the river without a licence is strictly illegal.

*　　*　　*

I drove back from South Molton in an elderly, pale blue Morris Minor convertible that seemed in good mechanical condition, though the bodywork showed a few signs of rust. Thumper had wanted me to buy a 1949 Bentley that was being sold very cheap but I had, with some reluctance, argued that I really needed something that was reliable and that could be driven around the village without having to be refilled with petrol more than once. Thumper had bid for the car for me. 'Don't worry about it!' he insisted, when I kept warning him that I didn't have any money. He said he had explained to the auctioneer (who was, I gathered, a friend of his) that I was a doctor who needed a replacement car urgently and that I was waiting for a cheque from an insurance company. 'Besides,' said Thumper, 'the guy owes me a favour.'

I couldn't think of any favour which would encourage a car dealer to allow a customer to take a car away without paying for it but I didn't want to know any more so I didn't ask.

And so we drove back in convoy. Thumper leading the way in his huge and powerful four wheel drive Ford and me following in the little Morris Minor.

My first task on getting back to Bilbury was to visit Patsy's father at his farm.

A small crudely made wooden sign, with the name of the farm painted on it in white, marked the long, narrow, heavily rutted lane which led down to the small valley in which the farm nestled. I drove down the lane carefully, wincing as rocks and stones crashed noisily against the underside of the car. The farm itself was one of the largest in the area. In addition to the farm house two small cottages and two huge stone barns helped to create a large courtyard area. A row of neatly painted bee hives stood alone in the corner of a nearby field. As I drove into the courtyard chickens, ducks and geese half flew and half ran out of my way.

'Thank you for coming,' said Patsy, opening the front door. She looked at the Morris. 'Is that a new car?' she asked.

I explained that I'd just bought it (with Thumper's help) and Patsy said suitably polite things about it. 'My father can be very difficult,' she warned, leading me into the hallway. 'Please don't take offence if he says anything rude.' She looked very worried.

I followed her from the hallway, which was cluttered with coats, sticks and boots, into a large, comfortable looking sitting room. The first thing I noticed was the heat. There was a huge, old fashioned wood burning stove in the hearth and although there was no sign of burning fuel the heat was coming out of the stove in waves. Homes in North Devon didn't usually have central heating but they weren't cold. The second thing I noticed was a man in his mid forties lying on a sofa. He was fully dressed, even down to his wellington boots, and he looked thoroughly miserable.

'I suppose you're the bloody doctor,' he said as I approached.

I admitted that he was right.

'Can't stand bloody doctors,' said Mr Kennett. 'They always think they know everything.'

Patsy blushed. 'The doctor has come to look at you,' she said. 'I asked him to come.' She looked at me and held her head on one side as though to say 'sorry'.

'What can I do for you, Mr Kennett?' I asked.

'You could try buggering off,' said the farmer belligerently. 'But I don't suppose you will.'

'Daddy!' said Patsy. 'Please!'

The farmer sighed. 'I've got a weak heart,' he said. 'But I'm not having any of your damned pills and I'm not going into hospital.'

'You might not need to take anything,' I told him. 'Do you mind if I examine you?'

The farmer sighed and with obvious reluctance started to sit up. 'I'm not peeing in no bottles!' he said vehemently.

'That's OK,' I agreed. Slowly I helped him unbutton his shirt and then I pushed his vest upwards so that I could get at his chest.

'Well?' demanded Mr Kennett, when I finally took my stethoscope away.

'You do seem to have mild heart failure,' I told him. I rolled his trouser legs up and pressed my thumb on each of his ankles in turn. Even though he'd been lying down for some time fluid had accumulated in his legs.

'Are you taking anything at all at the moment?' I asked him. 'Any pills? Even anything not prescribed by a doctor?'

'Only my heart tablets,' said Mr Kennett, nodding towards the mantlepiece. I got up, walked across the room and picked up the small glass bottle of pills that he had referred to.

'Where did you get these from?' I asked him. The label on the bottle announced that the contents were made with an extract prepared from the hawthorn plant.

'I prescribed them for him,' said a voice I recognised. I turned and saw the shepherdess who'd helped me deliver Anne Thwaites' baby.

'This is my sister Adrienne,' said Patsy.

'They're hawthorn tablets,' explained Adrienne. 'For his heart.'

'How long has your father had heart trouble?' I asked her.

'I first diagnosed it about six weeks ago,' said Adrienne.

'I get breathless,' said Mr Kennett. 'That's a sign of heart trouble isn't it?'

'How long have you been breathless?'

'A month or so.'

'He's been getting worse,' said Patsy. She looked across

at her sister. 'I know you've been doing everything you can, Adrienne,' she said, apologetically. 'But it's true. Despite your tablets he has been getting worse.'

'His chest pains have gone,' said Adrienne. 'You had pains in your chest didn't you, Dad?'

Mr Kennett nodded.

'What brought the pains on?' I asked him.

'Came on during the harvesting,' said Mr Kennett. 'I came home one evening with this terrible pain across my chest.'

'And that's gone now?'

He nodded.

I put my stethoscope on his bare chest again. His heart sounded strong but there was no doubt that he was in mild heart failure.

'I'm not going into hospital and I'm not taking any damned drugs,' said Mr Kennett emphatically.

'OK.'

'You're stumped, aren't you?' he said, sounding almost pleased.

'At the moment,' I admitted. 'But I'd like to come and see you again if I might.'

Mr Kennett started to object but Patsy intervened. 'Please, father!' she said. 'What harm can it possibly do?'

Eventually her father agreed to see me again.

'Thank you for being so patient,' said Patsy as she saw me out of the house. 'I did warn you!' She really did have extraordinarily beautiful eyes. I smiled at her and said good-bye. I wanted to do some checking but I had an idea that I might be able to help Mr Kennett get better without sending him into hospital or prescribing any pills for him.

*   *   *

After that evening's surgery had finished I went in search of Dr Brownlow and, on Miss Johnson's advice, found him pottering in the dark in his large, walled vegetable garden.

'How's it going?' he asked me, as he prowled between two large vegetable beds. He had a torch which he flickered from side to side as he walked, though the garden was quite well lit with moonlight.

'It's hard work!' I confessed.

'It never gets easy,' said Dr Brownlow. 'But it gets easier.' He pulled out a carrot that had been half eaten and tossed it onto a compost heap. Then he picked up a small snail and carried it carefully over to the side of the vegetable garden where he placed it in a ledge on the wall.

'It's daunting never knowing what you're going to see next,' I said.

'That's what makes it the most exciting job in the world,' said Dr Brownlow quietly. 'As long as you like people.' He straightened up and looked straight at me. 'Do you like people?' I started to answer but he held up a hand. 'I don't just mean do you enjoy being with people you like,' he said, correcting himself. 'I mean, do you enjoy watching, listening to and even being with people that you don't like?'

I thought about what he'd said for a moment. 'Yes,' I said eventually. 'I do find people fascinating.' I walked with him across to his greenhouse. 'In hospital,' I said, 'I never really had a chance to develop any sort of relationship with my patients. Patients in hospital don't really regard doctors as people – I suppose that's why there is so much camaraderie between patients – it's "them" and "us".' I watched as Dr Brownlow picked up some cuttings and examined them carefully. 'Here as a general practitioner I feel that everything is so much more real.' I paused for a moment. 'It's very nice,' I said. 'I like it. But it's also very frightening.'

'No white coat to hide behind?'

'Exactly!' I agreed. 'And no one else to help share the responsibility.'

'The stakes are higher in general practice,' said Dr Brownlow. 'People expect more of you but they'll give more of themselves too. You have to risk more, you have to give more of yourself, but you get more in return. Satisfaction, I mean, not money.' He picked a piece of parsley from a plant in a pot and handed it to me. Then he picked a second sprig and popped it into his mouth. 'What did you dream of when you were a kid?'

I looked at him for a moment before answering. 'It sounds a bit embarrassing, a bit too good to be true, but I wanted to do something to help people.'

'I can believe that. It isn't entirely altruistic to want to

96

help people. If you want to do something then you're doing it for yourself. Ultimately that's selfish. It just happens that while you're doing something selfish you're also doing something useful.'

'I've never thought of it like that before,' I said. I put my sprig of parsley into my mouth. I'd never eaten parsley by itself before. I liked it.

'Who was your favourite hero?'

It was such an odd question that I replied instantly, without thinking. 'Robin Hood.' I immediately felt embarrassed.

'Mine was Don Quixote.' Dr Brownlow sat down on the edge of a small wooden table. He looked thoughtful. 'You've picked the right job,' he told me. 'I enjoyed being a family doctor.'

'Enjoyed? That sounds final.'

'I'm getting old. My best days are over. General practice is a job for a young man. Thirty years ago I could stay up all night delivering a baby and then spend the whole of the next day driving around from farm to farm.' He paused. 'No more,' he said softly and rather sadly. 'No more.'

There was a long silence. Eventually I broke it.

'Talking of farms,' I said, 'I went to see Mr Kennett today.'

'There you are,' said Dr Brownlow. 'I looked after his father for thirty years. I delivered his two daughters. I've got old around here.'

'His one daughter seems to be a bit of a herbalist.'

'Daft business. Using crude, contaminated herbs doesn't make any sense to me these days.' He bent down, carefully picked up a moth that had got trapped in a spider's web and gently freed its wings. 'I told her off about it last year.'

'Adrienne is treating him for heart trouble.'

Dr Brownlow looked at me. 'Heart trouble? Kennett? No. He's got a heart like a Rolls Royce engine.'

'Not at the moment,' I said. 'His heart is beating irregularly, his chest is full of fluid and he's got ankle swelling. Classic heart failure.'

'When did all this start?'

'Haymaking. He got a pain in his chest.'

'What do you think?'

'I think he probably tore a muscle hauling bales of hay about.'

97

'And the heart failure?'

'That's what I wanted to ask you about. Adrienne is giving him something made out of hawthorn. Do you know what the toxic effects of hawthorn are? I think she might be poisoning him.'

Dr Brownlow looked at me sharply.

I smiled. 'Accidentally.'

Dr Brownlow carefully carried the liberated moth over to the greenhouse door. Once he was outside he opened his hands and held them out in front of him. The moth paused for an instant, fluttered its wings a couple of times experimentally, and then flew away into the night.

'Come with me,' said Dr Brownlow, turning and heading for the house. He led me into the surgery where he headed straight for a row of books on a bottom shelf. He pulled out a large, blue bound textbook and blew a thick layer of dust off its binding. Then he handed me the book. 'Have a look in there. I haven't got my glasses with me.'

The book was a textbook of herbalism. I opened it at the index and then flicked through until I found the entry for the hawthorn bush. There was a clear warning there that preparations containing hawthorn could cause heart failure; the very disorder that Adrienne thought she was treating. I read the passage out loud.

'Take him off the hawthorn and the chances are that he'll get better,' Dr Brownlow told me.

'Do you want to have a word with him?' I asked. I knew that there was a very good chance that Mr Kennett would make a fairly miraculous recovery if we stopped his pills. Most of the hospital consultants I'd ever worked for would have insisted on taking the credit.

'No!' said Dr Brownlow. He sounded surprised and looked puzzled. Then he understood. 'It won't do your reputation any harm if you can cure his heart trouble,' he told me. He took the book off me and put it back on its shelf. 'Do you know, I used to work with doctors who would have taken great advantage of a situation like this. They'd have prescribed some harmless sugar pills to replace the hawthorn and charged a fortune for them. Then they'd have told poor Kennett that it was their magic pills that had cured him. And they'd have carried on selling the damned things to him for years.'

'I know doctors who'd still do that,' I said quietly. I suddenly looked at my watch. It was ten to nine. 'I ought to be going.' I said regretfully. I liked talking to Dr Brownlow. I liked him. 'Mrs Parsons will have my dinner ready for me.'

'Are they looking after you all right?'

'Very well.'

'Good,' said Dr Brownlow, who seemed genuinely pleased. 'You must come and have dinner with me one evening.'

'I'd like that very much,' I told him. And meant it.

*　　*　　*

For the first time since I'd been in Bilbury the sun was shining brightly and it made a world of difference as my Morris Minor bumped and jiggled its way down the hill to the Kennett's farm. High overhead a buzzard circled slowly and patiently, floating on currents of air as it looked for food. I was so busy watching the buzzard that I didn't watch the road properly. The nearside of the Morris bounced down into a large pothole and then bounced out of it again; only with difficulty did I manage to hold onto the steering wheel and keep the car away from the stone walls which bordered the track. I drove a little more cautiously after that.

Seeing the farm ahead reminded me of Patsy. I liked Patsy. I wondered how she got to the Duck and Puddle every morning. I wondered why she was working at the pub when there must be lots to do at the farm. I wondered, idly, if she had a boyfriend.

It wasn't Patsy who answered my knock on the door. It was her sister, Adrienne.

'I've come to see your father,' I said. 'I promised I'd come back.'

'I know you did,' said Adrienne. She turned and walked back into the house. Silently I closed the front door and followed her.

Mr Kennett was sitting on the same sofa and in virtually the same position as the last time I'd seen him. But if anything he looked worse. His legs were more swollen and he was clearly having even more difficulty in breathing. I put my bag down on the floor, knelt down beside him and examined him.

99

'I'm not going into hospital,' said Mr Kennett forcefully. 'And I'm not taking any damned pills.'

I thought he ought to be in hospital but I didn't say so. No one seemed to want to go into hospital these days. 'I think you could be reacting badly to the hawthorn,' I told him, trying to be as tactful as I could. 'It sometimes happens,' I said, half turning and half addressing Adrienne who was, I knew, standing behind me.

Neither of them said anything.

'The pills stopped the pains in my chest,' protested Mr Kennett.

I suspected that the pains in his chest had been muscular, brought on by throwing bales of hay around. But I didn't think it would help to tell him that. 'But you've been getting all sorts of other symptoms since the pains went, haven't you?'

Reluctantly, Mr Kennett nodded. The movement started him coughing and Adrienne had to come forward and push a couple of cushions behind his back. I waited until the coughing fit had passed.

'Just try managing without the pills for a few days,' I said. 'That's all I want you to do. If the pains come back then by all means try taking the tablets again.'

'Do you think his breathing will improve if he stops the hawthorn?' asked Adrienne suspiciously.

I nodded.

'You think he could be allergic to it?'

'Yes,' I lied. I thought he'd been poisoned by it but I didn't think they'd believe me if I said that.

Adrienne looked doubtful.

'People can get allergies to anything,' I reminded her. 'You must know that.'

'Yes, I suppose so,' she admitted with some reluctance.

'Then what is there to lose by stopping the hawthorn for a few days?'

'I think he's right, Dad,' said Adrienne at last.

'OK,' grunted Mr Kennett. 'If you say so.'

Before I left Adrienne insisted on giving me a jar of their home made honey.

*   *   *

CHAPTER SIX

The arrival of Mike Trickle, the television celebrity, had caused a good deal of excitement in the village, though no one had yet seen him.

Mr Trickle had bought a house called Bilbury Grange that was situated about half way between Dr Brownlow's spacious home and the village green. It was impossible to see it from the road.

'Have you seen him yet?' asked Patsy, as I ate my breakfast. My mouth full of bacon I shook my head.

'We thought he might have rung the surgery to register as a patient,' said Mrs Parsons, who sounded disappointed.

'Has Mr Trickle been into the pub for a drink?' asked Miss Johnson half an hour later as I prepared to start the morning surgery.

I shook my head. 'Sorry. No sightings yet.'

I had little time for the exciting but invisible Mr Trickle because I was now discovering that one of the problems of general practice is that the number of problems to be sorted out seems to increase steadily with each new day.

I wanted to speak to Mr Kennett about stopping his hawthorn pills. I wanted to ring the hospital to find out what was happening to Keith Harper. And I was waiting for the X ray results on Lionel Francis and Hubert Donaldson.

It was the two sets of X ray results that came first, arriving at the surgery that morning in the same large, brown envelope. The results, which surprised me, showed that Hubert, the elderly tramp, had no more than a chest infection, while Lionel, the pompous chemist, had an inoperable carcinoma of the lung. I did the surgery that morning knowing that afterwards I had to go round to tell the pharmacist that he was dying.

At the end of the morning's surgery, before I could leave to do any visits, a stout man in a tweed suit walked into the consulting room accompanied by a tall, elegant looking woman wearing an open fur coat over a white dress. The man looked vaguely familiar though I didn't realise why until a few moments later. He wore a pair of gold rimmed half moon spectacles, an old university tie which I couldn't identify and had a Rotarians badge in his lapel. She wore a single strand of pearls round her neck and had a silk scarf draped around her neck.

She had the sort of bone structure that most women claim to envy but she also had small, rather mean looking eyes which meant that she didn't look as attractive as she might otherwise have done. He had an old fashioned hair cut that looked as if it had been done by an army barber and red, rather blotchy skin which suggested to me that he had a penchant for rich red wines. He looked like the sort of man who is never late for anything, the sort of man who always wears a clean shirt (and clean underwear), who always keeps his car clean and tidy (inside and out) and who always knows exactly how much change he's got in his pocket. He was a man I felt instinctively that I could safely distrust.

'I want to talk to you about my father,' said the man, shutting the door behind him. The woman with him, who was, I assumed, his wife, sat down without speaking.

I looked at him expectantly.

'We both think he's behaving irrationally,' said the stranger firmly. 'We think he needs to be looked after.'

I looked at the man and then at the woman, trying to remember if I'd ever seen them before. But although I half recognised the man I couldn't identify either of them. 'I'm sorry,' I said. 'Could you please tell me who you are? And who your father is? Do I know him?'

'My name is Simon Brownlow, Dr Simon Brownlow,' sighed the stranger rather impatiently. 'I'm a general practitioner in Barnstaple. You're working for my father.'

'Dr Brownlow?' It would be a fearsome understatement to say that I was surprised.

'This is my wife Dr Daphne Norman,' said Dr Brownlow junior, waving a hand airily in the direction of the woman in the fur coat.

'I'm an anaesthetist,' said Dr Norman. She spoke as though someone had rammed a large piece of fruit into her mouth.

I realised why I half recognised the man. He looked a bit like a younger and less cheerful version of his father. 'Oh.' I said. It was all I could manage.

'My father has always refused to register with another general practitioner,' said Dr Brownlow junior. 'So you are the closest thing he has to a family doctor.' I made one of those unintelligible, meaningless noises we all make when we want to indicate that we're listening but we don't want to commit ourselves.

'The thing is,' said Dr Norman, 'that we're worried about Simon's father. We're worried about him because he doesn't seem to be able to look after his own affairs properly.'

'This house is far too large for him,' interrupted Dr Brownlow junior. 'It is quite absurd that he should continue to try and live here at his age.'

'He seems to cope quite well,' I said. 'From what I've seen.' I looked at them both in turn. 'Have you noticed any specific problems?'

There was a silence and my two visitors looked at one another.

'To be frank,' said Dr Brownlow junior, 'the problem is largely a financial one. My father simply can't afford the upkeep of this enormous house but he won't accept that he needs to move to more suitable accommodation. I've already spoken to a property developer who's offered a very respectable sum for the house and grounds. The interest on the capital would give my father a good income. He would never have to worry about money again.'

'Nor would you,' I thought, wondering what plans the young Dr Brownlow and his wife had for the capital when old Dr Brownlow died.

'If father keeps on selling off bits of land the value of the site will fall dramatically,' said Dr Norman. 'The developer Simon has spoken to is interested in developing the whole site and turning the house and grounds into a holiday complex: hotel, chalets, restaurant, caravan park, you know the sort of thing.'

'There are some perfectly acceptable flatlets available in Barnstaple,' Simon Brownlow told me. 'My father would be much safer in one of them.'

'What happens if he falls in the night and breaks a leg?' demanded Dr Norman. She waved a hand around. 'Who'd find him in this massive barn of a place?'

'There's Bradshaw and his wife,' I reminded them. 'And Miss Johnson and I come in every day.' I didn't like young Dr Brownlow or his wife. I didn't like them quite a lot. They were talking about Dr Brownlow as though he had one and a half feet in the grave.

'That's another thing,' said Simon Brownlow. 'It's quite absurd for my father to have staff. He can't possibly afford them.'

There was another long silence. I looked at each of them in turn. 'What did you want me to do about it?'

'For a start you could have a word with him,' said Dr Norman. 'If he won't listen to you then I think you ought to consider having him taken into care.'

I was aghast. She was suggesting that I use the law to have her father-in-law locked away.

'It's going to come to it sooner or later,' she replied. 'It would be better for everyone if it were sooner.'

I stood up. 'This has all been a bit of a surprise for me,' I said. 'I'll think about what you've told me.'

'OK,' said Simon Brownlow. 'That's fair enough.'

'But don't take too long about it,' said Dr Norman.

They left without shaking hands or bothering with any of the other time wasting social niceties. I was glad. I didn't want to shake hands with either of them.

*   *   *

When they'd gone I stayed where I was for several minutes wondering what on earth to do. I'd been in the job for just a few days and already I was under pressure to have my employer taken into care. As if all the other problems I'd got weren't enough! What made the whole thing significantly more painful was the fact that I admired and respected Dr

Brownlow. And I liked him. Eventually, I decided that I'd have to talk to him and tell him what had happened.

I found him in the billiard room.

'I've never been able to make the cue ball swerve,' Dr Brownlow complained, without looking up from the table. He drew back his cue and stabbed at the white ball which travelled the length of the table in a perfectly straight line. 'Damn.'

'I think perhaps your contact point on the cue ball needs to be a bit further to the side,' I suggested. 'And you need to hit down into the ball a bit more too.'

Dr Brownlow stood up and handed me his cue. 'Show me.'

I bent down and, with that occasional spot of good luck that always fools me into believing that the fates aren't entirely conspiring to destroy me, succeeded in sending the cue ball skidding down the green baize in a perfect curve.

'I wish I could do that,' sighed Dr Brownlow. He retrieved the cue ball, bent down and tried again. This time there was a hint of swerve in the ball's path. 'Did you see that?' he asked, looking up with a broad grin on his face.

'Once you can curve it a little bit it's just a question of practising more and getting more power into the shot,' I assured him.

'I'm always frightened of jumping the cue ball off the table,' Dr Brownlow confessed.

'You won't if you hit it in the right place,' I said. It felt good to have found something about which I seemed to know a little more than Dr Brownlow. I reached over the table, picked up the cue ball, looked at it for a moment, wiped it on my sleeve and then put it back on the table and rolled it towards him. 'I've just had a visit from your son and his wife.'

'They came to see you?' Dr Brownlow sounded surprised.

I nodded.

'What on earth for?'

I shrugged and tried to smile. 'They think you ought to be living in sheltered accommodation,' I told him. 'Apparently they've found somewhere in Barnstaple that they think would be suitable.'

Dr Brownlow went pale and then started to redden with

what I suspected was suppressed rage.

'They suggested that I ought to consider signing a court order agreeing that you're not competent to manage your own affairs.' I felt embarrassed.

'Why you? You're not my doctor.'

'They say that since you're not registered with any other doctor and I'm looking after your patients I'm responsible for you.'

Dr Brownlow smiled at me. 'What are you going to do?'

I laughed. 'I'm not going to do anything.' I promised him. 'It's absurd.'

Dr Brownlow sighed. 'It isn't all that absurd,' he said sadly. 'At least, not from their point of view.' He picked up one of the red snooker balls and rubbed it against his waistcoat to get rid of a speck of dust that neither of us could see. He put the ball back down on the table. 'They've been nagging me for years to sell this house to developers. It costs a lot to run and to pay for the upkeep I've been selling off bits of land.'

He picked up another ball and fingered it lovingly. 'I suppose they can see their inheritance slowly disappearing and they don't like it.'

I didn't know what to say and so I said nothing.

'I bought this house in the 1930s,' said Dr Brownlow. 'I didn't have any money but my wife had an inheritance and doctors were quite well paid in those days. My income paid the bank and her income paid the staff we needed.' He looked around the snooker room. The oak panelling was richly decorated with wooden carvings. Suddenly he looked old and frail and weak and vulnerable.

'When I was a boy,' he said after a long pause, 'my parents were very poor. We only ever had milk in our tea when there was a baby in the house.' He walked across the room to a large, leather arm chair and sat down in it. The chair was one of a pair. I walked across and sat down in the other chair. 'My father was a farm labourer,' he said. 'When I was twelve he hurt his foot in an accident on the farm. The doctor said it was only bruised so he didn't get any compensation and he didn't get any sick money. So to get money for food he had to go to work. I watched him go out of the house limping. He had to walk six miles to work and six miles back again in the evening. That night he came back home and his foot was swollen up so much that he had to cut his boot off.'

There were tears in Dr Brownlow's eyes as he continued. 'He came into the living room and put his foot on the fender and got my mother to fetch him a hammer. Then he deliberately broke his big toe. He just smashed the hammer down on it right there in the living room. Then he went up to bed. Next morning the foot looked even worse and my mother called the doctor in. They gave him his sick money.' Dr Brownlow swallowed hard. 'He lost his foot two weeks later,' he said. He spoke so quietly that I could hardly hear. 'It got infected and they had to amputate it.' There were tears running down Dr Brownlow's cheeks as he looked across at me. 'He never worked again after that,' he said.

After a long, long pause he looked across at me. 'Have you ever known what it's like to be hungry? *Really* hungry?'

I shook my head.

'When I got a scholarship my parents were so proud they nearly burst with joy. But when I qualified as a doctor they wouldn't come to the university for my graduation ceremony. I begged them to but they wouldn't come. They said they had to stay at home to look after the chickens but they didn't. They stayed away because they thought I'd be ashamed of them. They thought they would let me down. They didn't want to risk damaging my career in any way.'

Dr Brownlow swallowed hard. 'When my wife and I bought this house I went and fetched them. I don't think they believed it for a while. I wanted them to stay here, to live with us, but they wouldn't.' The tears were rolling down his cheeks. 'Do you know,' he said quietly, 'they would never use the front door? They always insisted on coming round to the back.'

I looked around the huge billiard room. It was a wonderfully absurd room and a wonderfully absurd house. I tried to imagine how it must have looked to Dr Brownlow's parents.

'My wife and I loved it here. She's buried in the gardens,' said Dr Brownlow. 'There's a piece of consecrated ground that was used when the house had its own chapel.'

'When did she die?'

'Five years ago. March the 14th. She died upstairs in our bedroom.' He looked straight at me. 'When she was dying we talked about where she'd be buried. And I promised her that I'd be buried next to her.' He paused. 'If the developers buy the house and the land heaven knows what will happen to her.'

For a few moments neither of us spoke. It was Dr Brownlow who broke the silence. 'Logically Simon is right,' he said at last. 'I can't afford to run this place. It's crazy that I continue to live here.'

He stroked the leather of his chair. 'But this is my home. It contains all the things that make living worthwhile and it contains every happy memory I've got. I don't want to sell it. I don't want some barbarians turning it into flatlets or flattening it and covering the land with pre-fabricated chalets.'

I leant forward. 'Doesn't your son understand any of this?'

Dr Brownlow shook his head.

'Have you talked to him about it?'

Dr Brownlow thought carefully before speaking. 'I love my son,' he said slowly. 'I love him because he's my son.' He paused for what seemed a long, long, long time. 'But I don't like him,' he added. 'And I know I can't trust him.' There was another long silence. 'And I neither like nor love nor trust my daughter-in-law.' He looked across at me. 'Sad, isn't it? Does it shock you?'

'No,' I said slowly, after a moment's reflection. 'But it is sad.'

'Simon has never been able to forgive me,' said Dr Brownlow. 'He's always been intensely materialistic. I think it was something he picked up at school. When he was young he decided he wanted to be a doctor. I thought it was for the right reasons but it wasn't. He wanted to become a doctor because he knew that we lived in a big house and had a Rolls Royce and people to help look after us. He assumed that all doctors lived the same way.'

'I bought the Rolls very cheaply,' said Dr Brownlow. 'My wife loved it. It's cost me less to run than if I'd bought ordinary cars.'

I waited. I felt very close to him.

Dr Brownlow stared thoughtfully at the floor. 'Simon feels cheated and frustrated and he blames me.' He took out a large handkerchief and wiped his eyes then blew his nose. 'I don't think it's conscious,' he said. 'But deep down he blames me for misleading him. Part of his desire to make me sell this house – and it's something he's been trying to do for years – is inspired by the fact that he wants the money – and wants me to stop spending it on running the place – but part of it is inspired by the fact that he wants to punish me. He doesn't like the idea of me living here when he can't afford anything larger than a very ordinary four bedroomed, detached house in Barnstaple.' The bitterness came through in Dr Brownlow's voice. 'Still,' he said sadly, 'there is one thing. I may not be able to trust Simon but at least he's predictable.' He smiled. 'Funny thing, isn't it? The people in this world that you can rely on most are the people you know you can't trust.'

There was another long silence. Once again Dr Brownlow blew his nose.

'I suppose I ought to be getting on and doing some work,' I said quietly.

'Do you think I should sell?' asked Dr Brownlow. 'Do you think I'm crazy trying to stay here?'

I didn't need to think about it. 'No,' I said without any hesitation. 'No. I don't think you should sell and I don't think you're crazy at all.'

He smiled at me. I thought he looked much older and much more weary. 'Thank you.' He spoke so quietly that I could hardly hear him.

I started to move towards the door. 'I think it's a lovely house,' I told him.

Almost imperceptibly he nodded. Then he looked up at me and smiled faintly. When I left him he was chalking his cue.

*   *   *

Telling Lionel Francis that he had cancer that couldn't be treated was no easier than I had expected.

'There must be some mistake,' said Mr Francis defiantly, his face white with fear and his body trembling.

'I'm afraid not.' I showed him the X ray report with his name on it.

'But lung cancer,' said Mr Francis. 'It's not fair! I've never smoked a cigarette in my life.'

'I know,' I said quietly. 'It's not fair.' I really didn't know what else to say. No one had ever told me how to tell a man he was dying. Maybe there isn't any way to teach someone how to do that. Maybe it's something you have to learn the hard way.

'I want a second opinion,' insisted Mr Francis. Now there was anger in his voice. 'I want to see Charles Jarvis.'

'That's no problem,' I assured him. 'I'll fix it up for you.'

'Today!' insisted Mr Francis. 'I want to see him today.'

'I'll try,' I promised. 'Can I borrow your telephone?'

When I left him a few minutes later he was convinced that his appointment with Charles Jarvis later that day would confirm that he didn't have cancer after all.

*   *   *

I was far less apprehensive about my consultation with Hubert Donaldson that evening but in a way it was just as disturbing. Instead of being pleased when I told him that he simply needed to carry on with the antibiotics I'd prescribed for him Hubert looked glum.

'You don't seem pleased with the X ray results?' I said.

'I'm not afraid of death,' he told me. 'Why should I be pleased?' He coughed painfully. 'What is there about death that makes it worse than life?'

I didn't know how to answer him. There were too many good things in my life for me to ever understand him.

'There are three sorts of people in this world,' said Hubert. 'Those who are afraid of death. Those who are afraid of dying. And those who are afraid of living.' He looked straight at me. 'Once you know what someone fears most you'll know a lot about them.'

I looked at him for a long moment before I spoke. 'That's sad.'

'Life is often sad.'

'Isn't there anything you'd miss?'

'My dog. I'd miss my dog.'

'What sort of dog?'

'Welsh sheepdog. I found her when she was a puppy. I was passing a farm in Shropshire. She was a sorry little thing then. I bent down to give her a pat and she's never left me since.'

'Where is she?'

He jerked his head towards the door. 'Waiting outside.'

'What's her name?'

'Ben.'

'Isn't that an odd name for a bitch?'

He shrugged.

'Can I see her?'

He stood up and walked towards the door. I followed him. The dog, a young black and white collie was sitting patiently outside the surgery door. As soon as Hubert appeared the dog's ears pricked up. Her whole body stiffened with excitement and her eyes seemed instantly brighter.

Tentatively, I bent down to stroke her but she backed away, her eyes fixed firmly on Hubert. I turned and saw him nod to her. That was all it took. Then she kept still and allowed me to make a fuss of her.

I liked Hubert's dog. I wasn't entirely sure what to make of Hubert. But I liked his dog.

*　　*　　*

CHAPTER SEVEN

Penelope was coming to stay for the weekend and Dr Brownlow had agreed to give me two days off duty. At half past nine on Saturday morning I drove over to Barnstaple to pick her up at the station.

'God!' she said when she saw me. 'What an expedition!' She was dressed in a white trouser suit and had had her brown hair cut very short in a page boy style. She was carrying a small green leather handbag and didn't seem to have any luggage. She looked more elegant and more full of confidence than I remembered.

'I had to leave Bristol at 6.30 this morning!' she announced. She looked around the station as though trying to decide whether or not to buy it. I leant forward to kiss her but at the last moment she turned her face so that my lips collided with her cheek.

'I must find my luggage,' she said, turning round and searching the platform behind her. She didn't have to look far. A man in his late twenties, dressed in a rather scruffy grey suit, was standing behind her holding two suitcases; one small and one quite large.

She thanked him and the stranger put the cases down but didn't move away immediately. To my embarrassment Penelope ignored him and turned back to me. 'Would you bring my cases, please? Where's the car?' The man who'd carried her cases from the train stood for a few moments more and then walked away looking strangely alone. I felt sorry for him.

'He kept trying to chat me up on the train,' Penelope confided. 'So I thought he could at least help with my cases.'

'What on earth have you brought with you?' The cases were difficult to lift.

Penelope shrugged. 'Just a few clothes.' She paused to flick a speck of dust off her jacket. 'It's difficult knowing what to bring to the country.' I looked at the white trouser suit and thought about the inside of the Morris. I wished I'd remembered to give it a bit of a clean.

I opened the boot and just managed to fit Penelope's two suitcases into it. 'This is it!' I said rather proudly.

'Oh,' said Penelope, clearly disappointed. 'How sweet.' She walked across to the front passenger door and looked inside. A look of clear distaste appeared instantly on her face. For the first time I noticed that she didn't look anywhere near as pretty when her face showed any expression. She opened the door, brushed at the seat with her handkerchief and then sat down. I closed the boot lid, walked round to the driver's door and jumped in beside her.

'I'm so glad that you could come,' I said. I leant across to give her a proper kiss and this time she let me kiss her briefly on the lips before pushing me away. 'Not here. Not in public. Not now we're both doctors.'

I put the key into the ignition and switched on.

'Before we set off do you think we could have the hood up?'

I looked up at the sky. It was clear and cloudless. It was winter but it was a superb day for topless motoring. I got out of the car and put the hood up. While I did so Penelope took a small mirror out of her handbag and checked her make up.

It took no more than fifteen minutes to drive from the railway station in Barnstaple to the Duck and Puddle in Bilbury but during the journey I realised two things.

First, I realised that Penelope and I didn't seem to have anything much to talk about. At medical school we had, I thought, got on quite well. But now that all seemed a lifetime away. I tried to remember what we'd talked about then but could remember nothing that wasn't tied up with work. We had discussed difficult cases we'd both seen. We had talked about textbook problems we'd encountered. And we had moaned about consultants we didn't like. But it had all been practical work talk. We had never really bared our souls to one another.

Since moving to Bilbury I had begun to start to live and to enjoy my life in a way that had never really been possible when I'd been a student. Instead of working with cases and diseased organs I was working with people and it had made a difference to the way I looked at the world. I was working harder than ever but I enjoyed it.

Second, I began to realise that I might have made a mistake when organising the sleeping arrangements for the weekend.

'Will your girlfriend be sharing your room?' Mrs Parsons had asked me when I'd told her that Penelope was coming.

I'd blushed. 'I think so.'

But now I wasn't so sure. In the past we had fallen into bed together when we'd been too tired to think but had merely needed the physical release of making love and then falling asleep together. Somehow, things seemed different now. Going to bed together at the Duck and Puddle seemed cold blooded and I wasn't sure that it was what either of us wanted or expected.

With all this on my mind it is perhaps hardly surprising that I didn't speak during the journey to Bilbury. Penelope, too, was silent until I parked the Morris in the small car park outside the pub.

'Is this it?' she asked, looking around her at the village green, the cottages and the village shop. She sounded horrified.

'This is it! Home!' I looked round and tried to see it through her eyes; tried to remember how it had looked when I'd first seen it.

We got out of the car. I collected Penelope's suitcases out of the boot and we went into the pub. Gilly Parsons was hoovering the stairs. Frank was sitting in his trousers and vest in the bar drinking coffee and eating his usual bacon sandwich. In the kitchen I could hear Patsy singing. I put Penelope's suitcases down in the hall and introduced Penelope, Frank and Gilly to each other.

'Hello Penny!' said Frank, cheerfully. He held out his hand, thought about it, pulled it back and wiped it on his trousers. Then he offered it again.

'It's Penelope, actually,' said Penelope. Then she paused and corrected herself. 'Dr Shrewsbury.'

Frank looked as embarrassed as I felt. Penelope didn't take his hand so he withdrew it, sat down and picked up his sandwich again.

'Would you like a coffee, love?' asked Gilly. 'Travelling always makes me thirsty.'

'I'd prefer to freshen up a bit first,' Penelope answered. 'I've had an absolute nightmare of a journey. If you could show me to my room?'

Gilly looked at me and I looked back at her hoping that she had a spare room where she could put Penelope. She smiled at me and nodded to show that she understood. I was appalled at the way that Penelope was behaving. I thought of Frank and Gilly Parsons as my friends. Penelope was treating them as though they were servants.

Gilly didn't hesitate. 'I know how you feel, love. Follow me.' She lifted the vacuum cleaner out of the way and led the way up the stairs.

As she moved to follow Penelope turned to me. 'Would you bring my bags up?'

It made me feel slightly better to have her treat me like a servant too. I picked up her bags and followed her. As I did so I looked across at Frank. I thought he might have been cross but he wasn't. He was grinning broadly now and he pulled a face at me as though he had just tasted something sour. Since Penelope was my guest I suppose I should have been offended but I wasn't.

It was twelve o'clock before Penelope reappeared. I was practising pool in the bar when she came down. She had changed out of the trouser suit and had on a blue pleated skirt, a white blouse and a white cardigan. At first sight I hardly recognised her because in addition to changing her clothes she had also changed her hairstyle and now wore a blonde, shoulder length wig.

The wig was so good that for a while I wasn't sure which was real: the short, page boy style brown hair or the shoulder length blonde stuff.

'Would you like to go into Combe Martin for lunch?' I asked her. 'There's a super pub down by the harbour?'

'If that's what you recommend,' she said. So we drove into Combe Martin, which she thought was rather tired and grubby looking, parked overlooking the beach which she thought looked distinctly unsavoury and ate fish, chips and peas, which she thought rather ordinary at a pub which she said she wouldn't go out of her way to visit again.

I didn't know what to do with her after we'd finished lunch so for a while we sat in the car and watched the tide coming in.

'It's very quiet here, isn't it?' she said at last. 'Don't you get bored?'

I said I didn't get at all bored and that I liked living in the country very much.

'I don't think I could cope with it,' said Penelope. 'Apart from the fact that it's so damned boring don't you worry about your career?'

I genuinely didn't know what she meant. I said so.

'You're so far out of things here,' she explained patiently. 'Are you going to stay in general practice?'

I said I thought I probably was.

'But don't you think it's a bit second rate?'

'What do you mean?'

'Well, you're hardly practising high technology medicine in Bilbury, are you?' she laughed. 'You always were a bit of a dreamer. But you have to think about these things.'

'I enjoy the job. And I like the people.'

'But that's not everything is it?' Penelope said that most of the consultants she knew regarded general practice as very much a backwater. 'It's for the drop outs,' she said. 'The people who can't cut it in hospital.'

I didn't say anything. I knew she wasn't right, whatever the hospital consultants said. I liked living in Bilbury. I liked the smell of the log fire in the Duck and Puddle. I liked the countryside. I even liked the rain. And I knew that working as a general practitioner was hard, exacting, worthwhile work. My only doubt was whether I was up to it.

'I'm going into radiology,' said Penelope firmly. 'I've done some research and there's a shortage of consultant radiologists. I should be able to get a good consultant's post by the time I'm thirty.'

She stared out of the car windscreen for a moment. 'I did think about geriatrics but I don't think I could put up with the smell all day long.' She wrinkled her nose with distaste.

'Do you enjoy radiology?' I asked her. 'Isn't looking at X ray pictures all day long a bit tedious?'

Penelope shrugged. 'I'm staying in Bristol until the end of the year. And then I'm applying for a job in London. If you work in a stimulating city it doesn't matter too much if your job is a bit tedious.' She moved the driving mirror and checked her lipstick. 'Anyway,' she said, 'you can always come and work in the country when you're old if that's what you still want to do.'

I thought that she was wrong. I remembered a friend who wanted to get rich so that he could take off and ride his motorbike round the world. He didn't need to become all that rich. Just rich by our standards. He got a job with a small chemical company and made a fortune within five years. But by then he'd got so hooked by the system that he forgot his dreams. And he became just another man in a suit.

I started the car and we drove over to Lynton. I wanted to go for a walk on Lynmouth beach but Penelope didn't have any decent walking shoes with her so instead we walked along a cliff top path to the Valley of the Rocks. The path there clings to the cliff edge and there is a spectacular three hundred foot drop down to the sea below. It was a clear day and we could see the Welsh coastline in the distance. A family of wild goats stood on the path and stared at us in innocent curiosity as we edged our way past them. Suddenly something startled them and they fled up the rocky cliff face, springing from one small ledge to another with remarkable surefootedness.

We had a pot of tea for two and a plate full of buttered tea cakes in a cafe in Lynton. Penelope tried to persuade me to give up my job with Dr Brownlow and to go back to work in hospital. 'It may seem idyllic now,' she said. 'But you'll soon get bored with it. And how much money can you make in a place like Bilbury for God's sake?'

'I don't think I will get bored,' I told her. 'I've never done anything so challenging or so stimulating.'

'But you're not going to make any money, are you?'

'Enough.'

'But you're living in a pub!' said Penelope. 'You've got to get into the property market. Can you afford to buy a house on what you're earning? And what sort of houses are there round here, for God's sake?'

'I haven't even thought of buying a house,' I confessed. The truth was that I rather liked living in the pub. I wasn't ready for the responsibility of owning a house.

We drove back from Lynton to Bilbury in silence again. The relationship between us had changed. Both of us seemed to have changed. Penelope had become more professional and more ambitious. She seemed hard hearted. I wasn't sure exactly how I'd changed but I knew that I had. At medical school we'd had simple, straightforward things like passing exams to worry about. There had been no real competition between any of us. We had been united in our fear of the senior consultants and our determination to survive the system. There hadn't been time to formulate career plans or to worry about money.

'You're going to stay down here, then?' asked Penelope as I took a short cut through Parracombe. It wasn't a question so much as a statement and I couldn't help detecting a certain finality in the way she spoke.

I thought carefully before I answered. 'I hope so. I like it here.'

A car was parked outside the general stores in Parracombe and the road was blocked. I slowed down, pulled in behind it and waited for the driver to come out.

'I've been seeing someone else,' said Penelope unexpectedly.

I was surprised to find that I received this news with relief rather than dismay. 'Anyone I know?'

She shook her head. 'He's a surgical registrar,' she said after a moment. 'He's Greek,' she added inconsequentially.

A man in a green oiled jacket came out of the shop clutching a loaf of bread, a bottle of milk and a brown paper packet. He smiled and waved, opened his car door, put his purchases down onto the front passenger seat, climbed in and drove off. I followed. 'Is it serious? Do you love him? Why are you here?' The questions piled up but I didn't ask any of them.

'Aren't you going to say anything?' Penelope asked me.

I still didn't say anything. I was startled to realise that I felt strangely relieved.

'I imagine it's come as rather a shock,' said Penelope. She reached out and touched my hand. 'I'm sorry,' she said.

'Why did you come?' I asked her at last.

She paused for a moment. 'I had to see you. I'm not really in love with him.'

I slowed down as the car in front braked. It was dusk and his brake lights shone brightly. I switched on my side lights. There was another long silence. 'Won't you come back and work in hospital?'

I shook my head. 'I'm sorry,' I said.

'But there's no future for you here! Can't you see that?' She paused. 'I'll give him up if you come back to Bristol.'

Somehow it made everything very easy. I pulled the car into a gateway, put on the handbrake and turned to face her. 'I'm sorry,' I said, though I didn't really know why I was apologising. 'Shall I take you back to the station?'

'I think that might be a good idea,' said Penelope. Her face looked hard.

I hadn't even switched off the ignition. I took the handbrake off and drove straight off again.

Five minutes later we were back at the Duck and Puddle. I waited in the bar while Penelope went upstairs to pack her suitcases. While I waited I telephoned the station in Barnstaple. The man who answered told me that there was a train in twenty five minutes time that would connect with a main line express from Cornwall to Bristol. Frank looked at me while I made the call but didn't say anything. I went upstairs and knocked on Penelope's door.

'If we hurry you can just catch the last train to Exeter,' I told her. 'It connects with an express to Bristol.'

The door opened and Penelope came out. Her eyes were red and there were tear stains on her cheeks but she wasn't crying any more. I looked behind her and saw that her bags were packed. 'I can get a taxi.'

'Don't be silly. I'll take you.'

We got there with five minutes to spare. The train was already standing in the station waiting. I put her cases on and then climbed off and let Penelope climb past me. I stood on the platform and she stood at the open window.

'It didn't have to end like this,' she said. She took a small handkerchief out of her handbag. It had green and red embroidery around the edges. She blew her nose daintily and put the handkerchief away again. 'You're throwing everything away.'

'I hope everything goes according to plan,' I told her. 'I hope the Greek looks after you.' I felt bad about the fact that I couldn't wait for the train to start. I felt that Penelope and I had nothing at all in common. I didn't love her and I knew she didn't really love me.

'We had some good times, didn't we?'

I nodded. There had been good times it was true. But the good times were now a part of the past. In the future our lives would, I knew, go in very different directions. Penelope's was planned. I had no idea what was going to happen in mine.

The train started with a jerk and Penelope clutched at the door.

'Bye!' I said, waving a hand.

Penelope didn't say anything and didn't wave. Neither of us promised to write letters that we knew we'd never write. I thought she looked very sad and lonely and I couldn't help feeling sorry for her as the train slowly disappeared down the line towards Exeter. I felt sorry for her because I thought that her life contained no passion. She was doing things because she thought she ought to do them rather than because she wanted to do them. I stood there for a few moments, watching the train until it was out of sight. It was like watching my last connections with the past disappear. Then I turned and went back to the car and drove back to Bilbury.

I am slightly ashamed to admit that I sang all the way home. I didn't really know why but I felt happier than I had felt for a long time.

*   *   *

'He came home the day before yesterday,' said Mrs Harper. 'I thought the hospital would have let you know.'

They hadn't.

I followed Mrs Harper up the stairs to Keith's bedroom. 'What did they say when they let him come home?'

'They did all sorts of tests and said that he definitely hasn't got diabetes.'

'What has he got then?'

'They said they couldn't find anything wrong with him at all. But this morning he's as bad as ever.' She was right. Keith was lying in bed looking just as ill as he had when I'd sent him into hospital. I sat down on the edge of his bed and picked up his hand. His skin felt clammy and his pulse was racing. He looked weak and there were tears in his eyes.

'How did you feel when you came out of hospital?'

'I felt OK,' answered Keith. He spoke so quietly that I could hardly hear him and his voice shook, though whether it was with weakness or with anxiety I didn't know.

'He seemed right as rain when he came out,' said Mrs Harper. 'He was playing in the garden.'

'What happened?'

'It's difficult to say. He came in at tea time, had his tea, had a bath and came downstairs to watch a programme on television ...'

'It was Thundercats,' interrupted Keith.

'That's right,' agreed his mum. 'He came down to watch Thundercats. But he wasn't his normal self and then by the time he was ready for bed he was beginning to look queasy again.'

I took out my stethoscope and listened to Keith's chest. His heart was racing. I listened to his lungs, examined his abdomen, looked in his ears, tested his reflexes and asked him a hundred questions. At the end of it all I still didn't have the faintest idea what was wrong with him.

'I'm going to get you back into hospital, I'm afraid.'

Keith started to cry.

'We've got to get you better,' I told him. 'They can do tests I can't do.' I got up off his bed and moved aside so that Mrs Harper could hug her son. 'I'll go and telephone the hospital,' I said quietly.

*　　*　　*

'A girl's been on the phone after you,' said Frank Parsons

121

as I walked into the pub. 'A girl called Kim,' he added, concentrating hard on the pint of beer he was pulling. He took great pride in his work.

'New one, eh?' said Thumper who, as ever, was standing at the bar bent over a nearly empty glass. I once asked Thumper why his glass was nearly always empty and in a semi drunken moment he explained that it was a trick he'd learned from his father. 'Always drink two thirds of your pint the minute it arrives and far more people will offer you a refill than if you're standing there with a glass that's almost full.'

'I don't know anyone called Kim. It must be a patient.'

'It wasn't a patient,' said Frank. 'I asked her about that in case it was an emergency.' He handed the pint he'd just pulled to the customer who'd ordered it then reached behind him, took a scrap of paper from beside the till and handed it to me. 'That's her phone number.'

Curious, I rang her straight away. A male voice I half recognised answered the telephone and with bad grace agreed to fetch Kim to speak to me. A minute or so later a bright young female voice came onto the phone.

'Hello!' she said cheerily, when I'd told her my name. 'Thanks for calling back. Do you believe in the use of animals in medical experiments?'

The question caught me off guard. I hadn't expected it. But it wasn't a difficult question to answer. 'No!' I answered firmly and honestly.

'That's marvellous!' said Kim. 'I'm the secretary of the North Devon Anti-Vivisection Group. We're holding a public meeting in Barnstaple a week on Thursday. Would you come?'

'I don't know ...' I said hesitantly. 'I don't know if I can get away ...'

'Will you come if you can get away?'

I hesitated.

'Good!' said Kim firmly. 'Can I put you down to say a few words to our group?'

'Oh, I don't know about that!' I said, quickly. The thought of saying anything in public has always horrified me.

'It'll be a great boost to the group,' insisted Kim. 'You being a doctor.' She paused. 'And it would be a pity for you to be there and not to speak.'

'I'm not sure that I can be there,' I reminded her.

'You work for Dr Brownlow don't you?'

'Yes.'

'He's my grandfather,' said Kim. 'I'll have a word with him and ask him to make sure that you aren't on duty that evening.'

'Dr Brownlow is your grandfather?' I realised why I'd recognised the voice of the man who'd answered the phone. That must have been Dr Brownlow's son, Simon.

'Yes!' said Kim brightly. 'He'll do anything for me. Absolutely anything.'

'How many people will be there?' I asked her, becoming more and more horrified as I realised my escape route had been blocked.

'We usually get twenty to thirty,' answered Kim. 'But if they know we're getting a doctor to speak we'll probably be able to get more than that.'

'What do you want me to speak about?' Kim had totally out manoeuvred me and I had now accepted the inevitable.

'Anything you like!' said Kim brightly. 'As long as it's about why vivisection should be stopped.' She said that she'd send the details of where the meeting was due to be held in the post, thanked me for agreeing to speak and put the phone down.

* * *

At the end of the evening surgery I had a telephone call from the hospital to tell me that they were sending Keith Harper back home again.

'But he's only been in for a few hours!'

'He was ill enough when he came in,' admitted the doctor who phoned me. 'But he's perfectly OK again now. We can't find anything wrong with him at all.'

'And you haven't got any idea what made him ill?'

'None whatsoever,' said the hospital doctor cheerily. 'Let us know if he gets ill again and we'll take him back in.'

I thanked him, put the telephone down and wondered how long it would be before I heard from Mrs Harper again.

123

*　　*　　*

In the pub that evening Thumper handed me £20 in brand new notes.

'What's this for?'

'The insurance company have paid up for the Humber. That's your change.'

'Change?'

'After paying for the Humber and the Morris Minor.'

I looked at the four five pound notes and then I looked at Thumper. I was puzzled. 'You mean I don't owe you anything for the Morris?'

Thumper nodded.

'I've got £20 and a Morris Minor and I don't owe you any money?'

Thumper grinned. 'That's right.'

I didn't understand but I put the money in my wallet and told Frank to fill up Thumper's almost empty glass.

*　　*　　*

Lionel Francis had seen Dr Charles Jarvis but the radiologist had been unable to offer him the contradiction and comfort that he wanted. 'The X ray clearly shows a large cancerous growth which has already spread throughout one lung,' wrote Jarvis in a letter to me. 'I'm afraid that this man will probably not survive more than another six weeks.'

Every day Mr Francis's condition seemed to confirm the accuracy of that diagnosis. Within a few days of the diagnosis being made Mr Francis was virtually unrecognisable. The corpulent, arrogant man who had visited me in the surgery complaining of nothing more than a persistent and annoying cough had become a weakened and pathetic shadow of his former self.

'He won't eat and he hasn't got the strength to get out of bed.' his wife told me when I visited him one morning. 'He's fading away before my eyes.' I followed her upstairs to the spare bedroom which had been converted into a sickroom. The curtains were drawn and the room already smelt of death. I hardly recognised the grey skinned figure lying on the bed. His eyes were dull and full of fear and he looked

124

like a man who has given up the fight to live. In my clumsy, untutored way I tried to persuade him to fight but he would have none of it. He had accepted the sentence of death that Charles Jarvis had pronounced and he had always been far too much of a believer in the power of the modern medicine man to give credence to the thought that there might be hope.

* * *

If Lionel Francis's rapid deterioration was unexpected it was hardly inexplicable. The same could not, however, be said for the deterioration which had taken place in Hubert Donaldson's health. The penicillin that I had given Hubert seemed to have made no difference at all to his condition. On the contrary, instead of getting better, as I had expected, he seemed to be getting worse. When I persuaded him to undress again so that I could listen to his chest it was imposs- ible not to notice that he had lost even more weight and that his skin had acquired a greyish-yellow pallor.

'I want you to have another X ray. The antibiotic doesn't seem to be working.'

Hubert didn't seem too enthusiastic. 'I don't like hospitals,' he said simply. He breathed in deeply and leant back. 'But I'll go for another X ray if that's what you want me to do.'

I wrote out a request for a repeat chest X ray and handed him the form.

* * *

CHAPTER EIGHT

During the night I had been woken several times by the sound of rain lashing against my window. My room faced south west and the wind had clearly been coming from that direction. When my alarm clock went off at seven thirty I jumped out of bed, went over to the window and drew the curtains to see what damage the storm had done. I was glad I hadn't been called out to any emergencies; it sounded as if it had been a night for staying tucked up in bed.

The first person I saw was Frank Parsons. He was dressed in a green waterproof jacket, waterproof hat and wellington boots. The wind had died down but it was still raining fairly heavily. In his hand Frank held a large lump hammer and looking at the debris around him I assumed that he was struggling to do some emergency repairs. A wooden fence had been flattened and a small wooden tool shed had lost half its roof. Rubbish from an overturned dustbin was strewn around the garden. Across the road I could see Peter Marshall at the village shop. He too seemed to be struggling to do some basic repairs. I pulled on my clothes, shrugged into my waterproof jacket and hurried downstairs to see if I could help.

'It must have been pretty bad last night,' I said, approaching my landlord and picking my way through the broken fence panels. He turned and looked at me with some surprise.

'Didn't expect to see you out here!'

'I saw you out of the window,' I explained. 'I thought I'd come and see if you wanted a hand.' I looked around. A long ladder, brought out of the garage, had already been leant against the side of the house. 'Is there any damage to the roof?'

'Not yet.'

'It seems to have died down now,' I said, mistaking his meaning. 'It doesn't look as if the wind will be back for a while.' I looked around. The tree tops were still; though it was still raining hard there was hardly any wind and the heavy clouds hovering above looked to be almost stationary.

'You go and get your breakfast,' said Frank. 'There isn't anything out here that you can do.' He wiped his nose on the back of his hand. 'But thanks for the offer. Much appreciated.'

'I'll help you clear up some of this debris.' I bent down and lifted up a broken fence panel. 'Where do you want this putting?'

'It's OK,' said Frank. 'You can leave it there.'

'No, really!' I insisted. 'It's going to take you ages to sort this lot out.'

'I'd rather you left it where it is.' Frank seemed surprisingly firm and I still didn't quite understand. 'I've got the insurance assessor coming later on this morning.' He looked straight at me and winked. Before I could say anything he had started to climb up the ladder to the roof. I stood and watched.

'Stand clear!' he shouted, with the hammer in his hand. I stood back just in time as Frank brought the hammer crashing down onto the roof. A shower of broken slates crashed down to join the debris on the ground.

I still assumed that he was merely clearing away stuff that could be dangerous if it wasn't brought down and so out of curiosity I moved back even further to try and see the extent of the damage to the roof. To my astonishment the roof looked to be in virtually perfect condition. There were one or two gaps where slates were missing but judging by the growth of moss on the underlying slates the missing ones had been gone for some time. I stood and watched open mouthed as Frank crawled higher up onto the roof and carefully and systematically broke slates in all the areas where the roof was already damaged. Then I watched as he deliberately dropped a slate onto the flat roof of an outside lavatory. The slate smashed instantly, leaving a great shard sticking up out of the flat roof.

'The main roof has been leaking for ages and that damned outside lavatory always leaks like a sieve,' explained Frank when he had climbed back down the ladder.

Slowly, it dawned on me that my landlord was simply taking advantage of the storm to get some essential repair work done at the insurance company's expense. 'Aren't you worried that they'll find out?' I asked him in a whisper, looking around to make sure that no one was listening. 'Insurance fraud is illegal!'

'Fraud?' said Frank indignantly. 'What are you talking about?'

I looked around at the debris, the broken slates, the broken pieces of fence and the rubbish from the upturned dustbin. There was, it was quite true, no sign of any fraudulent activity; merely signs of storm damage.

Frank smiled at me and nodded towards the other side of the village green. 'Look!' I looked and could see at least half a dozen householders. At first glance each one seemed to be busy trying to repair the damage that the storm had done. But a closer examination showed that most were doing exactly what my landlord had been doing.

'In a way we're helping the insurance companies,' said Frank with a smile that rapidly grew into a broad grin. 'We're all getting rid of structural weaknesses and having essential repair work done before anything serious happens. That's just what insurance companies always advise people to do.'

'I've no doubt they'll be grateful,' I agreed.

Frank looked across to where Peter Marshall was working. 'OK Pete?'

The shopkeeper-cum-taxi-driver nodded cheerfully. 'New shed roof, new back porch and some body repair work on the taxi!' he shouted. He sounded very pleased. He waved and disappeared into the house. I'd never before seen people receive storm damage with such good grace.

'Let's get some breakfast,' said Frank. 'I don't know about you but I'm starving.' He led the way towards the back door, stopping only to pull a loose drainpipe away from the wall completely, letting it fall with a loud clatter across the tangle of broken wood and slate.

'Bilbury is an insurance based economy,' explained Frank

128

as, for the first time, we ate breakfast together. Normally he didn't get up until long after I'd left the pub for the surgery. 'We can't afford to get our properties repaired without help from the insurance companies.' He took a huge bite of his perennial favourite, a bacon sandwich. 'Insurance claims are second to tourism as a source of income round here.' As he spoke he sprayed crumbs around in all directions. Eating with Frank was always a hazardous business. When Frank ate it was the people around him who needed napkins.

'Don't the insurance companies ever complain?'

'They never notice anything,' said Frank. 'Apart from the fact that Bilbury seems to be a bit exposed to south westerly winds.' He took another bite and brown sauce dripped out of his sandwich and onto the back of his hand. He licked the sauce off his hand. 'They fix their premium rates for counties,' he explained, 'so as long as the people in other parts of Devon don't get too much storm damage we'll be OK.'

'Don't you have difficulty in finding workmen to do all the repairs?'

Frank shook his head and emptied his mouth before answering. 'We do all the work ourselves,' he told me. 'I have some notepaper printed up as GB House Repairs. Thumper is North Devon Repairs and Pete Marshall is Devon House Restorations. I'll quote for some of the work over the road and they'll quote for my work.'

'So you get the insurance companies to pay you for repairing your own houses?'

Frank nodded. 'It's the capitalist system and free economy working at its very best,' he answered, pouring himself another cup of tea.

*   *   *

I had left medical school rich with the arrogance of youth; an arrogance that had been blessed by the provision of a medical diploma and endorsed by the might of the medical profession which assumes that it is possible to turn an irresponsible, callow medical student into a responsible, all knowing medical practitioner overnight. But, as the weeks went by, I gradually began to learn the true extent of my ignorance. Gently, patiently and with a kindly sympathy Dr Brownlow's patients taught me that the human spirit is bewilderingly complex and reliably unpredictable. If I learnt one sure thing it was that making premature judgements about people was almost certain to lead to some modest embarrassment at best and, at worst, to an unforgettable humbling.

Few patients helped to illustrate my ignorance of the human condition more effectively than Thomas O'Donnell.

Born in Dublin around the turn of the century Thomas O'Donnell had migrated to Liverpool in the late 1920s in search of employment and, continuing his fruitless search, had drifted further and further south throughout the bleak years of the following decade. After surviving a number of close brushes with various part of the establishment he had ended up in North Devon in the 1950s. There he had finally come to terms with the fact that having been unemployed for so long he had become unemployable.

'If it'll be all the same to you I'll have another certificate for the sick, doctor!' he said, when I first visited him. He beamed at me from his huge, old fashioned, wooden posted bed. Like most ex patriots he had become far more Irish in exile than most Irishmen ever are at home and his accent, demeanour and habits were all quintessentially Irish in flavour. His voice rose and fell throughout each sentence as though in constant search for some satisfactory level.

Having been asked to visit him in his bed I innocently assumed that there was something wrong with him. So I asked him what else I could do for him. This was, for me, a polite, rather roundabout way of saying: 'What symptoms have you got?'

He looked at me uncomprehendingly, but with a growing look of alarm.

'Apart from the sick note,' I added quickly, realising the cause of his distress and wanting to reassure him that the sick note wasn't under any sort of threat.

'Nothing thank you, doctor,' said Thomas.

I waved an arm towards the bed and bluntly asked him what was wrong with him. I had no nasty motive. I just wanted to know.

'It's the weariness, doctor,' said Thomas, with a smile that would have charmed the devil himself. 'I have the weariness.'

He paused, as though temporarily overcome by exhaustion. 'And whatever can you do about the weariness?'

I opened my mouth but being unable to think of anything appropriate to say I simply wrote out the requested sick note, laid it on the edge of the bed with the reverence that seemed appropriate, replaced my fountain pen in my inside jacket pocket and closed my mouth. I did all this in silence. Thomas ignored the certificate in the same superior way that a waiter will ignore a tip. We nodded to one another and I left.

Gradually, I thought I was getting to know Thomas O'Donnell quite well. He seemed to have an insatiable need for documentary evidence with which to support his invalidity. Apart from the straightforward sick notes for the national insurance people he also seemed to have a variety of insurance policies which required some sort of paper work completing. Most of these certificates required me to confirm that Thomas was unable to work but one or two simply required me to confirm that he was still alive. 'It's the pension company,' explained Thomas, in his rich and soothing brogue. 'They'll only pay out for as long as I'm alive.'

On none of my early visits to Thomas O'Donnell's cottage did I ever see him out of his bed. Indeed, for all I knew there might not have been anything of him apart from a head and shoulders and two arms. The rest of him was invariably hidden beneath a double layer of heavy woollen blankets and a thick, richly embroidered red eiderdown. The front door was always open and a small sun faded post card thumb tacked to the front door invited all callers to climb the stairs if they wanted to speak to Mr O'Donnell.

'What do you do about food?' I asked him one day. 'Shopping, cooking and stuff like that?'

'I have the most wonderfully kind neighbours,' explained Thomas, with a firm nod of his head.

'People do your shopping and cooking for you?'

'They do.'

'And bring all your meals to you here in your bed?'

'They do indeed.'

And they did too.

Mr and Mrs Broadstone, the kindly couple who lived in the next door cottage clearly looked after him devotedly. They shared the vegetables they grew in their garden. They picked up his groceries and his tobacco and his pensions at the corner shop and they even did his laundry for him.

'Don't you ever feel, well, guilty?' I asked him one day.

'Guilty?' repeated Thomas, apparently genuinely puzzled. 'Now, why ever should I feel guilty?'

'Letting your neighbours look after you all the time,' I explained. 'They're old too.'

But Thomas just smiled. He didn't seem to know what guilt was. It was the first time I'd ever come across a Catholic whose life wasn't regulated by guilt.

'Don't you ever get bored?' I asked him on another occasion. 'Just lying in bed all day. What do you do?'

Thomas raised a firm, white forefinger and tapped it deliberately against his temple. 'I think!' he told me. 'I think.'

'But what do you think about?'

'I think about life, doctor,' said Thomas. He paused. 'And I think about death.' He smiled at me as though challenging me to admit that I didn't understand. The simplicity of his answer reminded me of the sort of alarming truth one comes across in dreams. It has happened to me several times. I wake up in half shock convinced that I have discovered the meaning of life. I write down the magic words and then I go back to sleep. When I wake up the following morning I find myself staring at a piece of paper upon which are written phrases such as 'love is beautiful' or 'death is the end'.

I arrived one Friday to give Thomas his sick note, bounded up the stairs and found the bedroom empty. The heavy mahogany wardrobe was still there. The small pine dressing table was still there. The oval handbasin was still there, with a bright red towel neatly folded on the rail underneath it. And the heavy wooden posted bed was still there. But the blankets and sheets were turned back and of Thomas himself there was no sign.

I assumed that he must have slipped out of bed to answer a call of nature and so I sat down on the edge of his bed and gazed out of the window. The window was low and from the bed it was possible to see a vast stretch of countryside. A group of hens were scratching at a bare patch of soil in a very desultory fashion. A pair of geese were strutting around as though they had inherited the earth. And a large black and white cat was asleep on a small grassy knoll behind the chicken shed.

'Hello, doctor!'

I recognised the cheery voice instantly and turned my head. I had trusted my ears but now I doubted my eyes. The figure before me had definitely not just clambered out of bed. He was wearing a dark, three piece heavy worsted suit, a white shirt with a stiffly starched collar and a plain, dark green tie. Balanced on the top of his head was a smart black trilby hat. His feet were encased in a pair of plain black socks. And inside all this stood Thomas O'Donnell.

'I've lost my shoes,' he announced sternly. He knelt down with surprising suppleness and peered under the bed. Then he squeezed past me, moved round to the other side of the bed and did the same thing there.

'Has the weariness gone?' I asked him. I didn't ask him the question with any mischief in mind and I don't think Thomas mistook my genuine curiosity for anything other than what it was. He turned, looked up and smiled at me. 'It has not, doctor,' he said sadly but firmly. 'The weariness has not gone.' He moved away from the bed and continued his search within the mahogany wardrobe. The single, shaped wooden hanger upon which the grey worsted suit had presumably rested hung naked from the rail. Below it Thomas rummaged around among a collection of untidily piled cardboard boxes. Eventually he pounced with some visible relief upon a white cardboard box which he seemed to recognise. He closed the wardrobe door, opened the shoe box and put on his shoes.

'Where are you going?' I asked.

'It's the hurling, doctor,' explained Thomas, as though that answered everything.

'The hurling?'

'The hurling,' Thomas confirmed. 'In Dublin.'

'What hurling?' I asked him, puzzled. Though I had never heard of it at the time I later discovered that although it is a game that has some passing similarity to hockey, it is played, apparently, without rules and at the end of each match every man on the field is invariably bloodied for there seem to be no constraints on the hitting of opponents with sticks. Hurling

133

is a game that makes rugby, American football and Australian Rules football seem effeminate in comparison and only the Irish seem to play it.

'It is the Championships, doctor!' explained Thomas, as though talking to a child. There was no doubting the fact that the word 'Championships' began with a capital letter.

'How are you getting to Dublin?' I asked. It seemed a long way to travel for a man who hadn't been out of bed since I'd been living and working in Bilbury.

'I shall take Mr Marshall's taxi to Barnstaple, then I shall take a train to Exeter where I shall catch the express to Birmingham,' explained Thomas. 'In Birmingham I shall take a plane to Dublin.' He turned his left wrist and looked at his watch. 'The taxi should be here soon.' It occurred to me, though I didn't mention it, that for a man who suffered so much from the weariness it was a fairly impressive itinerary.

'When will you be back?'

'I shall come back home on the Monday, doctor,' answered Thomas, knotting a shoe lace with precision.

'I hope you have a good time.'

'I shall do that, doctor,' said Thomas O'Donnell. 'Without doubt I shall do that.' He tied the second shoe lace with the same precision with which he had tied the first. 'Have you a sick note for me, doctor?'

I wrote out his sick note, laid it down carefully on the bed as usual and left him tying a luggage label onto a green leather suitcase.

The astonishing thing about Thomas O'Donnell was that no one seemed to regard him as unusual and no one uttered any criticism of his behaviour. Upon his return from the hurling Championships in Dublin he took off his suit, hung it up in the wardrobe and clambered back into his bed. He then stayed there while Mr and Mrs Broadstone continued to do his shopping, cooking and laundry and I continued to write out sick notes so that he could continue to lie in bed all day and think about life and about death.

*   *   *

'I've got Charles Jarvis on the phone for you!' said Miss Johnson, popping her head into the consulting room just as

I was about to start the evening surgery. She had that air of excitement about her that she always had when someone important was telephoning.

'Jarvis? Who's Charles Jarvis?' The name rang a distant bell but that was all.

'The senior radiologist at the hospital,' hissed Miss Johnson, as though afraid that he would be able to hear her through two solid stone walls.

I remembered and picked up the telephone. The voice at the other end sounded only slightly less than hysterical. 'I don't know how it happened,' he said, speaking rapidly. 'I've checked and double checked and it really can't be blamed on us.'

'What? What's happened?'

'There's been a mix up with some X rays,' said Dr Jarvis. 'It's never happened before. Never. I've been here for 27 years and nothing like it has ever happened.' He sounded very flustered.

'What sort of mix up? Which X rays?'

'One of your patients. Hubert Donaldson.'

'I sent him along this morning for a repeat X ray,' I confirmed.

'That's how we found out,' said Dr Jarvis. 'His last X ray showed a little bit of infection but the X ray we took today shows a disseminated carcinoma. He can't possibly have deteriorated that rapidly in a week.'

'So, what do you think has happened?'

'His first X ray must have got mixed up with someone else's,' explained Dr Jarvis. 'It's the only explanation. Heaven knows how we're going to find the identity of the patient who's got Mr Donaldson's report in his files. We've got thousands and thousands of files here. It could take months. It's terrible. Terrible.'

I knew instinctively the name of the patient with whom Hubert Donaldson's X rays had been confused.

'I've got a patient called Lionel Francis,' I said. 'I think you know him.'

'Vaguely,' admitted Jarvis, sounding slightly irritated at the sound of the name. 'He's a member of my golf club. He's a bit of a pain to be honest. Didn't he come to see me recently?'

'He did. You said he'd got cancer. Could his X ray have

got mixed up with Hubert Donaldson's?'

'I can't see how,' said Dr Jarvis. 'There isn't much similarity between Donaldson and Francis, is there?'

'They both had their initial X rays on the same day,' I pointed out.

'How is Francis now?'

'He's dying.'

'There you are then. His X ray results must have been right.'

I hesitated. I didn't like arguing with a hospital consultant. I'd been brought up to respect them. 'Not necessarily,' I said. 'He could be dying because he expects to die. He has a lot of faith in doctors. Maybe his body is just doing what it's been told it should.'

'Poppycock,' said Dr Jarvis baldly.

'I honestly think it would be worth checking him out,' I said. 'If I get him along to the hospital can you arrange an urgent check X ray?'

Reluctantly, Dr Jarvis agreed and so I rang for an ambulance to take Mr Francis to the hospital. Then I rang Mrs Francis to tell her that I wanted her husband to have another X ray.

'What's the point?' she whispered. Even two miles away, down a telephone line, the house smelt of death. 'Lionel knows he's dying and he knows that there isn't anything you can do. It seems cruel to drag him along to the hospital.'

'We mustn't ever give up hope,' I said and with some reluctance Mrs Francis agreed to let the ambulance men take her husband along to the hospital X ray department.

*   *   *

Dr Brownlow caught me as I was leaving the surgery. 'My grand-daughter rang me up last night,' he said. 'Only decent thing to have come out of my son. She says you want to have the evening off next Thursday to go and speak to some loony group in Barnstaple.'

'Well, that isn't exactly . . .'

'No problem,' said Dr Brownlow generously. 'I'll cover for you for the evening.'

He wasn't really being as generous as he thought he was. But I didn't like to say anything.

*   *   *

'I'm afraid I've got bad news for you,' I told Hubert Donaldson. 'Your X rays . . .'

'I've got cancer,' said Hubert bluntly.

I looked at him. 'How did you know?'

He shrugged. 'I just knew,' he said. 'It feels like I'm dying.'

'There was a mix up at the hospital,' I explained.

Hubert started to say something but began to cough. I gave him a handkerchief.

'The hospital consultant who saw the X rays says he doesn't think there is anything they can do. But I'd like to arrange for a second opinion.'

Hubert shook his head. 'No thank you.' He looked at me. 'But there is something you can do for me.'

'What? If I can I will.'

'Look after Ben when I've gone. I don't want her put down.'

'Of course,' I promised.

'Come and say "hello" again,' said Hubert.

We went out together. Ben was sitting patiently waiting for her master. Her ears pricked up when she saw him.

I'd never before seen a dog so clearly devoted to a human being.

*   *   *

'I feel like a duck!' complained Mrs Tate, leading a line of small children into the surgery and settling herself down on the other side of the desk.

I raised an eyebrow.

'I'm waddling like a duck and everywhere I go this lot follow me.' She put one hand on her tummy and stretched her back with the other.

'How many months are you?' Not even I could mistake Mrs Tate's pregnancy for a weight problem.

'Only five,' said Mrs Tate. 'I always carry a lot of fluid. When I had Kevin I put on over two stones and Dr Brownlow was talking about renting me out as a barrage balloon.'

I flicked through her medical records. 'Is this your first visit?'

Mrs Tate nodded.

137

'You really should have come a bit earlier,' I admonished her.

'Didn't seem a lot of point, I've had three so I know what to do.'

'Slip your things off, climb up onto the couch and I'll examine you,' I told her, expecting her to slip off her skirt and any relevant underwear.

While I waited for her I studied her medical records. She certainly didn't seem to have had any real problems with her previous pregnancies. When I looked up I had quite a shock. Mrs Tate was sitting on the edge of the examination couch absolutely stark naked. Her clothes were piled in an untidy heap on the chair she'd vacated. Her three small children were standing by the side of the couch looking up at her. The eldest had produced a gob stopper on a stick from somewhere and was licking it furiously and noisily.

With four pairs of eyes watching my every movement I got up and went over to the couch.

'Why is that strange man touching you there?' one of the children asked as I examined Mrs Tate's breasts.

I blushed so much that I could almost hear the blood pumping into my face.

'They're breasts,' said Mrs Tate.

'Daddy touches you there,' said another small voice.

'No he doesn't.'

'Yes he does. I've seen him.'

'Does Daddy know this man is touching you there?'

'Why is he going it?'

'Do you like it mummy?'

'I'd like to see you in a couple of weeks time,' I suggested.

'I've brought you a sample,' said Mrs Tate. 'Get the sample will you Daphne?'

Daphne rushed over to her mother's bag and produced a pickle jar.

'I washed it first,' Mrs Tate assured me. 'Wouldn't a month do?'

'I think a month would probably do,' I agreed, taking the pickle jar off Daphne.

'Why did that man touch them?'

'To examine them.'

138

'Is that why Daddy touches them?'

'Don't be silly. Daddy isn't a doctor.'

I tested the urine sample as rapidly as I could. 'You can put your clothes back on now,' I told Mrs Tate. 'Your sample is perfectly OK.'

'Does that man touch everyone's breasts?' I heard Daphne ask in a loud voice as Mrs Tate and her brood disappeared down the corridor.

*   *   *

When I had first taken the job as Dr Brownlow's assistant I had been promised that I could have half a day off a week. But it hadn't worked out quite like that until, at the end of one morning surgery, Dr Brownlow suddenly appeared.

'Have you got any visits?'

'Not yet.'

'Take the afternoon off. I'll hold the fort and do this evening's surgery. Take a bit of a break. Have a look at the countryside.'

I didn't wait to be told twice. Ten minutes later I was sitting in my Morris, with the top down, driving along the lanes with absolutely nowhere to go and nothing special to do. It felt wonderful. About half a mile out of the village I joined the main road between Barnstaple and Lynton. I turned left and almost immediately I saw a pedestrian walking along the side of the road. I slowed and recognised Patsy Kennett.

'Where are you going?' I asked, slowing to a halt alongside her.

'Watersmeet!' replied Patsy. 'Just up the river from Lynmouth,' she added when I looked puzzled. 'I've got to take them some honey from the farm and I promised a friend I'd help out this afternoon.'

'Do you want a lift?'

She hesitated. 'Are you sure?'

I opened the passenger door. 'Jump in!'

She thanked me with a glorious smile that I'd never seen before and climbed into the front passenger seat.

'Do you walk everywhere?' I asked her.

'I walk a lot,' she replied. 'But I was going to catch the bus to Lynton and then walk along the river to Watersmeet.'

'I'd have thought you'd have been kept busy on the farm!'

Patsy winced. 'Please don't you start! I get enough of that from my father.'

'I'm sorry! I didn't mean . . .'

Patsy smiled forgiveness. 'I know. It's all right. It's just that my dad is always moaning at me. He says I ought to work on the farm all the time.' She paused for a few moments. 'I like working on the farm but I like to get out a bit occasionally.'

I nodded and nearly ran into the back of a large tanker which seemed to be stuck. Its front end was half way through the gates that led into the drive up to Mike Trickle's house and its back end seemed to be stuck in a hedge on the other side of the road. I braked hard, stopped and waited while the tanker driver struggled to extricate his vehicle. We both sat and watched him.

'Do you like working at the pub?'

'I only do mornings,' said Patsy. 'Gilly asked me to help out and she's always been nice to me. I like her a lot.' The tanker driver managed to free his vehicle and I moved ahead again.

'You can take a short cut down there,' said Patsy, pointing to a narrow lane on the left. I turned off the main road and drove down a steep hill. 'How's your father?' I asked, driving slowly through a tiny hamlet. Half a dozen hens squawked and fluttered as I drove round a corner. 'I was going to visit a few days ago but when I rang to make sure someone would be in Adrienne said he was a lot better and there wasn't any need to call.'

'He is a lot better, thank you!' said Patsy. 'He was better within a day of stopping the hawthorn. His breathing is fine now and all the water swelling has gone down.'

'No more chest pains?'

'No.'

'Good.'

'Do you think he'll be all right now? He's working on the farm again.'

'I think so,' I said. 'Though I'd like to have a quick look at him sometime if you can persuade him.'

'I think he and Adrienne were both a bit embarrassed,'

confessed Patsy. 'I think we all know that the hawthorn was poisoning him.'

'Possibly,' I said cautiously. I swerved to avoid a rabbit that had run out onto the road.

'I hope Adrienne learns from it,' said Patsy. 'She's ever so keen on herbal remedies. I worry about it sometimes.' She pointed to the left again. 'If you turn down there we'll be back on the main road again.'

I turned left and five minutes later we came to a fork in the road. The left hand branch was signposted to Lynton. The right hand branch went down a narrow lane signposted towards Lynmouth.

'Right?'

'Yes, please!' said Patsy. 'Are you sure this isn't taking you out of your way?'

I shook my head. 'Dr Brownlow has given me the afternoon off.' I suddenly had an idea. 'You said you were going to walk up to Watersmeet. If I park in Lynmouth do you mind if I walk up with you?'

Patsy seemed surprised. 'Of course not!' she said. 'There's a car park right by the river. Turn right at the bottom of the hill.'

I hadn't been to Lynmouth before and I immediately fell in love with it. As I drove down the hill the view across the harbour and out to sea was breathtaking. 'Where does that go?' I asked Patsy, nodding towards a road that climbed up a long hill in front of us.

'That's the road to Porlock.'

'I wouldn't like to try and get up there in the mist,' I said. 'It must be pretty dangerous.' The road was unfenced and on the left there was a drop of several hundred feet down to the sea. I slowed down to wait for a coach to pass by before I turned right and then left into the riverside car park.

'The men of Lynmouth once dragged a lifeboat up that hill,' said Patsy. 'There was a storm at sea and a foreign ship was in trouble. They tried to launch the lifeboat in Lynmouth but the sea was too rough so they decided the only thing to do was to carry it up the hill and all the way to Porlock.'

I turned into the car park and reversed into a space.

'The lifeboat crew lashed themselves and all the horses they

141

could find to the boat and dragged it right across the moors,' said Patsy. 'They even had to knock down part of a cottage because the road was too narrow for the boat to go through.'

We got out of the car, Patsy clutching her bag full of honey. I looked up at the sky. It was clear but I knew how fast the weather in North Devon could change. 'I'll just put the hood up!' I said. 'Can I get some lunch at Watersmeet?'

Patsy nodded.

Together we climbed down the narrow stone steps that led to the riverside path and started to walk along the banks of the river to Watersmeet. The rugged majesty of it all impressed me enormously and I couldn't remember the last time I'd been for a walk with no purpose in mind. To spend a few hours doing nothing but walk alongside a beautiful river with a beautiful companion seemed exquisitely reckless.

As we walked on, in comfortable silence, I gradually began to relax more and more. The peaceful beauty of the river seemed to me to be a perfect antidote to the harsh realities of the real world. The river itself, tumbling over rocks and through fern and moss laden grottoes; the heavily wooded hills, laden with hundreds of silvery, stunted oaks; the wild flowers; the lichen; the fungi and the rays of golden sunlight which filtered through the branches of the trees all seemed soothing and relaxing.

Suddenly, Patsy reached out and touched me lightly on the arm. She stopped walking and pointed across the river. We had walked up a slight incline and the river was fifty to sixty feet below us. 'Look!' she whispered.

I stopped and looked in the direction she was pointing.

'A heron,' she said softly. 'On the bank. Looking for fish.' The tall, unlikely looking bird merged easily into its background of silvery oaks and stood with unnatural stillness. It looked more like a garden ornament than a real bird. Quietly and carefully the huge bird stretched its wings. Then, equally quietly and equally carefully, it folded them again and settled down to watch the river once more.

We walked on. Patsy pointed out a cormorant drying its wings, a dipper and a wild mink swimming silently and skilfully in a deep water pool. We both stood and watched two rainbow trout in a shallow pool.

A mile and a half up the river, as the path rounded a rocky outgrowth, I caught sight of a beautiful, fairy tale house. 'Is that Watersmeet?'

Patsy nodded. 'The house was built as a fishing lodge but it's a tea room now. It was built at the point where two rivers merge.'

'It looks like something that Hansel and Gretel might have lived in.'

'I love it up here,' said Patsy. 'Even in winter when it's quiet.'

'What time do you finish work?' I asked her.

'Six o'clock.'

'Can I walk you back and then give you a lift home?'

Patsy blushed. 'You don't have to. I can easily get the bus.'

'I'd like to.'

She hesitated. 'Thank you,' she said. 'That would be nice.' She stopped as something occurred to her. 'But what will you do between now and then?'

'I'll walk further up the river!'

She laughed. 'OK.'

'I'll see you at six then.'

We neither of us moved.

There was something else I wanted to ask her.

'It's very beautiful here.'

'Yes.'

Still she didn't move away.

'Very relaxing.'

She nodded.

'Do you have to go straight back home when you've finished work?'

Patsy looked down. For a moment I thought she seemed uncertain. 'No,' she said. 'Not necessarily.'

'Would you like to come out with me for a meal?' I could feel my heart pounding and my hands felt clammy. I desperately wanted her to say 'yes'.

'Where?' she laughed. 'There aren't any fancy restaurants round here, you know!'

'I don't care where. A pub. Fish and chip shop. Anything. Whatever we can find.'

She relaxed. 'I'd love to.'

143

I wanted to take her into my arms, hold her tight and kiss her on the lips. I held my hand out. She took it. We shook hands formally.

'I'd better go,' she said, not moving.

'OK.'

'Really,' she laughed. I loved the sound of her laugh.

'OK.'

'You'll have to let go of my hand.' I let go of her hand but still she didn't go.

'I'll have to ring my mum,' she said. 'To tell her not to expect me for my tea.'

I nodded.

Suddenly she turned and ran into the tea rooms. I stood still for a few moments and watched the door through which she'd disappeared. Then I followed her into the tea rooms and bought myself a cornish pasty, a huge piece of home made apple pie and a large glass of lemonade. Patsy had disappeared but it was good to know that she was close by.

*   *   *

'What's up?' asked Thumper in the bar of the Duck and Puddle much later that evening.

'Nothing.'

'You're quiet.'

'Just tired.'

But I wasn't tired. I wasn't tired at all. My mind was firmly fixed on the evening I'd spent with Patsy. And my memories of Patsy were dominated by my memory of our first kiss.

Some kisses are gentle and simply social; no more than a greeting, a brush on the cheek. Some exist only as a prelude to other activities. But our first kiss had a life and a meaning of its own. I felt that it marked the beginning of something important. I hadn't felt so excited by a single kiss since I'd been sixteen years old.

*   *   *

144

CHAPTER NINE

I had seen very little of Kay Wilson after our unconsummated evening meal but not long after that eventful evening I got an urgent telephone call asking me to go round to the cottage to see her husband.

'Come in!' I heard a voice call, when I knocked on the front door. I obeyed. Inside the sight of all that chintz and all those dried flower arrangements made me feel quite nervous again.

'I'm over here, doctor,' said a gruff voice.

I walked further into the room and saw that the owner of the voice was sitting on the floor on the other side of the sofa. There was a blonde, curly wig, a lot of eyeshadow, bright red lipstick and a heavy growth of beard. This was, I assumed, P.C. Wilson.

I introduced myself and tried not to look surprised.

'Thanks for coming, doctor,' said P.C. Wilson. 'I've got a bit of a problem, I'm afraid.' He was wearing a pale pink silk blouse through which a black brassiere was clearly visible, a very short black leather mini skirt, black stockings and a pair of bright red high heeled shoes.

'I've got my zip stuck,' the policeman explained. He moved slightly to one side so that I could see what he meant. A flouncy piece of material that hung in generous folds around the base of the sofa had become jammed in the zip of his mini skirt. P.C. Wilson and the sofa were as one.

I was proud of the fact that I didn't even blink. I bent down and tugged at the zip.

'It seems stuck,' I observed.

'Yes,' agreed P.C. Wilson. He looked as miserable as you

145

might expect a man to look under such circumstances.

'How on earth did you get like this?'

'The skirt is a bit tight,' the policeman explained. 'I find it easier to get into it if I'm lying down.'

I poked at the zip with the blade of my penknife. 'I think you're going to have to choose between the skirt and the sofa cover.'

'Don't cut my skirt!' cried P.C. Wilson. 'I don't care what you do to the sofa but don't cut my skirt.'

Delicately, I cut a small hole in the chintzy material covering the sofa, enabling P.C. Wilson to stand up. He rubbed his back and examined the skirt zip ruefully.

'You should be able to mend it,' I assured him with entirely spurious confidence. My knowledge of zip technology has never been encyclopaedic.

'I'm very grateful,' said P.C. Wilson. 'If ever I can ...'

I held up a hand, embarrassed. 'It was nothing,' I murmured.

Suddenly, P.C. Wilson seemed to remember something else. He hesitated, plucking up courage, and then spoke again. 'It's a bit of a cheek,' he said. 'But while you're here ...', he paused and swallowed noisily. His adam's apple bobbed up and down in a rather startling way. 'I've got a rash ...'

'Let me have a look,' I told him. 'I'll see what I can do.'

He took off his blouse, unfastened his padded bra and turned round to show me his back. 'It's very itchy,' he told me, reaching over his shoulder to point at a small red area in the middle of his back.

I leant forward and looked closer. 'Its a small patch of dermatitis,' I told him. I bent down and picked up his discarded upper under-garment. 'It's the nickel,' I explained. 'The nickel on the catch at the back of your bra.' I took out my prescription pad and wrote out a prescription for a small quantity of steroid cream. 'That should get rid of the rash. And to stop it coming back paint the metal catch with clear nail varnish.'

P.C. Wilson took the prescription I held out to him and smiled. 'That's wonderful!' he said. Suddenly he seemed to notice the watch on my wrist. 'Is that the time?'

I told him it was.

'I must rush and get changed for work,' P.C. Wilson said, striding out of the living room and heading for the stairs. 'Would you like a cup of tea? Coffee? Put the kettle on, will you? I'll have a black coffee.'

I didn't really want anything but he'd disappeared before I had a chance to say anything so I wandered into the kitchen, filled the electric kettle with water and switched it on.

'Splendid!' said the same gruff voice a few minutes later. I had made two cups of black, instant coffee which were standing steaming on the kitchen table. I turned round and almost didn't recognise P.C. Wilson at all. He was wearing thick soled black shoes, smart blue serge trousers with a razor sharp crease up the front, a blue jacket with shiny silver buttons, a blue shirt and a black tie. Under his arm he carried a blue helmet with a shiny silver badge on the front.

I handed him his cup of coffee.

'How are you enjoying life in Bilbury?' he asked me.

'Very much.'

My host attempted to drink his coffee, found it too hot and added a splash of cold water. 'There's a very low crime rate round here,' he told me. 'Good quality of life. That's what its all about isn't it?'

'Absolutely,' I agreed, trying to sip my coffee and burning my lips.

'Must go!' said P.C. Wilson, draining his cup and then rinsing it carefully under the tap before putting it down on the draining board. I followed his example and accompanied him out of the cottage.

* * *

Looking at Lionel Francis it was difficult to believe that he had ever been ill at all. He had regained all the weight he had lost and he looked as ebullient and as assertive as ever. His colour was still a little pale but he had lost the dreadful grey pallor that had made him look like a corpse in waiting.

'How's your chest?' I asked him. 'How do you feel?'

'I rather hoped that you might answer the first of those questions,' said Mr Francis with a sniff. 'The answer to the second question is that I feel angry and aggrieved.' He took

147

off his jacket, pulled his tie to one side and started to unbutton his shirt.

I told him how sorry I was about the mix up over the X rays.

Mr Francis said something that sounded like 'Hrmph!' and pulled off his shirt. He then pulled his short sleeved woollen vest up over his head. I picked up my stethoscope, moved round the desk and listened to his chest. It sounded good. I told him so.

'My solicitor tells me that I should leave this to him,' said Mr Francis, as he fastened up the buttons on his shirt. 'But I thought I'd let you know that I'm taking legal action against you and the hospital radiology department.'

I stared at him in disbelief. 'But why?'

'Because you and the hospital very nearly succeeded in killing me. I'm not sure who should take the lion's share of the blame but I'm happy to leave that to the lawyers and the courts.' He held his head back while he tied his tie. It bore a pattern designed to induce nausea. 'I know that your defence organisation will pay for your costs and for any damages that I may win,' he went on, 'so I won't have your bankruptcy on my conscience.'

'But it was all an accident,' I cried in disbelief. 'And things were sorted out in the end.'

'An accident?' Mr Francis sounded very bitter. 'Your "accident" very nearly killed me. And it caused a considerable amount of emotional damage.' He finished tying his tie and pulled his shirt collar back down. 'This isn't just a question of money,' he said, leaning forward as he pulled his coat on. 'It's mainly a matter of principle.'

Innocent though I was in the ways of the world I knew enough to shudder inwardly when I heard that word 'principles'. When people start talking about 'principles' they invariably mean that they are about to start behaving in a pig-headed, short-sighted and self-destructive way.

Mr Francis glowered at me. 'I hope that neither you nor Dr Brownlow take any of this personally. But this is something that has got to be done.' He fastened his coat, patted his right hand on top of his head to make sure that his hair had not been disturbed too much and left me to my private fears and apprehensions.

*   *   *

As if waiting for Mr Francis's writ to arrive wasn't enough
I was also constantly aware of the fact that I had to think
of something to say to the North Devon Anti-Vivisection
Group. I couldn't think why I had agreed to speak to them
(although I excused my folly to myself by arguing that I had
been neatly and professionally outmanoeuvred) and as the
date of my speech got ever closer I found myself hoping that
I might lose my voice, break a limb or acquire some fearsome
and outrageously infectious disease.

*   *   *

Nigel and Karen Woodloe both worked in London. He
had a job as a currency dealer in the City branch of an American bank and she had an equally prestigious and presumably
equally overpaid job with an English merchant bank. Each
week they spent Monday to Friday in their smart flat in Pim-
lico and then spent their weekends at their cottage in Bilbury.
    'I'm sorry to call you out at the weekend,' said Nigel Wood-
loe, genuinely apologetic. It was early one Saturday afternoon
and I'd been playing pool with Thumper in the bar at the
Duck and Puddle.
    'We've been decorating the bedroom,' said Karen. She like
her husband, was wearing an expensive pair of jeans and a
pale, polo necked sweater. His was blue, her's was green. She
wore yellow rubber gloves and held a wallpaper scraper in
her left hand.
    'We want to try and retain as many of the cottage's original
features as we can,' Nigel told me. 'We had the old fireplace
unbricked and we're having a woodburning stove put into
the kitchen.'
    'We're doing as much of the work as we can,' said Karen.
'It's very therapeutic.'
    'The problem is,' said Nigel, very seriously, 'that we hit
a bit of a snag in the bedroom.' I nodded, put on my most
experienced and unshockable look, put my black bag down
on the floor, folded my arms and prepared myself for a torrent
of personal secrets.

149

'You heard it first, didn't you darling?' said Nigel to his wife.

'I think I did,' Karen confirmed.

Puzzled, I looked from one to the other. 'Heard what?'

'The buzzing,' said Nigel. 'We've got bees nesting in our chimney.'

'Have you been stung?'

'Not exactly,' said Karen, emphasising the second word. 'Not yet.'

'Only by some of the local builders,' said Nigel with a hollow laugh.

Karen gave him a dirty look and then turned back to me. 'We really need your advice.'

'The thing is that we had to move them,' said Nigel. 'But we didn't want to hurt them.'

'Bees are very social creatures,' explained Karen.

I murmured something suitably appreciative. I'd won £2 from Thumper and was rather looking forward to getting back for another few games.

'We did try ringing the council to see if they could offer us some advice,' said Karen.

'But there was no reply,' added Nigel.

'It's the weekend,' I explained. 'They were probably closed.'

'They were,' nodded Nigel.

'So then Nigel had a brainwave,' said Karen. 'We used the vacuum cleaner to suck the bees down the chimney.'

'The vacuum cleaner?'

'It's an industrial one,' said Nigel.

'Got a very powerful suck,' said Karen. 'It's German.'

'So the bees are now in the vacuum cleaner?'

They both nodded. 'That's the problem,' said Karen. 'We're not sure how to get them out without getting stung.'

'We've tied a plastic bag over the nozzle to stop them escaping,' said Nigel.

'But we can hear them buzzing about inside the bag,' continued Karen. 'And to be honest they sound a little angry.'

'Hope you don't mind us ringing you,' said Nigel. 'But we thought that it might come under 'preventive medicine'.'

'Since if we don't do it right we'll get stung.'

I scratched my head. 'It's not really my field of expertise,' I confessed.

'We did try to find a vet,' said Karen. 'But we couldn't find one prepared to come out for bees at a weekend.'

I nodded. 'Maybe you could just poke the vacuum cleaner pipe out through the window, take the plastic bag off and then turn the cleaner onto "blow".'

'It doesn't do "blow",' said Karen sadly. 'We had thought of that.'

'Couldn't you just put the vacuum cleaner out onto the lawn and let the bees come out when they're ready?

'We did think of that too,' said Nigel. 'But then we thought that they would probably just all come back into the chimney again.'

'Where is the vacuum cleaner now?' I asked.

'Still up in the bedroom,' answered Nigel.

'I'd better go and have a look,' I said bravely. I got half way up the stairs but the sound the bees were making melted my courage. To describe them as angry did not seem accurate. I retreated. 'I can hear them,' I confirmed.

Suddenly I had a useful thought. They don't come all that often but when they do they're always welcome. 'Can I borrow your telephone? I've thought of someone who might be able to help.'

Nigel threw aside a dustsheet and revealed a telephone. I dialled Patsy's number.

'Is that you Mr Kennett?' I asked, when Patsy's father answered the telephone.

'Yes. Who's that?'

I told him. 'Would you like a swarm of bees?' I'd remembered that he kept bees and produced honey.

He grunted and sounded unenthusiastic.

'They'll pay you £5 to take the swarm away,' I told him, adding an extra incentive to the prospect of a free swarm of bees. I looked at Nigel as I spoke and raised a questioning eyebrow. He nodded furiously.

Fifteen minutes later Mr Kennett arrived. He collected the swarm of bees with consummate ease and pocketed Nigel Woodloe's five pound note with an equal lack of effort.

*   *   *

Hubert looked terrible. His face was pale and gaunt and

151

the skin over his cheekbones looked paper thin. But although his eyes were sunk deep into their sockets they still seemed to be full of wisdom. I felt that I could learn a lot from Hubert if only I knew what to ask him.

'You ought to be in hospital,' I told him.

'Why? What they can do for me if I go into hospital?'

I had no answer to that and he knew it.

'I know you have to offer and I know you want to help but all I need is a prescription for more morphine tablets for the pain.'

In hospital Hubert would have been sedated and drugged and deprived of his dignity. He would also have been separated from Ben.

'How many morphine tablets are you taking?' I asked him.

'Enough and no more.'

I hesitated. 'It's just that they're addictive.'

Hubert shrugged. 'I'll be dead before I'm an addict so what does it matter?'

He was right again. I wrote out the prescription he wanted and handed it to him.

*   *   *

Keith Harper was out of hospital again. I couldn't keep up with him. This time the doctors had kept him in the hospital for three days before discharging him.

'We can't find anything wrong with him,' an extremely puzzled but slightly snooty senior house officer told me, making it fairly clear that he didn't appreciate having his time wasted by patients who didn't have clearly defined symptoms.

Two days after Keith was sent home Mrs Harper rang me up again. He was, she said, as bad as ever. And she was right. Not only did Keith look terrible but a couple of quick tests that I did showed that he had acquired all the signs of diabetes again.

'He didn't feel at all bad yesterday,' said Mrs Harper. 'So he got dressed and I tried to make him do everything as normally as possible. He even went out for a ride on his bike. But when I got up this morning he was lying in bed looking terrible.'

I said I would ring the hospital and get them to admit Keith again.

*　　*　　*

Hubert was gradually getting weaker and weaker but he never showed any signs of fear or despair. I asked him how he could be so brave in the face of death but he insisted that he was not being brave.

'People are only brave when they have something to lose,' he told me. 'It's easy to seem brave when you've got nothing to lose.' He told me that he thought that people who had no hopes and no dreams found it easiest to appear brave while people whose lives were full of ambition and hope found it much more difficult to show bravery in the face of adversity.

There were many answers I wanted from Hubert but I wasn't clear in my mind about the questions I needed to ask.

*　　*　　*

CHAPTER TEN

If Patsy hadn't come with me I think I might well have run away. We sat together in the Morris outside the British Legion Hall in Barnstaple where I was due to lose my virginity as a public speaker and while I tried to stop my knees knocking and my teeth chattering Patsy did her best to fill me with confidence.

'You'll be super!'

I tried to say something but instead made a sound that would have embarrassed a frog with laryngitis.

'They're on your side!' Patsy reminded me. 'They already believe in what you're going to say. They aren't going to "boo" or anything like that.'

It wasn't any good. Nothing she said seemed to make me feel any better. I felt I knew just how the Christians must have felt while waiting to slip into the ring to do a Wednesday afternoon matinee with the lions.

Eventually, I decided that whatever happened inside the British Legion Hall nothing could be worse than waiting outside the British Legion Hall. I looked across at Patsy, crushed her hand in mine and tried to smile. Judging by the look that appeared on her face the attempt at a smile wasn't a total success.

'I think I'll go in.'

'You'll be fantastic,' Patsy assured me. She leant across and kissed me. 'Do you want me to come in with you?' She paused. Despite my terror, or perhaps because of it, I realised just how much I cared for her. 'Or would you rather I waited for you out here?'

'Come in with me!' I begged. 'Or stay out here,' I added,

154

not wanting to sound too demanding. 'If you'd rather.'

'I'll come in with you,' said Patsy firmly. So we went in together.

The British Legion Hall was built largely out of asbestos; the walls having been clad in flat sheets of the stuff and the roof built out of corrugated sheets. The front entrance, two doors wide, led into a small vestibule. On the right there were ladies and gents lavatories. On the left a counter separated off a small area which was equipped with coat and hat racks.

As Patsy and I walked in through the doors, past a small handwritten notice which announced that I would be addressing a meeting of the North Devon Anti-Vivisection Group at 7.30pm, I began to feel a few blood corpuscles struggling to make their way round my body and the usual small army of heavy footed butterflies getting into position in my stomach. I patted my inside jacket pocket to make sure that the speech I had worked on with such loving care was still there.

There were two people standing in the hallway. Both were about five foot eight inches tall; both had black shoulder length hair; both wore black corduroy jeans and black sweaters; both wore ear rings. One wore a beard. The other wore black lipstick. They were deep in conversation.

'Hello!' I suspect that I sounded even more timid than I felt. 'I've come for the lecture.'

The black haired stranger with the beard took a long drag on a home made cigarette and nodded towards another pair of double doors. 'There's plenty of room,' he assured me. 'Make yourself at home.'

I muttered 'thank you' and the two of us headed through the second set of double doors. These led directly into the main room – a surprisingly large hall that was filled with two large blocks of wooden, folding chairs. At the far end of the room there was a stage, complete with two rich velvet curtains. In the centre of the stage there was a table and half a dozen wooden chairs. I looked around. The room wasn't exactly full. There were seats for about 150 people but most of them were unoccupied. To be precise 143 of them were unoccupied. The audience consisted of just seven people. They were spread around as though determined to minimise the risk of cross infection.

'It's not too daunting a crowd, anyway,' whispered Patsy.

'I think I'd rather there were one or two more people in the audience,' I whispered back. 'It's a bit depressing isn't it?'

Still holding hands Patsy and I sat down at the back of the hall. I took advantage of the moment to take a close look at the audience. There were four men and three women. Three of the men were in their sixties and looked as though they'd probably come in to get out of the cold. Or maybe they thought it was a dominoes evening. The exception was a teenager who carried a large folder and a spiral bound notebook. Only one of the women looked as though she was there to escape from the cold. The other two were teenage girls who were giggling and nudging one another.

We sat there for what seemed like a short eternity but was in fact probably no more than about twenty minutes. I tried hard not to look at my watch more than once a minute. The other seven members of the audience seemed well endowed with patience. The only sounds to break the silence were the regular ticking of a large clock to the left of the stage and the intermittent giggling of the two teenage girls.

Suddenly, the peace was broken by the bursting open of the doors behind us. We all turned round and saw the girl and the man in black walking through. They walked straight down the centre of the room and climbed up onto the stage together. Once on the stage the man with the long hair tapped a microphone with his finger nail and when he was satisfied that it was working satisfactorily he leant forward and spoke into it.

'Can you hear me?'

The words boomed and bounced around the hall. The acoustics were terrible. No one replied, of course, but he rightly took our silence as confirmation that he could be heard.

'I'm afraid we've been let down by our speaker,' said the man with the beard.

I looked across at Patsy at the same instant that she looked across at me. As I stood up the man with the beard was saying something else. 'I'm the speaker!' I said, raising my hand like a schoolboy who wants to attract the attention of the teacher. I spoke so quietly that I wasn't sure that I'd actually said anything out loud. The man with the beard didn't seem to be aware that I'd said anything. I felt Patsy reach up, take my hand and squeeze my fingers. I knew she was trying to give me strength. I coughed loudly. The man with beard looked straight at me.

'Do you want to say something?' He frowned at me.

'I'm the speaker,' I said again. It came out much louder than I'd intended; uncomfortably close to a shout.

The small, slighter figure who had accompanied the man with the beard onto the stage, the one wearing black lipstick, got to her feet and moved to the front of the stage. 'I'm Kim!' She walked to the front of the stage and jumped down. Then she hurried up the central aisle to where Patsy and I were sitting. She held out her hand as she approached and I couldn't help noticing that her finger nails were also painted black. 'I'm so pleased that you could come! Why didn't you tell us that you were here?' She didn't wait for an answer but turned her head towards the man with the beard. 'That's Garth,' she said, nodding in his direction. 'He's our President.' She hadn't let go of my hand and she now started to pull me down towards the stage.

I turned to look at Patsy. She mouthed 'Good luck!' to me and blew me a kiss. I stumbled against one of the chairs in the row in front and only just managed to recover my balance. With the girl in black lipstick leading the way I followed. Suddenly, taken by a fresh moment of raw panic I patted my chest pocket to make sure that my speech was still there.

On the stage I shook hands with Garth who stared at me from underneath huge black bushy eyebrows and who seemed to me to have an almost demonic look. The only piece of pink flesh that I could see was his nose which was red rather than pink. The rest of his face seemed to be covered entirely by hair.

I can't remember much of what happened next. It all seemed to be over in an instant. One minute Garth was introducing me and I was pulling my speech out of my inside jacket pocket and the next minute I was refolding it and putting it back into my pocket, climbing down off the stage and walking back up the central aisle to where Patsy was sitting waiting for me. The only thing I was aware of was that most of the audience seemed to be clapping. There wasn't a lot of noise and they weren't exactly hysterical but they weren't booing either.

'Marvellous!' whispered Patsy as I sat down. 'You were terrific.' She leant across and kissed me on the cheek. It was what I wanted to hear and I believed every word of it. All the terror now seemed worthwhile.

After that Garth spoke for a while and then Kim read out a list of names and places and addresses and then the meeting was over.

'Was it really OK?' I asked Patsy, as the other seven members of the audience scraped their chairs across the wooden floor.

'It was wonderful!' said Patsy, beaming at me. 'Really,' she insisted. 'It was great.'

'I think the trick is to forget about the audience,' I whispered. Now that I was an experienced public speaker I felt I knew the tricks of the trade. We turned and started to make our way towards the exit and as we did so I felt a tap on my shoulder. I turned to find the young man with the file and the notebook standing behind me.

'I'm afraid I'm not very good at shorthand,' he apologised. 'But would I be right in saying that you feel that animal experiments are a waste of money?'

'Absolutely!' I agreed vehemently. It never occurred to me to ask him why the fact that he wasn't very good at shorthand was of any significance. And I was too thrilled by the fact that a significant part of the audience was asking questions to ask myself why.

'How would you describe the sort of doctors or scientists who perform animal experiments?' asked the youth with the notebook.

'Barbarians!' I said instantly. 'These are the evil men of science.'

'Thank you very much,' said the young man, carefully writing all this down in longhand. He closed his notebook and scurried away and as he did so Kim, the girl with the black lipstick, appeared in his place. 'I just want to thank you for giving such a stirring speech!' She held out a hand. 'You're very brave,' she said. 'We very much appreciate it.'

'My pleasure!' I said. I didn't quite understand why it was brave but I wasn't going to duck any compliments.

'I'm sorry there weren't any more people here tonight,' Kim apologised. 'But we clashed with a secret meeting of the Freedom For Animals Campaign.'

I smiled and shrugged aside the lack of an audience.

Garth, Kim, Patsy and I then all shook hands with one another and Patsy promised that we'd try to attend next month's meeting. Then Patsy and I drove back to Bilbury and I didn't know whether I felt so good because I was relieved that it was all over or because it had all gone reasonably well but I didn't care why because just feeling wonderful was quite enough. And when I dropped her off at the farm Patsy let me kiss her and that made two in one evening and I was so excited that I didn't get to sleep until three in the morning.

*   *   *

The call from Mrs Harper came just as I was sitting down to my dinner.

'I'm sorry to ring you in the evening,' she apologised. 'But the hospital said that I was to ring you at the first sign of anything being wrong.'

'Absolutely right,' I told her. I asked Gilly to put my dinner in the oven and then raced over to Mrs Harper's cottage. When I got there I found Keith lying on the sofa in his pyjamas and dressing gown. He had been crying but was trying hard to be brave. His mother looked as though she too was struggling to hold back the tears.

'It was almost exactly the same as last time,' she told me. 'He was fine when he came out of hospital. I thought I'd keep him off school for one more day – just to make sure that he was all right – and he spent the day playing.' Suddenly, she started to cry. 'Can't you find out what is wrong with him, doctor? Please. It's worrying me sick.' She bent over the sofa and cradled her son in her arms.

I swallowed and leant forward. 'Let's go through what you did today,' I said to Keith. It was clear by now that whatever Keith's problem was it was caused by something he did, ate or came into contact with at home. His symptoms weren't typical of an allergy reaction but I was beginning to think that that was the only possible explanation.

Painfully, slowly and in between moments when both of them were too tearful to talk, Keith and his mother detailed the day for me. I could detect nothing in what they told me that would explain Keith's condition and the more I looked at him and thought about it the more convinced I became that whatever Keith was suffering from it wasn't an allergy problem.

'Try to think back to last time Keith came out of hospital,' I said to his mother.

She nodded to show that she was concentrating hard.

'Has he eaten or done anything today that he ate or did last time he came out of hospital?'

There were, of course, quite a number of similarities. Keith had eaten toast on both days. He had watched television. And he had had his favourite meal of baked beans with a poached egg on top. But none of this explained his symptoms.

'I wore my new jeans,' said Keith suddenly. It was the first time he'd spoken for several minutes and both of us looked at him. 'My new blue jeans,' insisted Keith. 'I wore them both times.'

Mrs Harper smiled at her son and then looked at me and shrugged. Like her I wasn't immediately convinced that the jeans were relevant but then a question occurred to me.

'When did you buy the jeans?' I asked Mrs Harper. 'How long before Keith first became ill?'

'I bought three pairs on the market in Barnstaple,' said Mrs. Harper. 'They were quite cheap and he gets through clothes very quickly.' She stopped and thought for a moment. 'I bought them two or three days before he first went into hospital,' she said. She looked at me sharply. 'Could that be it?'

'He's worn them each time he's been taken ill?'

She nodded.

'Could I see them?' I had no idea how a pair of jeans could have made Keith so ill but it was too much of a coincidence to ignore completely. Mrs Harper got up and disappeared up the stairs. Moments later she reappeared clutching three pairs of jeans. Two pairs were folded and still had the manufacturer's cardboard label attached to the back pocket. The third pair were creased and had clearly been worn.

'These are the pair that Keith's been wearing,' said Mrs Harper, handing me the crumpled pair. 'I haven't washed them yet.'

I looked at the jeans. They seemed like a perfectly ordinary pair of jeans. But they were the only possible explanation I could think of for Keith's symptoms. When I spoke to the hospital I suggested that they run some tests on the jeans to see if they could find anything in them that would explain Keith's symptoms. The doctor I spoke to sounded sceptical but agreed that they had nothing to lose by trying.

*   *   *

Hubert should have visited me but I hadn't seen him for over a week and I was worried. What made it worse was the fact that I didn't know where to look for him. And then Miss Johnson took a telephone call from a Mrs Roberts who had, she reported, discovered an old tramp lying half unconscious in her summer house. I went round there straight away.

'It was a terrible shock, doctor!' said Mrs Roberts. 'I only popped in there to check on some flowers I was drying.' Mrs Roberts did not have the demeanour of a woman who copes well with the unexpected. I think that she would have probably panicked if she'd found mildew on one of the stored deckchairs. She led the way down the garden path towards a small octagonal summer house that stood on the bottom of the lawn.

Inside the summer house, wrapped in a rug and curled up on a small pile of hammock cushions lay Hubert. His dog Ben lay by his side. Both looked exhausted.

'I didn't know whether to ring you or the police,' said Mrs Roberts.

'You did right to call me,' I told her. I reached out and touched her arm. 'Thank you.' I smiled at her. Mrs Roberts wasn't used to people smiling at her and she scurried away up the garden path. 'I'll be in the kitchen if you want me,' she called as she retreated.

I knelt down and put a hand on Hubert's shoulder. He

didn't move. Gently, very gently, I shook him. Slowly, he stirred and opened his eyes. 'Are you OK?'

For a moment or two he looked confused, as though he wasn't certain where he was. He rubbed his chin, opened his mouth and licked his lips. Judging by the state of his beard and the smell coming from the rug he'd been wrapped in he'd been lying in the summer house for several days. He looked weak and dehydrated.

'I ...' he began. But nothing else came out of his throat. His voice had apparently disappeared. He rubbed the back of his hand across his mouth and tried again. This attempt was no more successful than the first.

'Can you move?'

He tried to sit up but didn't have the strength. I put an arm behind his shoulder and helped him first to a sitting and then to a standing position. I was astonished to find out just how light and thin he was. It was like lifting a bird.

'I ...' he tried again. I lowered my head so that I could hear better. 'I was tired. I had to lie down.' He tried to push me away so that he could stand alone but I held onto him. He would have fallen otherwise. I knew that however much he hated the idea he was going to have to go into hospital.

*   *   *

Just as I'd promised Hubert I'd taken Ben home with me to the Duck and Puddle. When she wouldn't eat properly I decided to take her along to see the local vet.

While I was sitting waiting in the vet's living room Mrs Wilson, the district nurse, came in. She was carrying her two cats in a wicker basket.

'I didn't know you'd got a dog!' She seemed strangely subdued.

I told her about Hubert and asked her what was wrong with the cats.

She looked down at the wicker basket as though surprised to see that she had them with her. 'They're just old,' she answered.

The vet didn't have a proper consulting room since most of his work was done on the local farms so he saw Ben and I in his kitchen. It was the grubbiest room I'd ever seen. It looked like a lending library for germs. The vet, though, was rather jolly. He was bluff, huge and well built. He wore a rusty brown coloured thorn proof tweed suit with a matching waistcoat. His jacket had leather patches on the elbows and leather guards on the cuffs. He wore a pair of heavy brown brogues that were caked with dried mud and manure. He had a thin thatch of ginger hair combed across the top of a freckled scalp and a lot of darker hair growing out of his nose and ears. He had the bushiest eyebrows I'd ever seen.

After examining Ben carefully he took a thermometer out of his breast pocket and put it up her bottom. Ben looked at me sadly, as though asking me if such an indignity were really necessary.

'There's nothing wrong with her,' said the vet, shaking the thermometer and putting it down on the top of the fridge. He hadn't bothered to wash it. 'She's just a bit miserable. Missing her master I expect.'

I had explained about Hubert.

'Lots of love and affection and a few long walks,' prescribed the vet. 'That's what she needs.' He picked up the thermometer and put it back into his breast pocket. He still hadn't washed it.

As I left I passed Mrs Wilson preparing to carry her basket of cats into the kitchen.

'I hope everything is OK,' I said.

She looked at me as though puzzled.

'With the cats.'

'Oh, thank you.'

Ben and I left and later that afternoon I took her for a long walk around Dr Brownlow's estate.

* * *

It would have been an exaggeration to say that Patsy's father and I had become firm friends but he no longer treated me with the contempt he'd originally shown and I wasn't quite as frightened of him as I had been. Those were steps forward in the right direction as far as I was concerned. No one had ever mentioned the hawthorn tablets and Mr Kennett was now quite well again; there were no signs of his 'heart trouble'.

I sipped at the glass of homemade parsnip wine which he'd

given me and listened as he told me about the case of shingles he'd had in 1963.

'The doctor was no bloody good at all,' Mr Kennett complained vehemently. Then he remembered who I was. 'No disrespect to yourself, of course.' For him that was quite a climb down.

'No offence taken,' I assured him.

'The rash was two thirds of the way round my waist,' continued Mr Kennett, pouring himself another glass of home made wine and offering me a refill. I put my hand over my glass and shook my head. I'd already explained three times that I had to drive but Mr Kennett was either unconvinced by the research showing a relationship between alcohol consumption and impaired reflexes or else he wasn't listening to me.

'Do you know what happens if a shingles rash goes completely round your waist?' He drew an imaginary circle around his waist as he spoke and spilt a large measure of his parsnip wine onto his trouser leg. He gazed down at the growing damp patch and then decided to ignore it. But he did refill his glass.

I said I didn't.

'Dead!' said Patsy's father emphatically. He slammed his fist down on the sofa and spilt more parsnip wine. 'When the rash meets you're as good as dead.' I nodded. He was convincing and I wasn't in the mood to start an argument.

'Dr Brownlow didn't know what to do!' insisted Mr Kennett. 'No idea!' he cackled. He seemed pleased at the memory. I half opened my mouth to defend my employer but thought better of it. I knew that Dr Brownlow would forgive me.

'Alf Watercombe got me better again,' insisted Patsy's father. 'He wrapped a fresh circle of bullrushes round my waist every morning exactly as the sun came up over Shapcott Hill.' He pointed towards the window but it was pitch black outside. As he pointed he spilt more parsnip wine. Suddenly he lunged forwards, eyes glaring. 'You wouldn't think that would work, would you?'

He had me on a hiding to nothing and we both knew it. Whatever I said the reputation of orthodox medicine was lost.

'No,' I said.

'Haaargh!' said Patsy's father. He shook his head and the combination of the sound and the noise made him look a

164

bit like a horse. I didn't have the faintest idea what to say to that but I was suddenly saved by an angel walking into the room.

'Hello!' said the angel. 'I'm ready.'

I could hardly believe my eyes. I'd never seen anyone so beautiful.

'You look beautiful.'

'Do you like it?' Patsy lifted the dress a few inches and pirouetted. The dress was calf length pale pink satin. Below her waist it billowed like a cloud. At and above the waist it fitted her like a glove. There were no straps and I had no idea what was holding it up. I hadn't realised before what a perfect figure she had.

'I like the dress,' I said. 'And you look beautiful.'

Her mother who'd been hovering in the doorway behind her came forward looking as proud as only a mother can look. She leant forward and whispered something in Patsy's ear. Patsy blushed. Patsy's mother then draped a silk scarf around her daughter's neck.

Patsy's father managed to suppress his romantic urges. 'You'll freeze to death. Going out half naked.'

'Dad!' pleaded Patsy. 'Don't spoil things.'

'I'll get your coat,' said Patsy's mother.

Patsy sighed. Her father repeated his impression of an unhappy horse.

Patsy's mother disappeared for a moment and came back with a dark grey woollen coat which she draped round Patsy's shoulders. Patsy looked embarrassed. I looked at her and smiled. She still looked radiant. But then I was biased. To me she would have looked good dressed in a cardboard box.

'Hadn't we better go?' asked Patsy.

I looked at my watch. There was plenty of time. 'Yes.'

Patsy kissed her mother and said goodbye to her father. I promised them both that I would look after their daughter. Patsy put her shoes into her coat pockets and put her wellington boots on to cross through the aromatic mixture of mud, silage and animal waste in the farmyard.

While she fastened her seat belt I turned the key to start the car. Nothing happened. I tried it again. Nothing. A quick glance at the dashboard instruments showed that I had left the headlights switched on while I'd been parked. The lights had drained the battery.

Angry with myself I explained what I'd done.

'Never mind,' said Patsy. 'These things happen.' She leant across and kissed me on the cheek. Suddenly I felt better. I loved her more every moment I knew her.

'You should be shouting at me,' I said. 'It was a stupid thing to do.'

Patsy shook her head. 'It was my fault. I took so long.'

I heard someone tapping on my window, turned and saw Patsy's father standing there looking puzzled. 'What's up?'

'The battery's flat,' I confessed, miserably.

'Stay there!' he said unnecessarily. He disappeared back into the house. Moments later he reappeared holding a large key carried on a piece of bent and rusty wire. 'You can borrow the second best tractor.'

Patsy and I both got out of the car. I thanked Mr Kennett and we crossed the courtyard to the open barn where the second best tractor was stored.

*　　*　　*

'Bring Patsy if you like!' Dr Brownlow had said when he'd invited me to join him and a few of his friends. 'I hear you two are something of an item these days.'

'An item?' I laughed, blushing. 'What's that supposed to mean?' I knew exactly what he meant.

'Going out together. Dating.'

'We are going out together,' I agreed.

'She's a nice girl,' said Dr Brownlow. 'I delivered her.' He remembered the name of every child he'd ever delivered. He was proud of them all and loved them too.

'I'll ask her,' I said. 'I'd love her to come.'

'We usually dress,' Dr Brownlow told me.

*　　*　　*

The gardener had hung candles in jam jars from the lower branches of the corridor of trees that lined the driveway. It all looked like something out of a fairy tale. There were already half a dozen cars parked in the large, rectangular gravelled area in front of the house. There was a Jaguar, two Rovers, a Mercedes, an Aston Martin and a brand new Rolls Royce Silver Shadow which was coloured gold and had a gold plated silver lady mounted on the radiator cap. I parked Mr Kennett's second best tractor in between one of the Rovers and the Aston Martin.

Dr Brownlow's butler, Bradshaw, opened the front door. He didn't seem to recognise me though this was probably because of the hired dinner suit I was wearing. I don't think I would have recognised myself.

Patsy and I were the youngest there by at least a generation and a half. Apart from Dr Brownlow there was no one else in the room that I recognised. Dr Brownlow introduced us to everyone but I have never been very good at remembering a dozen names in one go and I was too busy trying to decide which of the guests owned the Rolls Royce to pay proper attention. I had never seen anything quite so gloriously tasteless and it had made a lasting impression on me. The last couple he introduced us to were Dr Charles Jarvis and his wife Carolyn. 'Are you the radiologist?' I asked, relieved to find someone whose name I knew.

He said he was. He looked even older than he sounded on the telephone but seemed no less bad tempered. His wife was much more fun. She seemed about fifteen years younger and wore a tight pink dress that looked expensive but that was far too small for her. The dress had lots of ruffs and flounces but there weren't enough of these to disguise the rolls of fat around her waist. She had well used laugh lines around her eyes and seemed to take to Patsy straight away. 'We've had a writ from that damned patient of yours,' said Dr Jarvis gruffly. He sounded as though he blamed me for it.

'Lionel Francis?'

Dr Jarvis nodded. 'Have you heard anything?' he wanted to know.

'Not yet. But he did tell me he was going to send a solicitor's letter.'

We talked for a while about the possibility of Mr Francis winning damages and the rising enthusiasm of patients for legal action. It was a dull conversation which, I suspect, probably bored Dr Jarvis as much as it bored me but we seemed to have little in common other than this one rather sad episode. We were eventually saved from one another when Bradshaw came in to announce that dinner was ready.

I found myself sitting between Carolyn Jarvis and a woman of about seventy whose name I couldn't remember. She had a large, old fashioned hearing aid clipped to the front of a garment which looked as though it had been designed for bridal wear and she had brought with her to the table a large gin and tonic which Bradshaw refilled regularly and without being asked. Patsy was seated at the far end of the table, between Dr Brownlow and a grey haired old man whose slightly shabby evening wear was put into shadow by a bright red velvet bow tie.

Whatever financial problems Dr Brownlow was having there were no signs of poverty in the dining room. The room, which was as large as a barn, was warmed by a massive log fire in a great stone fireplace and lit exclusively by candles. The flickering lights and the smoke from the fire and the candles gave the whole room a romantic, mediaeval atmosphere.

Much of the meal is now but a blur in my memory. I tried to make polite conversation with the two ladies on either side of me but failed fairly miserably. The old lady with the deaf aid thought, for some reason, that I was her bank manager and spent most of the evening complaining about the quality of the bank's services and the unreasonable extent of its charges. I suspect that I probably added to her sense of confusion by agreeing wholeheartedly with all her criticisms of the banking system.

The radiologist's wife, on my other side, seemed unwilling to talk about anything that didn't involve her children. These were, I gathered with some surprise, grown up with offspring of their own, but she talked nevertheless with genuine passion about playgroups, infant schools and the quality of modern education. What I had mistaken for laughter lines around her eyes turned out to be lines made by squinting. Through vanity she had refused to bring with her the spectacles which she clearly needed.

Eventually, in some despair, I struck up a conversation

with a small, almost entirely bald man who was sitting quite near to me. He wore a smart, military style moustache and even while seated had an unmistakably military bearing. It was this conversation which led to something which was destined to change my whole life.

'Do you live in Bilbury?' I asked him.

'Good God! No!' he replied with some force. 'I live in town. I like the bright lights and the buzz.'

'Really?' I said. 'Have you come here specially for this evening?' I had assumed that by 'town' he meant London.

He, in turn, seemed surprised by my question but confirmed that he had indeed made the journey to Bilbury specifically to attend Dr Brownlow's dinner party.

'Are you staying the night?'

'I'm driving back home.'

'Isn't it a rather long journey?'

'Not particularly. It only takes twenty minutes or so.'

At this point I realised my mistake. 'Oh, you mean you live in Barnstaple?'

He looked at me as though I was mentally deficient and nodded warily.

'Do you work there?'

'I'm Robert Wallace. I run one of the local papers. The Barnstaple, Bideford and Bilbury Herald.'

'Oh, I know it!' I said brightly, though my recognition of his product didn't seem to excite him in quite the way I had hoped it would.

'You're the new apprentice, aren't you?'

I nodded. I hadn't thought of myself as an apprentice before but it wasn't an inaccurate description.

'Very pretty wife you've got.'

'Oh, Patsy and I aren't married,' I said, automatically, though I realised a split second later that I rather liked the way he'd assumed that we were.

'Very pretty girl anyway,' said the publisher. He pushed a large piece of parsnip into his mouth and chewed on it thoughtfully. The parsnips weren't very well cooked and the chewing took quite a lot of effort. 'Do you fancy writing a column for us?'

I didn't think I'd heard him properly. 'I beg your pardon?'

'A doctor column,' explained Mr Wallace. 'My wife's always on to me about it. She's been saying for years that we should have a doctor page.' He cut a roast potato in two and put half into his mouth. 'I did ask Brownlow,' he confessed, speaking with some difficulty. 'But he wouldn't do it. Too damned lazy.'

'I'm not sure,' I said, rather hesitantly.

'We'll pay you,' said the publisher. 'But six pounds a week is all we can manage.'

'Six!' I repeated. It sounded quite a lot.

'Eight then,' agreed the publisher. 'But that's it.'

'Would it have to have my name on it?' I asked warily. All the doctor columns I'd ever seen before had been written under pen names such as 'Dr Goodnight' or 'Dr Helpful'.

'Oh, I think so, don't you?' said the publisher. 'People want to know who is writing the stuff they read these days.'

'How many readers does the paper have?'

'We sell 30,000 a week,' replied Mr Wallace. 'But you can multiply that by three or four.'

'That's 100,000 people a week!' I said, horrified at the responsibility.

'More than you'd meet in a lifetime working as a GP,' agreed the publisher. He speared a piece of cauliflower and bit a chunk off. 'You could do a lot of good with a column in our paper.' He added two slices of carrot to the masticated cauliflower. 'I'll tell the editor to get in touch with you to fix things up.'

*　　*　　*

It snowed heavily while we were having dinner with Dr Brownlow and as we crowded together in the hallway staring out through the front door the night looked absurdly romantic. Everything was covered in a thick layer of soft snow and the silence seemed strange and all invasive. There was a full moon and the fluttering snowflakes were backlit by moonlight as they gently made their way earthwards. We'd only been indoors for four or five hours but already the snow was at least six inches deep. Trees, garden statues and cars were all outlined in snow.

170

'It's going to be a miserable journey home,' moaned Dr Jarvis, staring out gloomily.

'I hate snow,' said the publisher emphatically. 'Hate the stuff.'

I turned my collar up, slipped out into the snow and ran over towards Mr Kennett's second best tractor. Walking was difficult since with every step I took my feet disappeared entirely from view. I climbed up onto the tractor's outside step, opened the cab door and picked up Patsy's wellington boots. Then I ran back to the house. Moments later the other guests gazed in admiration as Patsy slipped off her delicate evening shoes and slid her feet into her boots.

'What a wonderful idea!' said Mrs Jarvis. 'How did you know it was going to snow, dear?'

'Do you want to borrow them?' asked Patsy.

Mrs Jarvis laughed uncomfortably. 'Oh, no thank you!' she said emphatically, as though she found the idea very slightly offensive.

'Is that yours? the publisher asked me, nodding towards the tractor.

I shook my head. 'I borrowed it off Patsy's father.'

'How *did* you know it was going to snow?' asked Dr Brownlow.

'Just an old piece of country folklore,' I told him. 'When ducks sleep in groups of three or more it means it's going to snow.'

Everyone seemed impressed. 'I hadn't heard that one before,' admitted Dr Brownlow, which wasn't surprising since as far as I knew it was entirely original.

'Looks a bit glum, doesn't it? said the old lady with the deaf aid. 'Has it been snowing?'

'Does anyone need a lift?' I asked. 'I'm sure Mr Kennett wouldn't mind if I did a bit of ferrying when I've taken Patsy home.'

'Oh, I don't think that will be necessary,' said Mr Wallace. 'Our cars should be able to cope with a bit of snow.' He tiptoed down Dr Brownlow's stone staircase and stepped warily over towards the gold coloured Rolls Royce.

The rest of us took this as a cue and seconds later we were all tip toeing our way through the snow towards our vehicles (all apart from Patsy that is – she was able to stride confidently through the snow in her boots).

As Patsy and I drove away I turned back for a second to watch the chaos developing behind us, as one after another, Dr Brownlow's guests discovered that expensive two wheel drive motor cars can be just as uncontrollable in the snow as cheap ones.

'Well, you did offer to help them,' said Patsy. 'I thought it was very nice of you!'

* * *

CHAPTER ELEVEN

Most of Dr Brownlow's patients either lived in the village of Bilbury itself or in one of the nearby villages such as Patchole, Shirwell, Kentisbury or Combe Martin but one afternoon I received a call asking me to visit a patient in Barnstaple.

'He's apparently a patient of Dr Brownlow's,' said Miss Johnson, who had passed the message on to me. 'He has collapsed.'

I drove to Barnstaple as fast as my Morris would go and was quite breathless when I reached the address I'd been given. I leant against the doorbell and waited. The door was opened a few moments later by a young woman in a quilted dressing gown. At the neck of the dressing gown I could just see a few wisps of nightdress. Her attire surprised me a little since it was still early in the afternoon. 'He's in the bedroom,' she said, with tears in her eyes. I followed her down the corridor and found my patient lying on his back on a bed.

He would never again have to worry about finding a tie to match his shirt. He would never again curse as he struggled to find the partner to a single sock. He was beyond my help. Apart from the sheet which covered his body he was as naked as he had been at the other end of his life and although I didn't know exactly why I thought he looked vaguely familiar.

The question I asked as I turned to the young woman in the doorway still haunts me occasionally. 'Had your father been ill?' That's all. Five words that at the time seemed to make a natural question. The man was clearly in his late fifties or early sixties. The woman could be no more than thirty. They both looked quietly respectable. The woman certainly looked more like a daughter than a lover. Or at least she

173

looked more like I thought a daughter ought to look like. I was too inexperienced to know that appearances can be very deceptive; the Don Juan may turn out to be a grubby little man with a thin moustache and a spray of dandruff on his shoulders; the wife beater may turn out to be a plump, jovial fellow with bifocals and a slight stutter.

'He wasn't my father,' said the young woman, blushing bright red. She paused and looked away. I understood instantly. 'He used to come here two or three times a week.' She sat down on the other side of the bed and took the dead man's hand in hers. 'He was a client. A regular.'

'Had he been ill?'

She nodded. 'He'd been very ill recently. Something to do with his chest.'

'What happened?'

'We were making love. Suddenly he cried out in pain. He fell back clutching his chest. That was it. He didn't say anything or do anything else.'

'Had he had chest pains before?'

'I don't know. I don't think so.'

'But he had been ill?'

'He told me that he nearly died.'

I turned and, for the first time, stared properly at the dead body. Suddenly I knew who it was. I was looking at Lionel Francis. I was astonished that Lionel Francis should visit a prostitute. He hadn't seemed the type.

'What are we going to do?' asked the woman. She looked lost and very alone, like a child in a crowd whose mother has moved ahead too quickly. There were, I noticed, tears running down her cheeks. 'It was the first time we'd seen one another for some time,' she told me. 'I wanted to make things special for him because of that.'

'Where are his clothes?' I asked.

She opened the wardrobe and showed me. Lionel Francis had hung his suit up neatly on a hanger. Even his shirt was on a hanger, with his tie draped around the collar.

'Help me dress him!' I told her, pulling his suit out of the wardrobe.

When we'd finished I told her to get herself dressed while I rang for an ambulance.

'Man collapsed in the street,' I told the ambulance controller. 'A woman took him into her house but he was dead by the time I got here.'

* * *

I hadn't forgotten about the column I was supposed to be writing for the local newspaper but I had rather hoped that Mr Wallace had forgotten. Or that he and his editor had had second thoughts when reconsidering the idea in the cold light of day. However, the newspaper editor who telephoned was in no doubt about the publisher's commitment.

'I gather you spoke to Mr Wallace and agreed to write a column on medical matters?' The caller sounded weary of life, weary of his job and especially weary of his publisher hiring inexperienced strangers to write columns.

'Yes. But I don't expect he intended me to take him seriously.' I thought I'd give them an easy way out.

'Mr Wallace always expects everyone to take him seriously,' said the caller very quickly. 'I hope you haven't changed your mind since the meeting.'

'Well, no, not exactly.'

'Good. We're looking for 1000 words or so once a week. We're going to put your column onto our Family Page so we'll need the copy every week by 4.00pm on Thursday afternoon.'

The idea of writing a thousand words on anything startled me. And the idea of producing a thousand words every week sounded daunting beyond belief. 'What did you want me to write about?'

'We rather hoped you'd come up with the subjects,' said the editor. 'You're the expert after all.'

'But I've got no experience . . .'

'Don't you worry about it,' the editor reassured me. 'We'll put all the commas in all the right places. You just deliver your copy on time.' The phone went silent though I could hear him scrabbling through papers and talking to someone else. 'Where is it that you live?'

'Bilbury.'

'Of course. I've got the address somewhere. Well, if you pop it in the post on Wednesday morning that should be fine.'

175

'When do you want to start?'

'Might as well start this week, eh? Get going with it.'

'This week?' It was Monday. I had less than two days to think of a subject and write a thousand words about it.

'Great!' said the editor. 'I gather the publisher fixed a fee with you?'

'Er ... yes.' I remembered him talking money but I couldn't remember the fee we'd settled on.

'I'll get our accounts department to put you on the contributors' list. If you haven't started getting cheques in a year let me know.'

'In a year?'

'Just joking. They're not quite that bad. Look forward to getting your copy then. Cheerio for now.' And he was gone.

*   *   *

Miss Thwaites sat down, leant across the desk and smiled at me. 'I must say just how much I admire you for speaking out the way you did.' I didn't have the foggiest idea what she was talking about but I felt a strange, empty feeling in the pit of my stomach. 'Needless to say I'm right behind you!' she added.

'I don't want to appear too stupid,' I said, cautiously, 'but could you please tell me what it was that I said and where it was that you read it?'

Miss Thwaites looked surprised. 'The story about the animals,' she explained. 'In today's Daily News.'

Part of me didn't want to know any more. But part of me knew that I had no option. 'I don't suppose you have the paper with you?'

Miss Thwaites shook her head.

Apart from me everyone in Bilbury seemed to have read the Daily News that morning. By the end of the first hour six people had congratulated me on my courage and had wished me all the best for the future.

'I'm not sure I agree with you but there aren't many people in your profession who'd have had the guts to say it,' said Thumper Robinson who'd come into the surgery to have some stitches removed. He'd fallen off a ladder while doing some building repair work at the Duck and Puddle and he had gashed his leg rather badly.

Eventually, I could stand it no longer. I dashed out of the surgery and popped my head into Miss Johnson's office. 'I shan't be a minute!' I promised. 'I've just got an urgent call to make.' Miss Johnson, who knew that there had been no urgent requests for home visits looked at me as if I'd gone mad. 'I'll be back in less than ten minutes!' I called over my shoulder, scurrying past the waiting room and out to where my car was parked. Ben was sitting on the front passenger seat. She pricked up her ears when she saw me coming.

'I thought you'd be in for a copy!' said Pete Marshall. He reached underneath the counter and produced a copy of the Daily News. 'I put one on one side for you,' he told me with a wink.

'I took the paper from him and, discovering that I didn't have any change on me, asked him to put the paper on my bill. 'Must go!' I said, desperate to open the paper and see what I'd said. I didn't like to open it in the shop. I wanted to read it somewhere private.

The story was on page three. 'DOC SLAMS RESEARCH BOFFINS' screamed the headline. I hardly dared look any further but I forced myself to read on. To start with I couldn't imagine how the Daily News could have possibly got hold of the story and then I remembered the scruffy youth who'd interviewed me at the end of my lecture. I closed my eyes and took deep breaths in an attempt to relax my body a little.

After a couple of minutes I felt strong enough to drive the rest of the way back to the surgery so I folded up the newspaper, put it into the glove compartment and started the car up again. I'm not sure how I managed to get through the rest of the surgery. It was all something of a blur. I had an awful feeling that I was going to regret giving that speech.

*　　*　　*

I was with Hubert when he died. I even managed to persuade the ward sister to let me smuggle Ben onto the ward. The two of them greeted one another with great joy.

'God is waiting for you, my son,' said the clergyman who had arrived uninvited at Hubert's bedside.

177

'Bugger God,' said Hubert. 'What did God ever do for me when I was alive and needed him? Why should I have anything to do with him when I'm dead?' He tried to lift himself off the bed but fell back in a fit of coughing. Shocked, the clergyman retreated.

'You will look after Ben, won't you?'

I promised again that I would.

Hubert died with one hand clasping mine and the other hand resting on Ben.

I took Ben back to the Duck and Puddle with me and had great difficulty holding back the tears. I've always wondered where Hubert Donaldson came from and how he came to be a tramp.

*   *   *

With Ben curled up at my feet I sat down at the small table in my bedroom and positioned the new foolscap note-book I'd bought from the corner store neatly in front of me. Then I lined up the three pencils I'd bought. I'd decided to work in pencil so that I could rub out any mistakes I might make. The three pencils were all painted yellow and all had tiny rubbers attached to them. They looked very smart. I arranged them carefully so that the names stencilled in black along their sides were all facing upwards.

It was while admiring their neatness that I noticed that the lead of one of the pencils had broken. Deciding that it would be sensible to make sure that all my equipment was in good working order before I started I felt in my pocket for my penknife. But it wasn't there. I got up from the table and looked in my jacket pocket. It wasn't there either. Nor was it in my black bag. Then I remembered that I'd used it at the surgery to help Miss Johnson open a parcel. I got up from the desk and walked down stairs. Ben came with me. 'Have you got a pencil sharpener?' I asked my landlady.

'A pencil sharpener?'

I nodded.

'I'll have a look.'

I thought that while I was waiting I might as well have a drink so I wandered into the bar and ordered half a pint of best bitter.

'Sorry!' said Gilly, when she returned a few moments later. 'I can't find a pencil sharpener anywhere.'

'Thanks anyway,' I said. It looked as though my column writing career was doomed before it had started. I wondered if I should ring up the newspaper editor now or if I should wait until the following morning.

'But I've got a penknife,' said Gilly. 'Will that do?'

'Thank you,' I sighed. 'That will do fine.' I took the penknife off her, emptied my glass and went back upstairs. I sharpened my pencil, took the penknife back down to Gilly and then sat down again at my desk. Ben curled up by my feet.

I picked up one of the pencils and wrote my name on the first sheet in the notebook. Then I underlined it. Then I underlined it again. Then I wrote the date. Then I put the pencil down and went downstairs to the kitchen where I made myself a cup of coffee. Then I carried the cup of coffee back upstairs.

I stared at the sheet of paper and waited for inspiration to strike. I even picked up one of the pencils and held it ready in my hand so that I would be ready to write down the words when the muse decided to arrive. It seemed exhausting work. Within minutes I felt physically and mentally drained. My eyelids didn't want to stay open and I had to prop my head up on my hands.

Then, out of nowhere, I had an idea. I picked up the pencil which had fallen out of my fingers and started to scribble my first column.

*   *   *

'There's a Mr Lister on the telephone for you,' said Miss Johnson. 'He's rung four times already but I've told him you're busy.'

'Mr Lister?'

'He says he's from the Herald,' said Miss Johnson suspiciously.

'Oh, *that* Mr Lister! He's the editor. I'd better speak to him.' I picked up the telephone expecting to have to fend off the compliments.

'We've got your first column safely.'

'Oh good. I was a bit worried because I didn't keep a copy. I'm glad it got there OK.'

'It's very good,' said the editor.

'Great. I'm glad you like it.'

'There are just a couple of problems.'

'Fine. I didn't expect to get things absolutely spot on the first time out. What adjustments would you like to make?'

'The first little problem is length,' said the editor.

'Did I do too much? I did get carried away a bit didn't I? Still, you can always cut things down a bit can't you?'

'No, it isn't too long at all,' said the editor. 'In fact we've got the opposite problem.'

'It's too short?'

'It is a little. We need another 600 words or so to fill up the space we've given you.'

'How much did I write then?' I asked, puzzled. I hadn't counted the words but there had been a lot of them.

'Four hundred and seventeen.'

'Oh.'

'Never mind. It's easily done.'

'What's the other problem?' I asked him.

'The subject,' said the editor bluntly. 'We discussed your piece at the editorial conference this morning and we felt that it was perhaps just a little bit too esoteric.'

I was startled by this. 'Really?'

'Afraid so. We felt that we might frighten some of our readers off if we devoted the whole of your first column to malaria.'

'It's a very important disease!'

'But is it important in North Devon?'

'Not very,' I confessed. 'It isn't terribly common.'

'That's what we thought. We felt it might be better to tackle a more popular subject.'

'Oh.' I had difficulty in hiding my disappointment.

'This isn't a criticism.' said the editor quickly. 'Please don't take it as such. Think of us as offering you constructive advice. We want to help you get this absolutely right. It's going to be a very important column.'

'Yes.'

'What do you think about devoting the first column to the common cold?'

'The cold?' I said, very disappointed. 'Isn't that a bit ordinary?'

'Ah. That's the point, you see. It's the sort of stuff our readers will love. Good solid, practical advice from you on how to treat a cold.'

'OK.'

'Do you think you could do something for us now?'

'Now?'

'It is Thursday,' said the editor gently. 'If you could dictate something to our copy takers before 4 o'clock this afternoon that would help us a lot.'

'Of course.'

'And we'll need a photograph of you,' said the editor. 'To put on the top of the column.'

'Is that absolutely necessary?'

'Absolutely!' said the editor, firmly. 'The readers will want to know what you look like. Can we send a photographer round?'

'Where?'

'The surgery would be nice,' said the editor. 'A nice shot of you with your stethoscope round your neck and lots of good, medical equipment in the background.'

I said that I had a couple of calls to do but that when I'd finished I'd write my new column and wait for the photographer. The editor said he was very grateful and that he'd like to take me to lunch sometime.

*   *   *

'Could I have a word with you about my feet?' asked Miss Johnson.

'Of course.'

Miss Johnson sat down in the patients' chair.

'What's wrong with them?' I asked her.

She carefully took off her shoe and rolled down her left stocking. 'How do you think it's coming along?' she asked, lifting her foot up into the air.

I leant forward and peered at it.

'Just there,' said Miss Johnson pointing. 'My verruca.' She gently prodded the sides of a large lump covered in yellow ointment. I leant a little closer. I'd never seen a verruca before. It looked like a small volcano.

'I'm putting some ointment on it that I get from the chemist. Do you think it's doing the job?'

I made some sounds which seemed suitably non-committal and nodded a lot. 'We'd better have another look at it in another week. Bit early to say now.'

This vague endorsement seemed to please Miss Johnson. She rolled her stockings back into place and then slipped her shoe on.

I felt quite pleased that she'd asked for my advice.

*　　*　　*

CHAPTER TWELVE

Followed by her three children and carrying the latest Mrs Tate headed for the door. Her pregnancy had been entirely uneventful and she had come into the surgery for her post-natal examination. 'Goodbye, doctor!' she said cheerily. 'See you next time!'

When Mrs Tate had gone I went over to the basin to wash my hands. But when I turned on the tap nothing came out but a little steam. Some distance away I could hear pipes shaking and rattling under the pressure from the central heating boiler but no water came out into the basin. I tried the cold tap with exactly the same result.

'What on earth is going on?' asked Miss Johnson, putting her head around the door. 'It sounds as if the whole house is about to blow up!'

I waved my hands in the direction of the sink. 'There doesn't seem to be any water in the system.'

'We'd better tell Dr Brownlow! Someone ought to turn off the boiler before it blows up.' Miss Johnson seemed very worried so since I was near the end of the surgery and feeling like a bit of physical exercise I offered to go and find Dr Brownlow. I found him in the conservatory attending to his orchids. He paled when I told him the news.

'Don't look so worried!' I said cheerfully. 'The water board is probably digging up the pipes. They'll have you back on again before long.'

Dr Brownlow shook his head. 'It's nothing to do with the water board,' he told me glumly.

Puzzled, I just stared at him. Being city born I'd always assumed that everyone got their water supplies through the local water board. After all, who else was there?

'We've got a private water supply here,' explained Dr Brownlow. 'Our water comes from a stream fed well in the north field.

'A well?' I repeated incredulously, struggling with visions of men and women drawing water up with the aid of buckets.

'There's a pump,' explained Dr Brownlow, noticing my surprise. 'But it's got nothing to do with the water board.'

'So, what do you think could have happened?'

He shrugged. 'The pump could have stopped, a valve could be blocked ...' he paused. 'Or the stream could have dried up.'

I was beginning to see why he was looking so glum. 'Streams don't dry up!' I said firmly. 'Do they?'

'They do sometimes,' said Dr Brownlow, miserably.

I went back to the surgery and left him setting off to try and find out what had happened to his water supply.

*   *   *

'You were right about the jeans,' said the doctor from the hospital. 'They were contaminated with phosphate. Keith has been suffering from phosphate poisoning. There's one patch of material on the right leg that's been soaked in a powerful industrial insecticide solution. Every time Keith put the jeans on his body absorbed more of the phosphate and his symptoms came back again.'

'But how on earth did the jeans get contaminated?' I asked. I'd never even heard of anyone suffering from phosphate poisoning before.

'That's what we hoped you could help us find out,' the doctor said. 'Do you think the jeans could have been contaminated at home? Maybe by a spillage from a can of insecticide?'

'I doubt it,' I told him. It didn't seem very likely that Mrs Harper would keep an industrial insecticide in the house. But when I rang her to tell her the good news that Keith's problem had been diagnosed I asked her if she had any insecticide stored in or near to the house.

'Good heavens, no!' said Mrs Harper instantly. 'I buy those sticky strips for flies in the summer but those are the only things I use.' There was a pause. 'When will Keith be able to come home?'

I told her that the hospital would probably let him home after another 24 hour observation. 'Have you still got the other two pairs of jeans that you bought?'

'Yes. Do you think I ought to throw them away? Or do you think it would be safe for him to wear them if I put them in the washing machine first?'

'I don't know. Do you mind if I get someone from the hospital to pick them up and have them tested?'

Mrs Harper said that she didn't so I rang the hospital back. 'Maybe the jeans were contaminated before Mrs Harper bought them,' I suggested. 'In which case it's possible that those aren't the only jeans that are dangerous.' I asked the doctor if he could arrange for someone from the laboratory to pick up the two remaining pairs of jeans and have them tested. He said he would. Then I told him the identity of the stallholder who'd sold Mrs Harper the jeans. 'It might be worthwhile getting someone to have a word with him,' I added.

* * *

I found Dr Brownlow standing in the middle of a large field to the north of the house. He was staring gloomily down a large hole in the ground. A large, metal manhole cover lay on the grass beside him.

'Have you found the problem?'

'The well is dry,' he said morosely, without looking at me.

'Have you checked the stream?'

'Not yet.'

'So it could just be a blockage?'

Dr Brownlow nodded but looked unconvinced.

'I'll come with you,' I volunteered. 'Where is the stream?'

We walked across to the edge of the field until we found a dry ditch running in the shade of a thick hawthorn hedge. 'There it is!' said Dr Brownlow, pointing to the ditch.

'That's your stream?'

'It was,' said Dr Brownlow. He walked along the bank for a dozen yards, then returned and walked a dozen yards in the other direction. 'It's unbelievable,' he said at last. 'That

stream has kept this house supplied for a hundred and fifty
years. I wouldn't have been surprised to see it running low
but to see it completely dried up ...' he shook his head as
if he found it all quite unbelievable.

'Which way does it normally flow?'

Dr Brownlow looked at me as if I was simple minded and
nodded to the left. I felt slightly embarrassed when I realised
that the field was on a slope and that the stream would have
found it difficult to flow in any other direction.

'Why don't we walk upstream a bit and see if it's dry all
the way?'

Reluctantly, Dr Brownlow agreed and we walked in the
direction that would have been upstream had there been any
stream. After about two hundred yards we came to a point
where the dry stream bed disappeared through a hedge.

'Whose land is that?'

'It used to be Lady Kentisbury's,' answered Dr Brownlow.
'Now it belongs to some fellow who works on the television.'

'Mike Trickle?'

'That sounds like it.'

'Not a very apt name if he depends on the same stream,'
I commented.

Dr Brownlow looked at me sharply.

'Sorry.'

'He's got a different supply anyway,' said Dr Brownlow.

I jumped down onto the still muddy stream bed, bent over
double and crawled forward through the hedge. About a yard
and a half into the hedge I came to a stop. 'Did you know
there was a wall here?' I called back.

Dr Brownlow jumped down into the mud behind me and
squelched his way forward. 'Wall? What wall?'

I pointed through the hedge at a very solid looking concrete
wall. Its foundations ran across the stream bed.

Dr Brownlow stared at the wall and banged his fist on it
in frustration.

It looked as though he was going to be without water for
some time.

*   *   *

'There are two registered letters for you this morning,' said

Gilly, putting my breakfast down in front of me the following Saturday morning.

I looked up at her in alarm. I couldn't remember ever having one registered letter before. And I knew instantly that they were both bringing bad news. Why would anyone spend extra money on registering a letter to bring me good news. 'Where are they?' I croaked.

'I think I put them on the hall table,' said Gilly. 'I didn't think you'd want to be bothered with them until you'd had your breakfast.'

I tried to forget about the mail and to concentrate on my bacon and eggs but I failed miserably. I got up from the table, went out to the hallway and collected the two letters. According to the franking marks one had come from a firm of solicitors in Devon and the other was from London. I picked the two letters up and carried them back into the bar. I put them down beside my plate and just stared at them for a few moments trying to decide which to open first and using the choice as an excuse to open neither.

'What's the matter?' asked Patsy, suddenly appearing from the kitchen and seeing that I had hardly touched my breakfast. 'Aren't you hungry?'

I lifted my head and tried to smile.

'What's wrong?' asked Patsy, immediately concerned. 'Bad news?'

I touched the two letters with the forefinger of my right hand. 'I think so.'

'What are they?'

'Trouble.'

'Haven't you opened them?'

I shook my head.

'Then how do you know that they mean trouble?'

'I just do.'

Patsy sat down on the edge of the chair opposite me. 'You're going to have to open them sometime,' she said quietly.

I nodded. After a moment or two I picked up the letter from London and used my knife to slit it open. My hands were trembling as I pulled out the letter that was inside.

'Is it bad?' asked Patsy.

'Yes.' I was still reading the letter but I knew that it was bad. 'Someone has reported me to the General Medical Council.'

'Why?' asked Patsy, concerned. 'Has a patient complained about you?'

I shook my head. 'Not a patient. I've been reported for advertising and bringing the medical profession into disrepute.'

'Advertising?' Patsy looked puzzled. 'What on earth does that mean? What have you done that's disreputable?'

'The complaint has come from another doctor,' I told her. I didn't really understand what it was all about either.

Patsy reached out and held my hand. For a few moments neither of us spoke. Eventually I handed Patsy the letter to read. I just couldn't believe it. I'd only been qualified for a few weeks and already my whole career was threatened. My mind was a maelstrom of confused and confusing emotions. All my life I'd wanted to be a doctor. And now there was a very real chance that it was all going to be taken away from me. I wanted to know who had complained about me to the General Medical Council. I felt angry with myself for being so stupid as to speak at the animal rights meeting. I felt angry with myself for agreeing to write a column for the local paper. I felt myself drowning in anger and bitterness.

'It doesn't say who has complained about you,' said Patsy, frowning. She was still reading the letter.

'They don't have to tell me who has complained,' I explained.

'So how do you know that the complaint came from a doctor?'

Because only a doctor would complain that I've brought the profession into disrepute or that I've been "advertising".'

'But you haven't been advertising!' said Patsy.

'Someone thinks I'm writing the newspaper column to try and attract new patients.'

'But that's daft!'

'And someone – probably the same person – thinks that I gave that speech about animal experiments to try to attract patients too.'

Patsy shook her head. 'It's not fair!' She looked at the letter again. 'What do they mean about bringing the profession into disrepute?'

I shrugged. 'That just refers to the speech about animal experiments.'

'But how did that bring the profession into disrepute?'

I shrugged. I didn't know whether to scream or to cry. I felt desolate, angry and violent all at once. I felt pleased that the letter had arrived on a Saturday morning and that I didn't have to do a morning surgery and grateful too that Dr Brownlow was on duty for the weekend.

'I'm going to organise a petition,' said Patsy. A tear was running down her right cheek.

'No!' I said sharply. 'I'm in enough trouble already.'

Patsy reached out to me. 'But I want to help you. It isn't right. None of this is right.'

I stood up. 'I know it's not right!' I said. 'It's bloody unfair. But organising a petition isn't going to help.' I could feel tears filling my eyes and suddenly I had a desperate desire to be alone. Like an animal who has been wounded I wanted to run away and hide. As I half turned to leave the table I remembered the second letter. I picked that up and tore it open. It was a letter from Lionel Francis's solicitor informing me that his client was taking legal action against me and demanding £500,000 in damages. I threw the letter down onto the table and walked out of the bar with tears of frustration, sadness, anger and bitterness filling my eyes. Behind me I could hear Patsy crying. I wanted to go back to her; to hold her and comfort her; to share my sadness with her.

But I didn't.

*　　*　　*

Outside the Duck and Puddle Ben and I got into the car. I felt as though I couldn't breathe. Everything had happened so quickly that I couldn't keep up. I felt as though I was running down an icy ski slope, totally out of control, with no idea how I'd got there and with no idea what was going to happen next. I felt lost, frightened and threatened. I felt as though my chest was in a vice.

For forty minutes I drove on automatic pilot. I drove without being conscious of anything else on the road. I drove without seeing any road signs and without knowing where I was or where I was heading.

I was awakened from this trance like state when I turned a corner, drove up onto a hump backed bridge and found myself bonnet to bonnet with a large Rover motor car that was towing a caravan. There was no room for our two cars to pass and the driver of the Rover, a blustery, red faced man who was surrounded by a car full of wife and daughters, waved imperiously and angrily at me, indicating that I should go back and get out of the way.

I had my hand on the gear lever ready to put the car into reverse when I stopped. I'd had enough of people pushing me about. I just sat there and did nothing and stared out, unseeing, into the distance.

Slowly, I became aware that there was someone knocking on the side window of the car. I turned my head and saw the red faced man from the Rover. The man's face was redder than ever and the veins on his forehead were pumped full of blood. The man's eyes were filled with frustration and rage and through the glass I could hear him shouting and swearing. I looked to the front. The Rover was still parked directly in front of me. In the front passenger seat I could see the man's wife. Her face was contorted with fury. She too was shouting but I couldn't hear what she was saying. Behind her I could see the faces of her two teenager daughters. Their faces, too, were full of anger.

If any of this had happened a day earlier I would have wound down my window, apologised profusely and backed my car up to a point where the Rover and its caravan could squeeze past. But I didn't. I switched off the ignition and took out the key. I then got out of the car. The red faced man was still shouting but, strangely, I couldn't hear what he was saying.

Ignoring him I then locked the car door and put the key in my pocket. I left the car where it was, walked down the road a few yards, climbed over a stile and walked into a field that stretched so far into the distance that it seemed to meet the horizon. Suddenly I became aware of Ben. She was bounding along beside me, never straying more than a yard or two from my side though there were exciting looking rabbit holes all over the place. I bent down, stopped and hugged her, and then walked on.

A few moments later I reached the cliff edge. Several hundred feet below me the sea was crashing on the rocks and I could feel sharp, salty spray being blown against my face by the wind. I turned and looked behind me. The Morris was still parked where I'd left it. The red faced man and his wife were standing on the road arguing. The man was pointing in my direction. I watched the scene dispassionately for a few moments. It didn't seem to have anything to do with me. Then I sat down on a rock and stared out at the sea.

Halfway across the Bristol Channel, maybe ten miles away, a tanker steamed slowly past. It moved with the grace that distance gives and I wondered what was happening on board. I wondered where the tanker was going. And I suddenly felt very small, very insignificant and very unimportant. Strangely, my problems felt small too and I realised just how little they mattered.

I closed my eyes and turned my head to face into the full force of the wind. The problems I had left behind seemed so insignificant that I couldn't understand why I had allowed myself to get so upset. I knew that I could live with whatever the lawyers and the General Medical Council did to me. I had done nothing to be ashamed of. I would not back down. I would not apologise. I would carry on doing what I felt was right. Ben, who was sitting by my side, rested her head on my thigh and I stroked her tenderly.

The wind got stronger and it started to rain. I shivered. I had no coat or jacket and I realised that I was cold. I stood and turned and looked back towards the road. It had taken them a long time but the bad tempered family had managed to push their caravan out of the way and someone, presumably the red faced man, had reversed and turned the Rover in a gateway.

Stuffing my hands into my pockets I strode back across the field to where my car was still parked on one side of the tiny bridge. By the time I got to it the red faced man and his family had hitched their caravan up to their car and were about to start retracing their steps. I waved to them as they disappeared. Then Ben and I got into the car. I reversed quickly and easily, turned in a gateway and started the drive back to Bilbury.

Above all else I wanted desperately to get back to see Patsy. I felt bad because I knew that I had taken out my anger and frustration on her; I wanted to see her to tell her how much it helped to have her around. I wanted to tell her how much it helped to be able to talk to her and share things with her. I wanted to tell her that I cared for her and that she was more important to me than the lawyers or the medical profession. And most important of all I wanted to tell her that I loved her. This final realisation surprised me somewhat but I knew without a doubt that it was true.

The only thing that frightened me now was that Patsy might no longer want to have anything to do with me.

I need not have worried.

*　　*　　*

Like all doctors I had joined an insurance society the moment I'd qualified. The payment of regular premiums entitled me to legal advice and protection if ever I got into trouble as a result of practising my profession – in exactly the same way that motor car insurance protects a driver from financial ruin in the event of an accident. The next Monday morning I telephoned the Doctors' Defence Association in London and told them what had happened.

'Let me get this straight,' said the plum voiced stranger on the other end of the line. 'You have received a formal notice of complaint from the General Medical Council and a formal notification of impending legal proceedings from a solicitor?' He said all this as though anxious to make it clear that he regarded any doctor who required so much help as deserving everything that the might of the law could throw at him.

'That's right,' I admitted.

'You'd better see one of our solicitors,' sighed the man with the plum stuck in his mouth. 'I'll ring you back with a name and an appointment.' With that the phone went dead. It wasn't quite the support I would have liked but somehow that didn't matter. I had Patsy and Ben for love and support and needed only legal advice from the Doctors' Defence Association.

*   *   *

After the Monday morning surgery had finished I set off in search of Dr Brownlow. I found him in the walled vegetable garden examining some cuttings that he had taken a couple of months earlier. I showed him the two letters I'd received on Saturday.

'What rubbish,' he said when he'd read them. He handed the letters back to me with earthy finger prints down both sides. 'You'll need the day off to see a solicitor in London.'

'I'm afraid so.'

'No problem,' said Dr Brownlow. He wiped his hands down the side of his trousers, put an arm around my shoulder and started walking towards the greenhouse. Once inside he sat down on the brick edge of one of the cutting beds. I sat down opposite him.

'The lawsuit is baloney,' he said. 'You can forget about that. Apart from anything else how can someone who's dead sue you? My guess is that the solicitor in Exeter is behind with his threatening letters. But the General Medical Council thing is a bit more serious. I suppose we'd better take that more seriously.'

I liked the way he said 'we'.

'Do you know who made the complaint?'

I shook my head.

'No idea?'

'None whatsoever.'

'Do you know if there are two separate complaints or if the same person has complained about the newspaper column and your speech?'

I shook my head again.

'My guess is that the two complaints came from the same person,' said Dr Brownlow quietly. 'And I think I know who it was.'

I was startled. 'Who?'

Dr Brownlow shook his head. 'I don't want to say anything yet. But I know who's likely to get up to tricks like this round

193

here.' Suddenly he stood up and looked down at me. 'Remember this,' he said very seriously. 'Whatever happens I'm with you.' He held out his right hand for me to shake. I stood up and took it. 'Everything will be OK,' he said confidently.

I found his support and comfort very touching but 'thank you' was all I could think of to say.

*   *   *

Ben still missed Hubert, I knew that, but we were close friends. She came with me everywhere; sitting underneath my desk in the surgery, travelling in the car with me and sleeping on the bottom of my bed. I never used a lead. She always stayed with me and I couldn't imagine what life had been like without her.

*   *   *

I had a telephone call from the hospital to tell me that they had tested over a dozen pairs of jeans from the market stallholder who'd supplied Mrs Harper. In addition to the two brand new pairs that Keith had never worn they'd traced several other customers and tested their jeans too. None of them were contaminated with phosphorous. 'The only explanation we can think of is that someone walked past the jeans stall carrying a leaky insecticide container,' said the doctor from the hospital.

'And spilt some of the solution on one of the pairs of jeans that Mrs Harper bought?'

'Exactly. Once the spillage had dried out there wouldn't be anything to see,' the doctor went on. 'But the jeans would be soaked with phosphorous.'

I telephoned Mrs Harper right away and told her that the hospital would be posting the two new pairs of jeans back to her. 'How is Keith?' I asked her.

'He's fine!' said Mrs Harper. There was a long silence. 'I really can't thank you enough, doctor,' she said. 'You were marvellous.'

'I'm just glad that Keith is OK,' I said, self-consciously.

*   *   *

The receptionist was busy with her nails and her tongue peeped out between her lips as she concentrated on what she was doing. She finished painting the nail on the little finger of her left hand, held her hand at arm's length to examine her work and then blew gently on the nails a couple of times. Then she shook her fingers gently. Satisfied, she carefully transferred the brush with which she was painting her nails from her right hand to her left hand. She gripped it tightly but carefully between her thumb and forefinger so as not to smudge the polish that she had already applied. Then she started on the nails of her right hand.

I stood and watched her. I had been standing in front of her desk for what seemed like hours. It seemed to take her another hour to paint the nails on her right hand. Then she carefully screwed the cap back on the bottle of bright red nail varnish that she'd been using, waved both hands in the air a few times and looked up. She seemed genuinely surprised to see me standing there and raised a neatly manicured eyebrow.

I told her my name. 'I've got an appointment to see Mr Wellings.'

The receptionist carefully picked up the grey telephone on the desk in front of her and used a pencil to dial a three figure number. She held the telephone cautiously, taking care not to smudge her nails. It made her look as though she found the telephone offensive or distasteful in some way. She listened for a moment and then dropped the telephone back down onto its rest. 'He's got someone with him,' she said. 'You'll have to wait.' She nodded towards a pair of low black, imitation leather chairs on the other side of the narrow reception area. A low, glass topped coffee table stood in front of the two chairs. Upon it lay a pile of magazines and a single, slightly untidy copy of the Financial Times.

I wandered across and sat down. The building looked as if it had been converted from something much larger. The ceiling was high and vaulted and numerous tall partitions divided up the room into a number of small units. Whoever had organised the conversion had clearly had a limited budget. The partition walls were poorly made and all the furniture that I could see was cheap and slightly battered. I moved the Financial Times and flicked through the magazines. They were all, with a single exception, ancient copies of a legal journal. The exception was a copy of a giveaway magazine telling young couples how to get a mortgage for their first home. I flicked through it. It was full of photographs of luxury flats in central London and spacious country mansions with huge, colourful gardens. Real life.

Suddenly, I heard someone shouting my name. I looked across at the receptionist who was sitting staring at me. She had her arms folded in front of her. 'I've had to call you three times,' she complained. 'Mr Wellings is waiting for you.'

I stood up. 'Where is his office?'

'Through that door over there,' said the girl, pointing to a door at the far end of the reception area. 'Turn right and it's the second door on your left.' She sounded as tired and as bored as she looked.

The office was nine, maybe ten, feet square. It had no window and contained one filing cabinet, one artificial teak desk and three tubular metal chairs. That made it crowded. One of the chairs was behind the desk and sitting on it was a small bespectacled man in his late sixties. He wore a shabby, plain, grey suit, a faintly striped white shirt and a badly knotted brown tie with a swirling pattern in the material. This was Mr Wellings. The solicitor whom the Doctors' Defence Association had retained on my behalf.

'Sit down, sit down!' said Mr Wellings, lifting himself up a couple of inches from his own chair and waving a hand at the two chairs in front of his desk. An unpleasant cloud of after shave almost suffocated me. I though he looked very frail.

I pulled one of the chairs back and sat down. The office was bleak. On top of the filing cabinet there was a pile of papers and a dying cactus in a brown flower pot. The flower pot stood on a patterned saucer. There were more papers stacked up on the floor by the side of the cabinet. The floor was covered in dark green carpet tiles. There was no radiator but a small electric fire stood in one corner of the room. The room was lit by a fluorescent tube attached to the ceiling. The walls were painted white and the only relief came from a diploma in a black bordered frame that was hung on one wall. On top of Mr Wellings' desk there was a telephone, a blotter, a chipped mug used to store pens and pencils, a dirty mug that had had tea or coffee in it and now had a dark stain around the inside, a tray marked 'in', a tray marked 'out' and a small dictating machine. In front of him Mr Wellings had a foolscap pad of lined notepaper and a cheap ball point pen that advertised a firm of legal stationers. The 'in' tray was empty. The 'out' tray was full – though it contained but a single, thick, blue cardboard file. It looked a miserable place in which to work.

I introduced myself.

Mr Wellings looked up. 'You're a little late, aren't you?'

I started to protest then decided that there wasn't any point and stopped. Mr Wellings had looked down again and was now studying a letter from the Doctors' Defence Association. 'How long have you been in practice in Devon?' he asked me without lifting his head.

'Four months.'

There was a long silence during which Mr Wellings incessantly clicked the retractor button on his ball point pen. 'And now you've received a complaint from the General Medical Council and a writ from a firm of solicitors acting on behalf of one of your patients?'

'Mr Francis wasn't actually my patient,' I corrected him. 'Dr Brownlow is the principal. I'm employed as his assistant.' I said this not in an attempt to evade responsibility but merely because I felt I ought to put the record straight.

'And what does Dr Browning think of all this?' asked Mr Wellings. He put down his pen and started cracking his knuckles.

'Dr Brownlow has been very supportive.'

Mr Wellings snorted and picked up his pen again.

'Dr Brownlow doesn't think that I need worry too much about the letter from Mr Francis's solicitors,' I said, rather hesitantly.

'I see,' said Mr Wellings. 'Dr Browning is a qualified solicitor, is he?'

It's Brownlow,' I corrected him. 'No. He isn't a solicitor. But sadly Mr Francis is dead.'

Mr Wellings sat up sharply at this piece of news. 'Dead?

197

When did he die?'

I told him.

Mr Wellings sniffed at this, pulled his legal pad towards him, picked up his pen and wrote something down. While he wrote I looked around. The room was small without being cosy, scruffy without being friendly and untidy without being relaxed. It looked as though it was a temporary office, borrowed for the day, though the nameplate on the door assured me that it wasn't. There were no signs of personal occupancy; no photographs; no knick-knacks; no souvenirs; no evidence of humanity. 'Is there any chance that the survivors may hold you responsible for the death?' asked the solicitor.

'I don't think so.'

'This other charge,' said Mr Wellings, 'the one from the General Medical Council. Do you have any idea where the complaint may have originated from?'

I shook my head.

'None whatsoever?'

'No.'

'It's a very serious charge,' said Mr Wellings sternly. He looked at me. 'You do realise that, don't you?'

My mouth felt dry. I tried to speak but my voice seemed to have disappeared. I nodded.

'If you are found guilty your name can be removed from the medical register.'

'Yes,' I managed to say. 'I realise that.'

'To all extents and purposes your career, your professional life, would be over.'

I swallowed hard. The solicitor seemed to be trying to frighten me but he was having the opposite effect. 'It all seems a bit daft,' I said. 'I had no intention of trying to attract patients. As I've already explained the practice isn't mine. It belongs to Dr Brownlow. I had no intention of advertising and I had nothing to gain by it.'

Mr Wellings sniffed. 'Are you still writing the newspaper column which features in the complaint?'

I nodded. I was getting slightly better at it too. I'd talked it over with Patsy and with Dr Brownlow. They'd both agreed with me that I shouldn't let myself be bullied. I wasn't doing anything wrong. 'There's no way that I could gain professionally by writing the column,' I insisted. 'It's a good way to help people with information. I've had a lot of nice letters from readers thanking me for the advice I've given.'

Mr Wellings frowned. 'That's not how the General Medical Council will see it,' he said. 'In their view you are enhancing your reputation among members of the public. You would, I think, be well advised to stop writing the newspaper column if you wish to remain on the medical register.' He glowered at me. 'And I certainly wouldn't advise you to tell anyone that you've received grateful letters from readers.'

I was beginning to wonder whether Mr Wellings was really on my side.

'Have I made myself clear?'

'Yes. Perfectly.'

'May I then write to the General Medical Council on your behalf to tell them that you apologise for your actions, you withdraw your allegations about animal experimentation and that you will cease to write your newspaper column?'

'Why do I have to apologise for my comments about animal experiments?'

Mr Wellings sighed. 'I understand that the official, establishment viewpoint is that animal experiments are worthwhile and important. Your views are likely to annoy and embarrass the establishment.'

'What are my chances if I fight?' I asked him. 'If I don't apologise or withdraw the comments I've made?'

'Very slim, doctor,' said Mr Wellings. 'Very slim indeed.' He stood up. 'I suggest that you go back to Devon and that you think very carefully about what you're going to do. When you've made up your mind perhaps you'd be kind enough to give me a ring and let me know?'

He didn't shake hands but made it pretty clear that the interview was over so I stood up and left.

*　　*　　*

One thing I did learn from my visit to the solicitor's office was that I never wanted to work in London.

Living in the country for a few months I had forgotten just how noisy, dirty and inhospitable cities are. Everything seemed so grey, so dreary and so unreal. I had arrived at

Paddington station and found it a deeply depressing experience. I had travelled from Paddington to the part of London where Mr Wellings had his cramped office by underground train and had found the journey had enhanced my sense of depression.

In Devon the air was clean and the pace of life was slow. In London the air was foul and everyone seemed to be rushing. Thousands spent much of their lives underground or in offices shut away from the fresh air. In Devon I could dawdle in the lanes and watch buzzards, swallows, badgers, foxes and rabbits. In London I had to keep my wits about me to avoid being crushed by the traffic.

In Devon there was time to think and to enjoy life. In London there was no time for thinking and no time for enjoying life. In Devon I felt alive and close to nature. In London I felt suffocated and too far from the things I had learned to value most. In Devon people smiled at one another and wanted to share their thoughts and experiences. In London people only seemed to scowl at one another and to covet one another's belongings.

*　　*　　*

When I got back to Bilbury Dr Brownlow had had his well filled with a tanker full of water that he had bought from the water board. 'It's disgusting stuff,' he complained. 'It stinks of chlorine.'

In the surgery water was strictly rationed and two house bricks had been put into all the lavatory cisterns together with notices requesting everyone to flush only when absolutely necessary. 'The water is cheap enough,' explained Dr Brownlow. 'But getting it here costs an absolute fortune. I had to get one of the local milk lorries to bring it in.'

'Did you find out why Mr Trickle had built a dam?'

It wasn't the wisest of questions for it turned Dr Brownlow bright scarlet and his face became unpleasantly contorted. 'Damn that Trickle!' he said angrily, banging his fist down on the nearest available surface which happened to be the desk. A half empty mug of coffee jumped two inches into the air and spilt most of its residue.

'He's building a trout pond in his garden,' complained Dr Brownlow. 'So he's diverted the stream.'

'Can't you stop him?'

'I might be able to if I could find him,' complained Dr Brownlow. 'No one ever sees him. And the workmen he's hired have come from London. They all seem to be staying in caravans.'

'But you must have some sort of legal rights! He can't just stop you using a stream that you've been using for years.'

'He can until I serve him with a writ,' growled Dr Brownlow. 'And I hate solicitors.'

'I'm sure Thumper would go in there one night and take the dam down,' I suggested.

Dr Brownlow looked truly horrified. 'That would be illegal. I couldn't countenance that.'

'So what alternative do you have? You can't keep hiring milk lorries to bring you tankers full of water.'

'I've got a dowser coming tomorrow,' said Dr Brownlow.

My sense of puzzlement clearly showed.

'A dowser,' repeated Dr Brownlow. 'A water diviner.'

I nearly laughed but stopped myself just in time. 'Do you really believe in all that? Hazel twigs and unseen forces?'

'That was my first reaction,' sighed Dr Brownlow. 'But everyone I've spoken to says that the only way to find water is to use a diviner.'

'But how on earth can it possibly work?'

Dr Brownlow shrugged.

'Do you mean they haven't yet got machines that can find water underground?'

Dr Brownlow shook his head. 'They all say that the most effective way to find water is to use a good dowser.'

'What time is he coming?'

'It's a she and she's coming in two days.'

'Do you mind if I come and watch?'

'As long as there's no sniggering,' said Dr Brownlow firmly. 'I don't want her going off in a huff without finding me some water.'

'You really do believe in it, don't you?' I was astonished that a man of science should believe such mumbo jumbo.

'I'll tell you whether I believe or not in two days,' said

201

Dr Brownlow. 'If they could find me water I'd believe in fairies.'

* * *

'There was a message for you from Mrs Francis,' said Miss Johnson. 'She asked if you'd be kind enough to give her a call.'

For a moment I hesitated. I felt sure that my lawyers would not have wanted me to telephone a woman whose late husband had started a legal action against me. That, I decided, was a good enough reason to call her.

'I'm glad you phoned,' said Mrs Francis. 'Really glad. I was afraid you might not want to speak to me. I wouldn't have blamed you.' She spoke in a rush.

'I was very sorry about your husband's death.'

'Thank you,'said Mrs Francis. There was a pause. 'I wanted to speak to you about two things,' she said. 'First I want to thank you for the tactful way you handled my husband's death.'

I started to say something then stopped.

'I knew all about his lady-friend,' said Mrs Francis. 'And I can guess how he probably died. I'm very grateful to you.'

I mumbled something.

'Second,' she went on, 'I want to let you know that I've instructed my husband's solicitors that they are to withdraw the lawsuit against you immediately and to pay any costs that you might have incurred. I didn't want him to bring the case in the first place and I'm certainly not going to consider letting them carry on with any legal action now.'

'Thank you,' I said.

'You don't need to thank me,' said Mrs Francis. 'The case should never have been brought. You never did anything wrong and even if someone at the hospital was at fault it was never fair to drag you into it.' She paused. 'I'm instructing the solicitors to drop the lawsuit against the hospital too. I don't care whether or not I could have sued them.'

As soon as she'd put the phone down I rang Patsy to tell her the good news. Then I rang Dr Brownlow to tell him the good news too.

They were both delighted.

Even Ben seemed to suspect that something good had happened.

*   *   *

CHAPTER THIRTEEN

'I'm sorry to interrupt,' said Miss Johnson, poking her head
round the surgery door, 'But there's been an accident on the
Barnstaple road.'

I stood up. 'I'm sorry,' I said to Mrs Jones, the vicar's
wife. 'But I'll have to go. If you'd like to wait?'

'Don't you worry, doctor,' said Mrs Jones. 'You go and
see to the accident. I'll wait here.'

I turned to Miss Johnson. 'Where exactly is it?'

'Near the junction with the road into the village.'

'Do you know who's involved?'

'The caller just said that someone had been knocked off
a bicycle.'

'Have they called an ambulance?'

'They said they had but I'll ring and check when you're
on your way,' said Miss Johnson. Her efficiency never failed
to amaze me. Somehow she seemed to get calmer and more
authoritative the more threatening the emergency.

The junction between the Bilbury road and the main Barnstaple to Lynton road was no more than three quarters of
a mile from the surgery and I was there less than five minutes
after Miss Johnson had interrupted the surgery.

I knew the moment I arrived that there was no hope. Young
Keith Harper must have been killed instantly. Judging by the
tyre marks on the road the car that had killed him had been
travelling far too fast for the fairly narrow road. Keith was
lying in the middle of the road: his chest was crushed and
both his arms were clearly broken. His neck was broken too.
Strangely, apart from a trickle of blood at the corner of his
mouth and another trickle coming out of his nose his face

was unmarked. His bright red bicycle, buckled into waste metal, was lying at the side of the road twenty yards away. I felt for a pulse but could feel none. Gently, I pulled up his jumper and then unfastened his shirt and tried to listen to his heart. But it was no longer beating. With tears in my eyes I knelt beside him and took hold of one of his hands. It seemed such a cruel, cruel waste.

Someone spoke behind me. 'Is he dead?'

I turned round. It was Thumper. His truck was parked a few yards down the road.

I nodded.

'Poor little beggar.' Thumper had tears in his eyes too. 'I wish I could get hold of the bastard who killed him.'

I nodded towards Keith's body. 'Did you find him?'

Thumper nodded and wiped his nose with the back of his hand. 'I just came round the corner and there he was – lying in the middle of the road. There was no sign of any car.'

I looked past him. A small queue of vehicles had built up on the road out of Barnstaple. I turned round and looked the other way. Another small queue of vehicles coming from the Lynton direction had also built up. 'Let's move him to the side of the road.'

Thumper and I picked up Keith's body and carefully lifted him over to the side of the road. We were about to lie him down on the grass when I heard a voice shouting. 'Don't you know you're not supposed to move accident victims?' The owner of the voice was a small, squat man in a three piece grey suit. 'I trained in first aid!' he announced firmly.

'I'm afraid he's dead.'

'This is the doctor,' said Thumper.

The stranger stared at me and then at Keith's body. He paled. 'Are you sure?'

I nodded. 'I'm afraid so.'

The small man turned away and a few seconds later I heard him retching in the hedge.

'Someone's got to tell his mother,' said Thumper. 'I don't envy anyone that job.'

I knew the moment he said it that I had to do it.

I waited until the ambulance came and I stood there while they loaded Keith's body into the back. A police car and two officers from Barnstaple came with the ambulance. They took charge of everything with quiet efficiency; measuring tyre marks and taking a statement from Thumper. 'Do you mind if I go?' I said to one of them.

He looked at me.

'I've got to go and tell the boy's mother.'

Thumper looked at me but didn't say anything.

'Thank you, doctor,' said the policeman, undoubtedly relieved that someone else was doing the job.

'I want to go before she hears it from anyone else,' I said quietly but I walked to my car with leaden legs. I didn't want to go. I would have given anything in the world to have been somewhere else. I had told relatives in hospital that patients had died but I'd never done anything like this before and I knew it was probably going to be the most difficult thing I'd ever done.

Those next few minutes scar my memory. I can remember every instant, every feeling and every tear we shed together. I sat in my car for nearly five minutes outside Mrs Harper's cottage trying to pluck up courage to ring her doorbell and tell her that her son, the one person who meant anything in her life, was dead.

I can still remember the smell of the nearby fields where a farmer had been spraying fertiliser on his pastureland. I can remember the sound of seagulls perched on the roof of the house; seagulls which flew away when I shut my car door and walked across to the front door. I can remember Mrs Harper opening the door and smiling at me, unaware that I had called to draw the curtains on her life and cast her into a gloom and deep despair that might lighten but that would endure and to some degree be with her always.

I can remember making her sit down before I told her. I can remember the look on her face when she knew that I had called with bad news and I can remember the instant of realisation when she knew, even before I had told her, that Keith was dead. I can remember the primeval scream of anguish which leapt from her body when she understood what had happened. I can remember the tears and the sobbing and the time when there were no more tears left and she was crying silently and tearlessly.

I don't remember how long I was there with her but after a while there was a quiet knock on the door and I took my arm away from around her and went and answered the door. It was Thumper.

'I've been waiting across the road,' he said. I had never heard him speak with such gentleness before. 'You have to look after other patients but she can't be left alone.'

'No.' I said. 'She can't.'

'I'll take her home with me,' said Thumper. 'Anne and I will look after her.' It was an act of simple, thoughtful generosity which sealed for ever my love for Bilbury and its villagers; people who would always look after one another, like members of some large, extended family.

I drove back to the Duck and Puddle, checked that there were no calls for me and then went around to the back of the pub where I could hear Frank chopping wood. He knew about Keith Harper and he knew where I'd been.

'Can I do that for a while?' I asked him.

He handed me the axe without question and for twenty minutes my unaccustomed muscles swung the heavy axe without skill but with a violence that would have frightened me if it had been expressed in any other way.

Only then did I remember that I still hadn't finished the surgery I'd been doing when Keith Harper had been killed. I hurried back and found Mrs Jones still sitting waiting patiently for me.

*　　*　　*

The death of Keith Harper cast a cloud of depression over the village. I had never lived in a small community before and had never before experienced this type of shared loss. It is one of the paradoxes of modern living that the larger a community is the fewer friends and acquaintances each individual will have. In the town where I'd been brought up there was no community spirit. There were people living less than a hundred yards away from us whose names we did not even know; there were people whom we saw every morning about whom we knew nothing. But in Bilbury everyone knew everyone else's name. The easiest place in the world to hide is the busiest apartment block. In a village nothing is secret.

Everyone shared Mrs Harper's loss. Each man, woman and child suffered with her. In the Duck and Puddle that evening there was no laughter, no jolly banter and no cheerful exchange of gentle insults. A visitor from South Molton called in on the way back from delivering some sheep to a farm near Croyde and was insensitive enough to atmosphere to tell a joke he'd heard. The silence embarrassed him so much that he left with his pint virtually untouched.

The whole incident was made worse by the fact that the police had no idea of the identity of the hit and run killer. There was, therefore, a communal sense of frustration. There was no outlet for our anger. And without any outlet anger built up and festered inside each one of us.

*　　*　　*

The dowser had arrived and was already at work when I found her, the mining engineer who had come with her and Dr Brownlow prowling around in a paddock near to the house. The mining engineer and Dr Brownlow were walking together, watching carefully, as the dowser, a rather good looking middle aged woman in a tweed skirt and a hand knitted jumper, walked slowly but steadily from one side of the field to the other. She carried a forked hazel twig in her two hands, was clearly concentrating hard and every few steps she would stop, hold her head to one side like a bird who thinks he may have heard something, and then carry on again.

'Any luck yet?' I asked Dr Brownlow in a whisper.

'No. Not yet!' muttered Dr Brownlow, who looked rather unhappy and embarrassed at the whole thing, as though he'd been caught at a black magic ceremony.

'Had a couple of false alarms,' said the mining engineer.

'Do you always use dowsers to find water?'

'Always use the same one,' said the engineer, nodding towards the woman with the forked hazel twig. 'She's marvellous.'

'How often does she succeed in finding water?'

The engineer looked at me as though surprised. 'She's never missed yet.'

'Never?' I said, emphasising the word. I assumed that he had been exaggerating in the way that people often do.

'Never!' said the engineer firmly. 'You wait and see.' Then he fell silent again. Dr Brownlow looked at me and frowned as though telling me to shut up so I said no more but I was still unconvinced.

It was another fifteen or twenty minutes before anything happened. And then quite suddenly we all heard the dowser cry out. It was as much a cry of pain as a cry of success. The mining engineer rushed over to where the dowser was standing, more or less in the centre of the field.

'It's a strong one,' she said confidently. Her face was contorted and she seemed to be struggling to hold the hazel twig horizontal. Her fingers were white with the effort.

'What do you reckon?'

'It's a gusher!' the dowser told him. 'Running at about 120 feet.'

The engineer turned to Dr Brownlow. 'You're in luck,' he said. 'You've got a good supply here.'

'What's a gusher?' asked Dr Brownlow.

'You won't need a pump to get the stuff up,' explained the engineer. 'When we drill into the supply the water will come shooting out of the ground.'

'Like an oil well?' Despite my doubts I was beginning to get excited.

'Like an oil well only it'll be water,' agreed the engineer patiently.

I turned to the dowser, who was still struggling to hold her hazel twig under control. She had dropped her scarf on the grass and was now walking across the spot in every possible direction.

'What are you doing now?' I asked her.

The mining engineer took me by the arm and pulled me away from her. 'In a minute,' he whispered. 'You can ask her questions in a minute.' I moved away with him. 'She's marking the exact spot for me to drill,' explained the engineer quietly. 'She needs to find the strongest force so that we can decide where to sink the shaft. If we get it six inches out we might miss the supply completely.'

This sounded to me like an excuse in the making and my cynicism flooded back. The engineer must have sensed this and he moved away from me. Dr Brownlow had said nothing but had been watching the dowser's activities with great interest. Suddenly, the dowser stopped moving and released her grip on her twig. It immediately bounced so that it was pointing straight at the sky and she dropped it onto the grass. She then massaged each of her wrists and fingers in turn. I noticed that most of her fingers were covered in bits of sticking plaster and that several of the plasters were blood stained. 'That's the spot!' she announced, pointing to a place on the grass with the toe of her shoe.

The mining engineer moved forward, took a small wooden stake out of his pocket and stuck it into the ground and then picked up her scarf and handed it back to her. 'Don't touch that whatever you do,' he said to Dr Brownlow and myself. Then he scurried off towards a Land Rover that was parked at the entrance to the field.

'It's all very impressive,' I said to the dowser. 'Do you mind if I try?'

'Impressive but you don't believe in it at all,' said the dowser, looking straight at me and smiling.

'I didn't say that!' I protested.

'I know you didn't,' said the dowser. She held her hand out to me. 'Come here,' she said. As I walked over to her she bent down and picked up her hazel twig with one hand. She then walked away from the spot she'd marked and beckoned to me to follow her. 'Hold this,' she said, giving me one of the forks of the hazel twig to hold in my right hand. 'Are you right handed?'

I confirmed that I was.

'Good,' she said. She took the other length of twig in her left hand. 'Now, walk with me!'

We walked together towards the site of Dr Brownlow's underground river and I must say I felt extremely foolish for about twelve paces.

Then, in an instant, I stopped feeling foolish and started to feel ashamed of my lack of faith. I couldn't believe what was happening. The twig I was holding had suddenly started to bend upwards so violently that I couldn't hold it down.

'Keep hold of it!' said the dowser firmly. I tried and looked across. Her hand, much smaller than mine, was white as she struggled to hold the twig horizontal. I was quite unable to stop my part of the twig from bending upwards.

'What on earth . . . ?' I began.

'It's the force of the water,' explained the dowser. 'Let me take the stick from you.' As she spoke she reached out and took hold of the stick. Then when she had it firmly in both hands she walked briskly away from the spot she'd already marked. She dropped the hazel stick onto the grass and massaged her wrists and fingers again. 'I'm sorry,' she apologised. 'But the stick was going to break.'

'Can I try it on my own?' I asked her.

'You can if you like,' she said. 'But it may not work for you.'

I tried and was very disappointed. However much I tried and however often I walked across the spot she'd marked I could get no response at all from the hazel twig. By this time the engineer had returned with a massive iron rod and a large sledgehammer. He hammered the iron bar into the ground at the exact spot that the dowser had marked.

'We'll be back to start drilling tomorrow,' said the engineer to Dr Brownlow.

I had never seen Dr Brownlow look so excited. He looked like a child who'd been told that he's going to have an unexpected birthday party.

'Well?' he said, as we walked back towards the house. The dowser and the engineer had left in the Land Rover.

'I don't know,' I said honestly.

'But you felt the force of the stick!'

'I know,' I admitted.

'Were you holding the stick firmly?'

'Yes.'

'She couldn't possibly be strong enough to make the stick move against your will simply by using her own strength.'

'I know. But I still can't believe that they're going to find water there when they drill tomorrow.'

'I do,' said Dr Brownlow. 'I believe they're going to find water at 120 feet and I'm quite certain that it's going to be a gusher.' And he beamed at me with delight.

* * *

The next day Dr Brownlow's confidence in the dowser was

211

entirely justified. The engineer and his drilling team hit water at 115 feet and when the drill broke through the rock into the underground river that flowed beneath Dr Brownlow's field water shot into the air like a fountain.

*　　*　　*

P.C. Wilson took off his helmet and put it down carefully on my desk. Then he stared at it as though he had never seen it before. His face was drawn and lined and there were large dark patches under both his eyes.

'What can I do for you?' I asked him, following the trite but necessary ritual designed to bring each consultation to life.

P.C. Wilson didn't seem to hear me. Instead of answering he reached out and picked up his helmet and held it in his lap, nursing it as a mother might hold her baby.

'You look depressed,' I said quietly. 'Do you want to talk to me about it?'

'I had a car crash,' said P.C. Wilson. He didn't look at me but kept his eyes fixed firmly on his helmet. 'It shook me about a bit.'

'What happened?'

'I lost control and crashed,' answered the policeman.

'Did you injure yourself?'

'No.'

'Have you been to hospital?'

'No. There's no need.'

'What happened to the car?'

'There's a big dent in the front?'

'Was this your car or a police car?'

'Mine.'

'The Ford?'

He nodded. He had a maroon Ford Zephyr.

'Was anyone else involved?'

A shake of the head. This time slightly more emphatic.

'What did you hit?'

'Just a grassy bank,' said P.C. Wilson. 'There was no damage to the bank. There's nothing to see.'

'When did it happen?'

'A day or two ago.'

212

'Are you insured?'

There was a pause. 'Yes. I suppose so.'

'Haven't you made a claim?'

P.C. Wilson seemed surprised at the question. He thought for a moment and then shook his head.

'It's not unusual to feel some shock after an accident,' I told him. 'It can come on several days afterwards and last for a week or so.'

Instead of answering P.C. Wilson picked up his helmet and turned it round, slowly and carefully examining it from all angles as he did so. Suddenly he asked me a question I wasn't expecting. 'Do doctors still have a rule of confidentiality?'

'Yes. Nothing you tell me here will go any further.' I wondered what new peccadillo he wanted to confess. I thought I knew all his secrets.

'Like a priest?'

'Exactly like a priest.'

There was a long, long pause. Suddenly, to my horror I knew what was coming next.

'I've got to tell someone,' he said. His face was etched with pain.

I didn't want him to tell me. I didn't want to know. I didn't want to be drawn into his dark secret. I didn't want to know what he wanted to tell me.

'I killed Keith Harper,' said P.C. Wilson and then he started to cry.

I waited for a moment but his tears didn't stop. I stood up, walked round the desk, handed him a box of tissues and put my hand on his shoulder. He pulled out one of the tissues, wiped his eyes and then blew his nose. 'I didn't see him,' he said.

'But you didn't stop,' I said quietly. 'Why?'

The tears started again. His body shook with the sobbing. At last he said something that I didn't hear. I asked him to repeat it. 'I was frightened,' he whispered. 'I know it isn't enough.'

'Have you told anyone else?'

He shook his head. 'No,' he whispered.

'You must.'

'I can't.' He looked at me in sudden terror. 'You said you

wouldn't tell anyone,' he reminded me. 'You won't will you?'

I shook my head. 'Of course not.' It was not a responsibility I wanted. I knew that Mrs Harper desperately wanted to know who had killed her son. I knew that everyone in the village wanted to know. I knew that the police wanted to know. But P.C. Wilson had come to me as a patient. I owed him secrecy and I knew I had no choice in the matter.

'What am I going to do?'

'You won't go to the police?'

He put his head in his hands. 'I can't,' he whispered. 'I can't.'

'Can you live with what you have done?'

He looked up, looked me in the eye for the first time. 'No,' he said simply.

'You might feel better if you confessed,' I told him. I honestly didn't know if what I was saying was true or not. I didn't know what else to say to him.

'Maybe,' he agreed. There was a long silence. 'But perhaps my punishment is that I don't have the courage to confess. I have to try and live with my conscience.'

It seemed a wise but sad thing to say.

Slowly, I moved back behind my desk and sat down.

'Can you give me something to help me sleep?'

I nodded and wrote out a prescription for half a dozen sleeping tablets. I didn't want to give him more because I was frightened that he might take them all.

'What am I going to do?'

I hesitated before answering. 'I don't know!' I said honestly. I paused before continuing. 'You aren't going to do anything silly, are you?'

'No.' He spoke quickly and firmly, almost defiantly. He picked up the prescription and stood up. 'Can I come and see you again? You're the only person I can talk to.'

I nodded. 'Of course,' I told him. 'Of course you can.' I looked at him. 'Can't you talk to your wife?'

He shook his head. 'Did you know my wife had my cats put to sleep?'

I looked at him, horrified.

'There was nothing wrong with them. She just took them to the vet's and had them put down.' There was nothing but sadness in his eyes.

I remembered seeing Mrs Wilson and the two cats at the vets when I'd taken Ben along. 'I'm sorry . . .'

'I know it sounds silly but I loved them like children,' he said and then he left.

*   *   *

It took the engineer and his team less than a day to cap the water geyser in Dr Brownlow's field and to connect the supply to the system which supplied the house and surgery. Three days afterwards Dr Brownlow met me outside the surgery door with an enormous grin on his face. He was clutching an opened envelope and a large sheet of paper. 'I've just had the report back from the laboratory,' he said. He couldn't have looked happier if he'd just won the football pools.

I didn't know what he was talking about and I assumed that he was talking about a report concerning a patient. I asked him who he meant.

'The water,' he explained. 'I had the water tested.' He pushed the sheet of paper towards me. 'Read it!' he insisted. 'We've got the cleanest, purest, best water they've ever tested!' He was almost dancing for joy. 'It's got plenty of minerals in it but nothing to excess and no bugs at all.'

'That's good news!' I agreed. 'It's nice to know that we won't get poisoned when we drink our mid morning cup of coffee.'

'You don't understand, do you?' said Dr Brownlow, impatiently. He snatched the laboratory report back off me and read it again though I suspected that he already knew the contents off by heart.

'No,' I admitted, 'I don't understand.'

'Our geyser supplies 600 gallons a minute of pure spring water,' said Dr Brownlow. 'We need less than a hundredth of that to supply the house and garden.'

'So you've got nearly 600 gallons of spare water . . .'

'Per minute!' Dr Brownlow reminded me.

'Per minute,' I agreed.

'I'm going to bottle it and sell it,' announced Dr Brownlow.

'But who will buy bottled water?' I asked him innocently.

Dr Brownlow stared at me open mouthed. 'Haven't you heard of Perrier?'

Slowly the light began to dawn.

'And Buxton Water and Malvern Water?' Dr Brownlow went on.

'You're going to . . .'

'Bilbury Water,' said Dr Brownlow excitedly. He took a pencil out of his pocket and began to scribble feverishly on the back of the opened envelope.

'Just look!' he said, showing me the back of the envelope as he scribbled. 'The water costs us virtually nothing and I reckon we can make ten pence a bottle profit. We're producing 4800 pints a minute so that's £480 a minute profit. In an hour that's . . .' he scribbled again '. . . £28,800.'

I stared at him open mouthed. He was still scribbling. 'In a year that's *millions*!'

'But can you sell that much?'

'Probably not to start with,' admitted Dr Brownlow. 'But if we can sell just 1% of what we produce I'll be rich.'

'Won't you have to buy lots of expensive equipment?'

Dr Brownlow shook his head. 'That's the beauty of it,' he said. 'I can buy a second hand milk bottling plant for next to nothing. With a little adjustment it'll take the right sort of bottles and then all we have to do is get the labels printed and stuck on.'

I was beginning to see why Dr Brownlow was so excited.

'Doctor!' I heard someone calling. I turned. It was Miss Johnson. 'Doctor!' she said to me, 'It's a quarter past nine. You've got seven patients waiting already.'

I congratulated Dr Brownlow and started the morning surgery.

*　　*　　*

CHAPTER FOURTEEN

The human spine is a truly remarkable structure. Made up of thirty three separate bones it supports and balances the weight of the trunk, the head and the arms; it acts as a shock absorber; it provides an anchorage for many of the body's most powerful muscles and it provides the delicate spinal cord with vitally important protection. The spine is as essential to the structure and shape of the human body as a tent pole is to the structure and shape of a tent.

There are many ways in which the spine can be damaged. A sudden movement or a blow may fracture one of the vertebrae and damage the spinal cord. The higher up the spinal cord that the damage occurs the greater will be the harm done. Of course, if the damage to the spine is serious enough then the owner of the spine may die. This is particularly likely if the damage occurs right at the very top of the spine, just below the base of the skull, just where a hangman's rope would sit if tied firmly around a man's neck.

I doubt if P.C. Wilson was aware of all this. But he knew that one of the most effective ways to remove the life from a human body is to tie a rope around its neck.

A farmer found him on the cliffs above Combe Martin. Or, to be more accurate, the farmer found his head. Nearby, a noose and a long length of rope still hung from a massive oak tree. It took the police another three hours to find his body, still strapped inside what was left of his motor car, smashed into wreckage on the rocks below. And it took them several hours more to work out exactly what had happened.

Wilson had tied a rope around his neck. He had used a pale blue, nylon climbing rope with a breaking strain of 2,000 pounds. Since he had weighed well under 200 pounds he must have felt comfortable entrusting his death to the rope.

First, he had tied one end of the rope to the largest tree he could find, wrapping the rope around the trunk of the tree and tying it with a reef knot. Then he had brought the free end of the rope into the car with him and he had tied the other end around his neck. Again he had used a reef knot that wouldn't give under the strain. A long, loose length of rope had been left uncoiled in a free tangle on the grass between the car and the tree. Next the policeman had fastened his seat belt. Finally, he had started the engine. He had put his left foot on the clutch and slipped the car into first gear. His last action had been to wedge a three foot long piece of fence post onto the accelerator.

As the car accelerated towards the cliff edge so the climbing rope gradually uncoiled.

The police spent a long time trying to work out how fast the car had been going when their colleague had died. But in the end they gave up. Wilson's head had been torn clean off his body by the rope and the noose on the now loose length of rope was left lying on the grass, pointing in the direction that the car had gone; pointing like a long, accusing finger of fate.

The police had come to me afterwards.

'Do you have any idea why he might have killed himself?'

I asked them if they knew that he was a transvestite.

They said they did.

And then I told them about Keith Harper.

In a way I felt guilty about breaking the confidence. But I thought I owed it to Mrs Harper and the rest of the village to tell the truth. And, rightly or wrongly, I felt that P.C. Wilson's death had freed me from my promise not to tell. I knew there was no one else I could ask for advice but in my heart I felt that my allegiance to the living had, in this case, to outweigh my allegiance to the dead.

* * *

An old unused stone barn behind Dr Brownlow's house had been cleared out and redecorated and the bottling plant was being installed. Labels had been designed and Dr Brownlow had signed a contract with a distributor who had already arranged a deal with a chain of up market grocery shops. Bilbury Water seemed to be heading for success. The villagers were delighted. Apart from the employment prospects at the bottling plant Dr Brownlow's discovery was attracting visitors to the village. Not too many, but just enough. An article in an up market posh Sunday newspaper had described the discovery in glowing terms and the Duck and Puddle was having to turn away potential customers because of lack of room.

'I'm thinking of having an extension built,' Frank Parsons told me one evening. 'What we really need is a good wind to take some of the slates off the north side of the roof.'

I looked at him and raised an eyebrow.

'That's where the extension will have to go,' he explained. 'We might as well get the insurance company to help with the building costs.'

Every evening he settled himself down in front of the TV weather report like a man checking his football pool coupon.

Dr Brownlow himself seemed to have gained a new lease of life from the discovery. He looked younger and always seemed full of energy. Every day he could be seen bouncing around supervising the improvements in the bottling plant or showing people forecasts he had made on the basis of the latest orders his distributors had taken.

But as far as I was concerned one of the most important events occurred late one Thursday afternoon just as I'd finished the evening surgery and was about to go back to the Duck and Puddle for my dinner. 'Have you got a moment?' asked Dr Brownlow, as I said goodnight to Miss Johnson.

I said I had.

'Come and have a drink.'

I followed Dr Brownlow through the house and into his living room. The table was covered with trade journals and piles of paper.

'What would you like?'

'I'll have a whisky, please.'

'Glenmorangie?'

'Great!' I agreed. I'd acquired a taste for malt whisky but couldn't always afford it.

Dr Brownlow poured a generous measure into an antique cut glass tumbler. 'Water?'

'Yes, please. Just a drop.'

Dr Brownlow smiled with childish delight, walked across the room, bent down and took a bottle out of a cardboard box. 'Here it is!' he said, holding up the bottle with a flourish. 'The first bottle of official Bilbury Water!' He held the bottle out to me, holding it in the same way that an oenophile might hold an ancient and valuable bottle of port or claret.

I don't really know what I'd expected but I was immediately impressed by how *professional* the bottle looked. It was properly labelled and the screw cap was sealed with an impressive looking strip of paper and fake sealing wax. The label bore a drawing of Dr Brownlow's house and I think this was probably the first time I'd realised just how serious the whole venture was. With a flick Dr Brownlow opened the top of the bottle and handed it to me. I inspected the label carefully and then added a splash to the Glenmorangie in my glass.

'It's in production, then?'

'Not properly,' admitted Dr Brownlow, taking the bottle off me and adding a little water to his own whisky. 'Not until next Monday. But they've been trying out the machinery.' He sat down in a massive leather arm chair near to the fireplace. Two huge logs had been burning for some time. He waved to the other chair and I sat down opposite him.

'I haven't felt so excited by anything since I first started out in practice,' he told me.

'You look well on it all.'

'It's exciting!' said Dr Brownlow. 'Not just because I can make money and keep the house going but for a dozen other reasons.' He waved a hand around airily as though uncertain which reasons to choose. 'It helps the village,' he said. 'I like that. And it's fun to see a new business growing.'

I nodded and sipped at my whisky.

'The thing is,' Dr Brownlow went on, 'that the water bottling is taking up all my time.'

'I realise that,' I said. 'It's OK. I seem to be able to manage now.'

'No!' said Dr Brownlow, shaking his head. 'I'm going to have to resign from the practice.'

It didn't sink in for a minute. And then, slowly, I realised that this meant that I was going to be out of work.

'It isn't fair to anyone for me to carry on pretending that I'm a GP,' Dr Brownlow continued. He stared into the fire for a moment, then drank half the remaining whisky in his glass. 'I've enjoyed it,' he said. 'But being a GP is a young man's job. And I'm too old for it.'

I started to protest but he raised a hand to stop me then got up and fetched the bottle of Glenmorangie and the bottle of Bilbury Water. He offered the whisky bottle to me first.

'I'd better not,' I said. 'I'm on duty. And I've got to drive home.'

'Sorry,' Dr Brownlow apologised. 'You're right.' But he took the stopper out of the whisky bottle. 'Do you mind if I have another?'

'No, of course not.' Although I didn't want to show it I was feeling empty inside. I had grown to love working in Bilbury. I liked the patients. I liked the job. I liked the practice. I liked the countryside. And I loved Patsy. A thousand questions were struggling for my attention but none of them were getting answered.

Dr Brownlow added water to the generous measure of whisky he'd poured himself and sat back down again. 'The patients like you very much,' he said. 'You care for them and they know that.' He sipped at his whisky and looked across at me. I didn't know what to say. It was a compliment I cherished and I felt myself blushing with surprise and embarrassment.

'So, there's only one solution!' said Dr Brownlow.

I looked across at him.

'You'll have to take over the practice,' he said. He raised his glass to me. 'What do you say?'

I opened my mouth and sat there for a few seconds giving a passable imitation of a goldfish.

'Will you take over the practice for me?' asked Dr Brownlow, repeating his offer.

Again, I tried to speak but again my throat seemed to have gone on strike. So I simply nodded furiously. Now another thousand questions were struggling for space in my brain. Again none of them looked like getting answered.

221

'What about the General Medical Council?' I reminded him at last. 'I've still got to face that advertising charge.'

'You can forget about that,' grinned Dr Brownlow. 'It's being dropped.'

I stared at him uncomprehendingly.

'It was that damned son of mine,' explained Dr Brownlow. 'He was trying to get at me by attacking you. I think he thought that if you had to leave I wouldn't be able to cope and he'd be able to get me into that retirement home.' He paused and drank some of his whisky. 'I guessed it was him and when I rang him up he confessed.'

'But how can you be sure that he'll drop the complaint?'

Dr Brownlow grinned at me. 'I told him that if he doesn't tell the General Medical Council to get off your back then he'll be out of my will for ever.' He raised an eyebrow. 'Can you imagine how much that frightened him now that I look like getting rich?'

I had to smile.

'So?' asked Dr Brownlow. 'What's your answer?'

'Yes!' I said simply with a word that was to change my life. 'Yes! Thank you!'

'Good!' grinned Dr Brownlow. He took another sip out of his glass and leant forward. 'I'll send in my resignation tomorrow and with it I'll send them a note telling them that you'll be taking over.'

I nodded. Half an hour earlier I'd been a temporary assistant. Ten minutes earlier I thought I'd been facing unemployment. Now I was about to become self employed with my own list of patients. It was all a little too much to cope with.

'If you want to carry on using the surgery that'll be fine,' said Dr Brownlow. 'I'll work out some extortionate rent and you can carry on just the same as you are now.' He sipped more whisky. 'But now that you're staying in Bilbury you'll probably want to find your own place to live and if you find somewhere big enough to house a surgery that's no problem at all.'

'They've been very good to me at the Duck and Puddle,' I said. 'I wouldn't want to just go and leave them in the lurch.'

'Don't you worry about that,' said Dr Brownlow. 'Frank and Gilly can let every room they've got these days – and for more than you're paying them.' He picked up the poker and gave the logs a shake, then he lifted a huge log out of the wicker basket that stood beside the hearth and threw it onto the fire. A cloud of sparks lit up the room. 'Did you know that Bilbury Grange was on the market again?'

'Mike Trickle's house? Is he leaving?'

'He's apparently decided that country life isn't for him,' said Dr Brownlow.

My mind was buzzing with so many ideas that I couldn't think about any of them clearly. I stood up. 'I ought to be getting back to the Duck and Puddle,' I told him. I fiddled with my watch. 'Gilly will have my dinner ready.'

Dr Brownlow stood up too and held out his hand. 'Thank you,' he said, as I took his hand in mine. 'I'm very fond of this village. I'm glad you're going to look after it.'

I found myself blushing again. 'I like it too,' I said. I felt a lump in my throat. 'And I'm honoured that you're letting me take over your practice.' It sounded corny but I meant it.

'Just make sure that you ring Patsy and tell her the good news,' said Dr Brownlow with a twinkle in his eye. 'She's a lovely girl. She'd make a great doctor's wife.'

I wouldn't have thought that my blush could get any deeper but I'm sure it did.

Dr Brownlow smiled at me. 'You do love her, don't you?'

'Yes,' I replied, without hesitation.

'Do you like her? Do you get on?'

'Yes.'

'Marry her,' said Dr Brownlow. 'If you've found someone you can like and love then grab her with both hands.'

*   *   *

Patsy and I sat in the Morris Minor staring through the windscreen. Two workmen were busy erecting a huge 'For Sale – By Auction' sign by the side of one of the two huge stone pillars which guarded the entrance to the drive up to Bilbury Grange.

I opened my car door. 'Let's go in and have a look around.'

'But we can't!' said Patsy, horrified.

'Of course we can,' I told her, with a confidence that surprised me. 'If we walk in as though we're buying the place no one will dream of stopping us.' As we passed the two workmen I nodded. One of the men waved a hammer in our direction and shouted a cheerful greeting.

Neither Patsy nor I had ever seen Bilbury Grange before. It looked as if it had been built in the last decade or so of the 19th century. Massive red brick chimneys towered high above the roof and two huge stone lions guarded the front door. Walking round to the side of the house we saw that the back part of the building made up one quarter of a cobbled courtyard. A derelict coach house, complete with its own clock tower, and a row of stables bordered the rest of the courtyard.

'I never knew any of this was here,' whispered Patsy. 'It's huge!'

The house and out buildings were all deserted and Patsy, Ben and I wandered around for the best part of an hour, trying doors and peering through windows. Inside the house the rooms were massive, with an impressive, swirling staircase and a beautiful stained glass window dominating the hallway.

Although Mike Trickle had owned the house for several months his workmen seemed to have done very little to restore the house to its former glories. The brickwork needed pointing, the window frames were rotten, many panes of glass were cracked and the whole of the outside of the house clearly needed decorating. Outside, the gardens, once landscaped, had been allowed to fall into terrible disrepair. The croquet lawn had been cut but the stable roof needed repairing and a small lake that we found in a copse behind the house was stagnant and choked with weeds.

But the house had enormous potential and the views across the North Devon countryside were magnificent. Hand in hand Patsy and I sat on a moss covered stone bench that overlooked the croquet lawn and looked out across the fields. We could see Dr Brownlow's house in the distance.

'It's wonderful, isn't it?' sighed Patsy. 'It would make a marvellous home.'

The coach house could be converted into a surgery,' I said.

'And there are enough bedrooms to take in paying guests during the summer,' said Patsy.

'I've always dreamt of owning a house with a billiard room.'

'I'd love to get the walled garden back into production.'

'I wonder how much it will go for?'

Patsy looked at me. 'You're serious, aren't you?'

I nodded. 'Yes. I am.'

'But . . .' began Patsy.

'No "buts".' I said. 'Let's buy it. Let's make it work. It's a wonderful house.' I dropped onto one knee in front of her. 'Patsy, will you marry me?'

Patsy was in tears when she said 'Yes.' She threw her arms around my neck and held me so tightly that I could hardly breathe. Then, when I finally stood up and she saw the damp, muddy patches staining my knees she started to laugh.

'Can we afford it?' she asked me a few moments later.

I kissed away a leftover tear that was running down her cheek.

'Dr Brownlow has asked me to take over his practice.' I told her. 'My income will pay the mortgage and we can live on what we make from holiday makers in the summer.'

Patsy started crying again. She kissed me full on the lips for what seemed like an eternity but still leant back from me far too soon. 'I love you!' she said.

'I love you too!'

*   *   *

An hour later we were parked outside the farm where Patsy and her family lived. 'Are you sure I've got to do this?' I asked her.

She nodded.

'I'm terrified.'

'He won't eat you.'

'Maybe not,' I said, unconvinced. I kissed Patsy, got out of the car and walked alone across to the front door. Patsy remained alone in the car.

'Could I have a word with you, Mr Kennett?' I asked. I probably sounded calmer than I felt. My heart was beating as fast as if I'd just run a mile. What, I wondered, would I do or say if he said 'No!'?

Patsy's father scowled at me. 'What have you done?'

'I haven't done anything.'

'You want to borrow the tractor?'

I shook my head. 'Not just at the moment, thank you, sir.'

He stared at me for a long few seconds. 'You'd better come in then.'

I followed him into the living room, which was empty.

'Sit down,' he said. It was an order, not an invitation. 'Do you want a drink?'

'I'll have whatever you're having,' I told him. I needed some Dutch courage but I didn't want to ask for an alcoholic drink if he thought it was too early in the day.

I needn't have worried. Mr Kennett poured us both very large whiskies.

'What do you want, then?' he demanded. He had huge, bushy black eyebrows which seemed to roam around his forehead without any planned direction in mind. I'd never noticed how mobile they were before. It was not, however, possible to make any accurate deductions about his mood by watching the position of his eyebrows.

I had, in my mind, a carefully rehearsed speech which was designed to win him over gently. On the journey over from Bilbury Grange I had thought up a number of strong reasons why he should say 'yes' and I had thought up a cleverly structured strategy to help me persuade him to say 'yes'.

'I'd like to marry Patsy,' I blurted out.

For a moment Mr Kennett looked startled. But he recovered quickly. 'I like a man who speaks his mind without beating about the bush,' he said. He sniffed at his whisky and then sipped at it cautiously. Then he looked directly at me. It was unnerving. 'Do you love her?'

'Yes, sir.'

'Can you look after her?'

'Yes, sir.'

'Have you asked her?'

'Yes, sir.'

'What did she say?'

'Yes, sir.'

Mr Kennett grunted, nodded, drained his glass and got up. He walked across the room to the cupboard where he kept his booze. He took out a bottle of 20 year old malt.

'Drink up!' he instructed me as he walked back.

I emptied my glass and held it out. Mr Kennett half filled it. 'You're not a bad bloke,' he said. 'Considering you're a doctor.'

I didn't know what to say to that so I kept quiet and sipped at my whisky. I gathered that getting the expensive stuff out was his way of giving us his blessing.

Mr Kennett still hadn't sat down and now he walked over towards the door into the kitchen where he called for his wife. She appeared in the kitchen door almost instantaneously.

'Patsy and the doctor are getting married,' he told her bluntly.

Mrs Kennett said nothing but burst into tears and buried her face in her pinafore.

'Don't be so bloody silly, woman,' he told her but Mrs Kennett disappeared back into her kitchen. I realised that I still hadn't ever spoken to her.

'Where are you going to live?'

I swallowed hard. 'We want to try and buy Bilbury Grange,' I said. 'It's in a pretty terrible state. It's for auction on Friday.'

'Can you afford it?'

'I don't know,' I said honestly. 'It depends on how much it goes for.' I paused. 'But we both like it.'

When I left twenty minutes later the malt whisky bottle was nearly empty and I could hardly stand. I staggered out to the car where Patsy was still waiting.

'Well?' she whispered as I climbed in beside her. 'What did he say?'

I turned and smiled at her. 'I think he said it's OK.' I murmured before falling unconscious into her arms.

*　　*　　*

The auction of Bilbury Grange was attracting far more attention than Patsy and I had hoped it would. The auctioneers handling the sale for Mr Trickle put large advertisements in several national newspapers as well as in all the local papers and on the morning of the auction the lanes around the house were clogged with traffic.

The day before I'd visited my bank manager in Barnstaple to find out how much money the bank would lend me and had been startled to find out just how little we could raise.

'Do you want me to stand surety for you?' asked Dr Brownlow. 'I'm not exactly drowning in cash at the moment but I might be able to help gouge a few more thousand out of the bank.'

I shook my head. 'You've done quite enough for us, thank you. If I can't buy it with what the bank is prepared to lend us then we'll just have to accept that it's too rich for our blood.'

Dr Brownlow agreed to look after the morning surgery for me and although the auction wasn't due to start until 11.00am Patsy and I and Ben left the Duck and Puddle with an hour to spare. We were both so nervous and excited that we knew very well that we wouldn't be able to relax wherever we were and whatever we were doing. Because we'd already heard about the heavy traffic we left the Morris parked at the pub and walked across the fields to the house. Ben thought it was marvellous fun.

We were climbing over a stile into a meadow that lay next to Bilbury Grange's gardens when, in the distance, between us and the house, we both saw building going on. I could just make out a couple of lorries, a tractor, a pile of wood, some massive sheets of corrugated iron and a group of workmen.

'What on earth is going on?' asked Patsy.

I shrugged. 'Maybe it's something to do with Mr Trickle,' I suggested. 'He had been building a wall around the estate to protect his privacy.'

'If we get the house we ought to knock the wall down,' said Patsy.

But as we walked on I began to realise that what was going on was nothing to do with Mr Trickle. I could see men still working though I felt sure that Trickle would have called his men off.

When we got closer we could see that the work wasn't going on in the grounds belonging to Bilbury Grange but in another field and we could see that quite a crowd of prospective buyers were collecting in the Bilbury Grange gardens. We hurried to get closer and to take a good look.

'Look at the workmen!' said Patsy, putting a hand on my arm and pulling me to a halt. I stopped and looked hard. Ben's ears were pricked.

'Isn't that your father?' I asked her, screwing up my eyes.

'Yes,' answered Patsy. 'And several of his men are with him.'

'What the hell is going on over there?' called a large, red faced man in a worn Barbour coat.

Patsy's father stopped what he was doing and stared at the man who had called. 'I don't know what business it is of yours,' he said sourly. 'But I'm building a barn and a slurry pit.'

'How big is it going to be?' asked the stranger anxiously. 'I'm the auctioneer. I'm selling the property over here.'

'About eighty feet long,' answered Mr Kennett.

'You can't build it there!' complained the auctioneer. 'You'll ruin the view from the house. And a slurry pit will stink.'

Mr Kennett shrugged his shoulders. 'That's your problem,' he said. 'I'm not bothered about views.'

'I could have almost kissed him.

'But ... but ...' stuttered the auctioneer furiously. 'You'll ruin the value of this property.'

'I can put up whatever I like,' said Mr Kennett bluntly. All around him the activity continued furiously, with men sinking posts into the ground and dragging corrugated iron sheets off the back of a flat bed lorry. Among the men working there I recognised Thumper Robinson.

'Doesn't he need planning permission for all this?' demanded a man in a grey suit.

Mr Kennett shook his head and glared at the man who'd interrupted. 'I don't need planning permission to do anything,' he said. 'I'm a farmer. I can put up whatever I like.'

'Is that true?' the man in the grey suit asked the auctioneer.

'I'm afraid it is,' admitted the auctioneer ruefully.

There was a murmur of dissatisfaction among the prospective purchasers of Bilbury Grange and many of them started to drift away back towards their cars.

'What on earth is my father up to?' asked Patsy in a whisper.

'I knew he was going to start work on a new barn today – but not here!'

'I think it's his way of helping make sure that we buy Bilbury Grange at a reasonable price,' I whispered back. I helped her climb around the impromptu building site. We both refrained from speaking to Mr Kennett, Thumper or any of the others and they ignored us.

'Watch out!' I cried suddenly, pointing to a large red painted sign that had been stuck on a post in the garden just outside the billiard room window.

'What's the matter?' demanded Patsy.

I read out the sign. 'BEWARE OF ADDERS NESTING'.

Patsy laughed. 'There aren't any adders around here. Besides it's not their nesting season.'

We walked on up through the garden towards the house that we'd both fallen in love with just in time to see the man in the grey suit and most of the other potential bidders getting into their cars and driving away. There was much unhappy muttering among those who were left behind.

Ninety minutes later Patsy and I bought Bilbury Grange for considerably less than we'd expected.

'There's even going to be some cash left over from the loan to pay for some of the repairs we need to do,' I told Patsy.

She threw her arms around my neck and kissed me firmly on the lips. 'Isn't it exciting?'

Exciting just didn't sum it up but I knew what she meant. I'd been in Bilbury for less than six months and I was about to become a fully fledged general practitioner, buy and rebuild my own house and get married!

'Let's walk round and plan what we're going to do first,' said Patsy.

'In a moment. There's just one thing I've got to do.'

Patsy looked momentarily disappointed. 'What's that?'

'Tell your father and Thumper that they can stop putting up that barn!'

*   *   *

Bilbury Grange

The second novel in the Bilbury series sees the now married doctor moving into his new home - a vast and rambling country house in desperate need of renovation. With repair bills soaring and money scarce, the doctor and his new wife look for additional ways to make ends meet. Another super novel in this series - perfect for hours of escapism!

Price £12.95 (hardback)

The Bilbury Revels

Disaster strikes in this the third Bilbury novel when a vicious storm descends on the village. The ensuing snow storm cuts off the village and blankets the whole area in a deep carpet of snow. Much damage is done to the village as a result of the storm and the locals band together to undertake the repair work. Money, as ever, is tight and fund-raising is of prime importance. Money-spinning suggestions are sought and so the idea of the Revels is born - a week of fun and festivities to raise the money needed to repair the local schoolteacher's cottage.

Price £12.95 (hardback)

Also available by Vernon Coleman

Bilbury Country

The fourth book in the Bilbury series set in idyllic Exmoor village. This novel sees the usual peace and tranquillity enjoyed by the locals destroyed by an invading army of tourists.

Does this invasion of holidaymakers mean financial reward for the locals - or will it threaten their much-loved way of life?

All the familiar and colourful characters are here to tell yet another spellbinding tale in this ever-popular series.

Price £12.95 (hardback)

Bilbury Pie

A delightful collection of short stories based in and around this fictional Devon village.

Every community has its characters and Bilbury is no exception! Thumper Robinson is the local "jack the lad" and Pete is the taxi driver, shop owner, funeral director and postman all rolled into one. Patchy Fogg dispenses advice on antiques to anyone who will listen and Dr Brownlow is the eccentric and rather elderly, retired local doctor

Price £9.95 (hardback)

All published by Chilton Designs Publishers
Order from Publishing House, Trinity Place, Barnstaple, Devon
EX32 9HJ, England